# CHAMPAGNE, MISFITS,
## *and other*
# SHADY MAGIC

CHAMPAGNE, MISFITS, AND OTHER SHADY
MAGIC (DOWSER 7)
Copyright © 2017 Meghan Ciana Doidge
Published by Old Man in the CrossWalk Productions 2018
Salt Spring Island, BC, Canada
www.oldmaninthecrosswalk.com

Library and Archives Canada
Doidge, Meghan Ciana, 1973—
Champagne, Misfits, and Other Shady Magic/
Meghan Ciana Doidge—PAPERBACK EDITION

Cover design by: Elizabeth Mackey

ISBN 978-1-927850-72-5

— *Dowser 7* —

# CHAMPAGNE, MISFITS, *and other* SHADY MAGIC

Meghan Ciana Doidge

Published by Old Man in the CrossWalk Productions
Salt Spring Island, BC, Canada

www.madebymeghan.ca

# Author's Note:

*Champagne, Misfits, and Other Shady Magic* is the seventh book in the Dowser series, which is set in the same universe as the Oracle and Reconstructionist series.

While it is not necessary to read all three series, *in order to avoid spoilers* the ideal reading order is as follows:

Cupcakes, Trinkets, and Other Deadly Magic (Dowser 1)
Trinkets, Treasures, and Other Bloody Magic (Dowser 2)
Treasures, Demons, and Other Black Magic (Dowser 3)
I See Me (Oracle 1)
Shadows, Maps, and Other Ancient Magic (Dowser 4)
Maps, Artifacts, and Other Arcane Magic (Dowser 5)
I See You (Oracle 2)
Artifacts, Dragons, and Other Lethal Magic (Dowser 6)
I See Us (Oracle 3)
Catching Echoes (Reconstructionist 1)
Tangled Echoes (Reconstructionist 2)
Unleashing Echoes (Reconstructionist 3)
Champagne, Misfits, and Other Shady Magic (Dowser 7)

Other books in the Dowser series to follow.

More information can be found at
www.madebymeghan.ca/novels

**For Michael**
For supporting my choices, even the ones you knew
would bring me harm.

*I* had everything I'd ever wanted—a successful business with a second bakery in the works, a sexy fiance who I adored, and good friends who loved to laugh almost as much as I did.

So of course it couldn't possibly last.

Unfortunately, this time the trouble was home-grown in Vancouver, threatening my own backyard and those who were under my protection—whether they wanted to be or not.

I was, after all, the wielder of the instruments of assassination.

Apparently, cutesy cupcakes and being nice only stretched so far.

# Chapter One

The green-haired werewolf handed me a broken stick of bright-pink chalk, fishing a crumpled wad of paper out of her backpack and halfheartedly smoothing it out on her blue-Lycra-clad thigh. The fake leather backpack was dyed bright purple and adorned with puffy leather spikes, mimicking some sort of dinosaur. It clashed spectacularly with the lithe werewolf's deep-green-dyed hair and orange T-shirt.

I had needled Kandy about the backpack when she'd shown up wearing it, just before she dragged me from the comfort of my apartment fifteen minutes before midnight, forcing me to jog to one of the many parks along Kitsilano Beach. But needing to deflect the tension I was feeling over the spell I had been asked to cast, I couldn't resist teasing her again.

"So … did you lose a bet? Or what?"

Once again, Kandy refused to engage on the backpack topic. Instead, she offered me a deeply disapproving glower and the still-wrinkled piece of paper. Of course, I might have been reading the judgement into the look.

I glanced at the carefully printed design, noting the handwriting of both my grandmother, Pearl, and my mother, Scarlett. Apparently, I was now expected to chalk the ornate circle they had scribed on paper onto the seawall. At exactly midnight. With only a smoke-shrouded sliver of a moon overhead for light.

"Runes?" I moaned dejectedly. "I thought it was just supposed to be a simple circle. And, like, just standing here."

Kandy shrugged her backpack-laden shoulder. "The witches decided you might need some help. You know, focusing."

I eyed her snottily. "I'm one of the most powerful Adepts in North America. A renowned dowser and skilled alchemist. I can tear down wards with my bare hands!"

"And you bake the tastiest cupcakes," Kandy said mildly. Then she glanced at her phone. "You've got ten minutes."

Still grumbling under my breath about my magical prowess, I surveyed the well-worn concrete path under my feet. Then I glanced to either side of the seawall running along the edge of Kits Beach Park. The Maritime Museum was just a short distance away, but this part of the seaside park was pretty much just a wide stretch of trimmed, mostly brown grass. So other than a large-leafed chestnut tree to our left, we were standing out in the open.

The eclectic mix of homes across the swath of grass behind Kandy were mostly dark, though I could see that someone was watching TV in the uppermost window of a Spanish-villa-inspired converted triplex on the eastern corner.

Those houses along Ogden Avenue rarely came on the market, as teardowns or otherwise. Hence the mixture of architecture. Practically every decade since Vancouver had been established was represented in this one residential block, from the fairly modern sandstone-clad mansion on the western corner, to the untouched

Cape Cod. Across from where I was supposed to be chalking a rune-marked witches' circle, a recently painted Craftsman stood, which I vaguely remembered was one of Godfrey Properties' long-term rentals.

So yeah, I was dithering. Over architecture.

"Nine minutes," Kandy said.

I jutted my chin out. "This isn't the right spot."

The werewolf bared her teeth. "It's exactly the right spot, dowser."

Belligerently, I took two wide steps to my left. I might have been only half-witch, but I could still feel the slumbering current of magic that I was about to try to tap into underneath my feet.

Kandy narrowed her eyes at my position adjustment, but she didn't comment.

"We could have at least set up distraction spells." I gestured around the empty park. "People jog at night around here. Chalking runes on the seawall is going to look weird, even in Vancouver."

"You know that any other spells might interfere with the casting of the grid." Kandy's tone was unusually cajoling. She was babying me in response to the baby I was being.

I exhaled harshly. No matter my previous bravado and declaration of might, in truth, I was worried that I was going to ruin the intricate spell that my grandmother and Kandy had spent six months planning and constructing. Twelve witches—most of whom had flown into the city for the occasion—were currently set up all around the borders of Vancouver, waiting for the stroke of midnight. Because together, we were going to attempt to raise a magically triggered boundary around the city.

In its primary phase, the grid would help the witches track magic users within a wide area—from the north edge of the Lions Gate Bridge to the property that Rochelle, the oracle, owned in Southlands; from the western edge of the University of BC to three eastern points along Boundary Road, the border between Vancouver and Burnaby. And if that initial grid held and functioned properly, the witches had plans to expand the coverage to include all of Greater Vancouver—aka all of the territory held and regulated by the Godfrey coven.

"Eight minutes."

"Screw you, werewolf."

"Any time, any place, dowser."

I laughed. Kandy flashed her teeth at me.

"Fine. I'll give it a go." I glanced down at the runes carefully printed on the paper Kandy had given me, wishing I had more light and that the paper wasn't so crumpled. "Why is it all wrinkled? It looks like someone balled it up and threw it away."

Kandy shrugged.

All right, then.

I hunched down to chalk the first rune, copying it as precisely as I could from the paper onto the concrete. It looked a little like a—

Kandy cleared her throat expectantly.

I cursed under my breath. "What? Do you have a freaking checklist?"

"Hand them over, Jade."

"You know it doesn't matter if I'm wearing them, right? They are me."

"Illuminating."

"You know what I mean. What if I told you that you were going to have to take off the cuffs?"

"I refer you to the T-shirt," Kandy said, her tone deceptively mild. She was pointing at her chest, where the words *I do bite* were emblazoned in thick black lettering on orange cotton. The aforementioned cuffs—gold, rune carved, and three inches across—adorned her wrists, creating a perpetual aesthetic conflict with her sporty outfits.

The cuffs were magical artifacts that not only imbued my werewolf BFF with a massive amount of strength, even above and beyond what her shapeshifter magic provided, but also afforded her some magical resistance to malicious spells. It was a resistance I'd been layering into them with my own alchemy. But carefully, so I didn't disrupt the magic already embedded in the gold, diamonds, and runes.

See? I was learning subtlety. At least when it came to wielding some of my power.

I pointed at my own chest. The werewolf had insisted I wear a specific bright-green T-shirt for the occasion of raising the magical grid. Etched across my ample assets was the phrase: *Never mind the cupcakes. I can totally kick your ass.*

"That doesn't apply to me," she said, beckoning in my direction.

Fine. I could decide that being a big girl, trying to cast the spell properly, and failing was better than being subjected to snide sneers from the twelve other witches for not even trying. I called my jade knife into my right hand, flipping the magic-imbued blade twice. Energy flashed around my hand and forearm, streaking through the night air. I couldn't see or taste the magic I'd accumulated in the weapon, cementing it with my own alchemy, but I could certainly feel it. Revel in it.

"Yeah, yeah," Kandy said. "Very pretty."

I carefully placed the hilt across her open palm, whispering, "Stay."

Kandy didn't bother reacting to my addressing an inanimate object. My attachment to my creations … well, two of my personal artifacts at least … wasn't news to her.

"Six minutes."

I let out a long, suffering sigh, then reached up and untwined the wedding-ring-laden gold chain I'd wound twice around my neck. My necklace also held the three instruments of assassination—aka the only three ways to kill a guardian dragon. The silver centipedes were clipped to wedding rings. The braids were encased in gold and twined throughout the thick links of the necklace. The leaves and flower petals representing the phoenix had transformed into an embossing over the entire chain when I claimed the instruments for myself.

I never took the necklace off.

Not even to shower.

Not even to have sex.

The artifact felt benign right up until the moment I shifted it away from my body, holding it out to Kandy. Then the magic held within it contracted, bristling with power.

Kandy sucked in her breath. Her hand, still extended toward me, shook slightly. Almost imperceptibly. But I could see and sense such things now. Perhaps I had always been able to, but absorbing the magic of Shailaja, the daughter of the former treasure keeper, had sharpened my abilities. So much so that after a year and a half of training, paired with meditative yoga, I was as much a weapon as the instruments themselves. Bound by the magic that ran in my veins, in my every cell, we belonged to each other. For better or worse.

"It's just for a moment," I murmured, more to myself than to the necklace.

Kandy gnashed her teeth at her own reaction to the power of the instruments. Then she took a deep, fortifying breath and her hand steadied.

I slung the necklace across her open palm, forcing myself to let it go. Then I immediately crouched, chalking the runes in a tight circle around my feet rather than giving in to the intense emptiness that accompanied being parted from the necklace. It felt as though I'd handed a piece of my soul to the wolf for her to hold. But that was fine, actually.

Because I would trust Kandy with my life, my very essence. Any day.

Kandy didn't sling the necklace around her neck, which was probably wise. She also made sure to avoid any direct contact between it and the magical cuffs.

"Three minutes," she murmured, but more out of duty now than any need to egg me on.

I could already feel magic blooming underneath the chalked runes as I etched them into the cement. Witches didn't often work with runes, and I certainly never did. They were more of a sorcerer thing. But Gran occasionally used them to anchor specific spells. And that was what I was currently doing—physically anchoring my own magic to this time and place. This moment.

I connected the last two runes, trying to replicate the complicated swoop that had been rendered on the paper I held in my left hand. Then as I straightened, magic rushed up all around me, taking my breath with it as it beamed upward into the dark sky.

I blinked at the few stars I could see through the smoky haze that had plagued Vancouver for most of the summer, the aftereffect of rampant wildfires burning throughout British Columbia. I wondered how high the thirteen points of the grid were now beaming above the city. If I were at a lookout point on Cypress Mountain, would I be able to see those beams of magic streaming up into the sky?

Kandy grunted with satisfaction, backing up a few steps until she stood on the dry grass. Then she peered down at her phone intently, most likely watching the countdown she'd coordinated. Each witch was paired with a companion who stood outside the magic at each individual anchor point. My own phone was in my satchel a few feet away from me, but even with the protection of the lead-lined case I usually kept it in, I wasn't foolish enough to risk using it around this much magic. I was actually lucky that my own magic didn't fry electronics, though I kept the bulk of my power tucked tidily away behind my necklace and my knife.

The magical grid was rooted at Gran's house in Point Grey, from where its power radiated. She, Scarlett, and some of the other Godfrey coven witches had been testing it for months, painstakingly tweaking the spell. Their idea had been to fortify the grid, so that even if any one of the twelve anchor points were compromised, the overall power would still hold. Assuming that we managed to get it up and activated in the first place.

"Ten … nine … eight …" Kandy whispered.

Ah, crap. I scrambled to take off my socks and shoes, completely forgetting that portion of Gran's instructions. The runes had been distracting.

"… seven … six …"

I had one foot bare. The concrete was colder than I expected.

"… five … four … three …"

"You're speeding up," I growled, hopping on one foot.

"Am not."

Magic crashed into the circle, hitting the rune-marked boundary from two directions. The flavors and scents of lilac … strawberry … citrus … rosemary … and nutmeg flooded through my senses, overwhelming the individual tastes until it resolved into a single potent grassy note.

Witch magic.

The pink-chalked runes flared with blue light, setting me aglow from my painted toes—a bright coral shade from OPI called *Me, MySelfie & I*—to my jeans to my T-shirt. My hair lifted up, spreading out like a golden halo of curls all around my head and shoulders.

I spread my arms within the field of energy swirling all around me, desperately trying to relax. I needed to let its power flow through and around me, rather than greedily absorbing every last potent drop. Completely contrary to my natural instincts, this energy wasn't for me to collect and hold.

"Not mine … not mine …" I whispered.

"It's not working, Jade." Kandy called out to me from somewhere beyond the maelstrom of magic. "It's supposed to flow out, not just in. Yes?"

Yes. Damn it.

And, of course, I didn't have my knife. It was going to be difficult to perform potentially illegal blood alchemy without being able to cut myself.

Reacting instinctively—which had never gotten me into any trouble before, right?—I clenched my right hand, crouching and slamming my fist down onto the concrete between my feet in the same motion. The seawall pathway cracked under the blow, though not enough to interfere with the runes. I'd barely scratched my knuckles, but it was enough of a scrape that blood welled. Quickly, before my skin could heal, I pressed a practically microscopic drop of blood into the center of the circle.

"Well, Pearl is going to love that," Kandy muttered.

Yeah, witches weren't really cool with anything that even hinted at blood magic. But since the runes appeared to be pretty useless, at least when it came to my attempt to use them, the magic carried in my blood would anchor me instead.

I straightened up, closing my eyes and imagining myself floating within the energy. Visualizing it flowing through me, then out into the invisible grid. I fueled the magic of the grid, combining my power with that of the twelve other witches. I visualized all that power streaking out over streets, the bakery, houses, skyscrapers, parks, and all the people of Vancouver.

I lost my footing within the buoyant magic, slipping up into it. Then I was floating about a foot off the ground, suspended within the power pouring through me.

"Shit!" Kandy said. "Is that supposed to happen?"

I didn't answer. I couldn't answer. Because for one breathless moment, I was the magic, the energy. I was all of the twelve witches, some of whom I hadn't even met yet.

I was Gran … Scarlett … Wisteria … Olive …

And they were me.

Our fingers were reaching for each other, our minds connected, our strength spread across the city.

Then my feet touched the ground. The magic remained, but the feeling abated. And I was myself within the steady stream of energy once more.

I opened my eyes.

Kandy grinned at me, almost manically. "Wicked cool."

I laughed. In that moment, that single breath of time, I was utterly at peace. Utterly full and fulfilled. My pure joy was reflected back and around me, my voice shared with every other witch anchoring the grid.

Then it was over.

The energy we'd collected together receded into the runes as their glow faded. I could still feel the anchor point I'd held, and the web of witch magic we'd raised, but I was just me again.

I stepped from the circle, still grinning madly in response to the mutual joy I carried with me. The bliss that always accompanied the use of my magic, but multiplied by twelve.

The moment I cleared the rune-marked boundary, my necklace settled around my neck and my knife slipped into the invisible sheath on my right hip. Both returned to me without being consciously summoned, as if the runes I'd chalked were more effective than I'd thought. But then, Gran was particularly savvy about magic. She had to be to head the witches Convocation, never mind being the architect behind something as powerful as the magical grid that now surrounded Vancouver.

Still riding the euphoria of the casting, I flung my arms around Kandy before she could dodge me, lifting her up and twirling her around. She gripped my shoulders harshly, first with the shock of being lifted, then in discomfort because she didn't much like being off her feet. The werewolf was a control freak, through and through.

"Dowser," she snarled, but I could hear the laughter underneath her protest. "Put me down, you twit. Someone will see you flinging me around."

I set her on her feet, even as I continued to spin around and around myself. Luxuriating in the magic. Drunk with it.

Kandy shook her head at my antics, fishing a water bottle out of her backpack and splashing it over the chalked runes. Even though the Adept population of Vancouver was small, it wasn't a good idea to leave magic lying around, spent or not.

I fell back onto the brown grass, watching the stars seemingly twirl overhead through the haze. The magic I'd inadvertently collected, but which wasn't mine to keep, slowly seeped out into the ground. I traced it by feel more than taste, sensing it feeding back and adhering to the anchor point, and then into the invisible grid that now surrounded us.

Kandy crouched beside me, grinning. "We need dessert."

I sat up swiftly at the mention of potential chocolate. Even with my head still spinning and possibly drunk on magic, I had my priorities straight. "Nothing will be open."

Kandy pulled two chocolate bars from her backpack. The single-origin bars—Fleur de Sel and Hispaniola—were encased in pale-yellow cardboard wrappers and sported an intricately scribed hummingbird logo. The Hispaniola was an award-winning 70 percent cacao from the Dominican Republic and a new favorite of mine from Hummingbird Chocolate Maker, small-batch chocolatiers out of Almonte, Ontario, near Ottawa.

"You were holding this entire time?" I cried, making a grab for the chocolate.

Kandy easily evaded my thievery attempt. Apparently, my depth perception was a little off. "Sometimes rewards should be actual rewards, dowser. Not just daily indulgences."

I smiled. "Fine. But I'm only agreeing so I get the chocolate."

Kandy tugged open the Hispaniola bar, careful to not rip the side flap, while I salivated. The werewolf snapped a generous piece from the bar and dangled it in front of me. Grinning, I opened my mouth obligingly. She placed the chocolate on my tongue. Then I lay back in the grass while it slowly melted in my mouth, savoring the deep, buttery-smooth cacao with hints of raisin and cherry.

A light breeze reminded me that I was lying on the ground in only a T-shirt and bare feet, with less than a week to go before the autumn equinox. We had suffered through an unusually hot summer that had left Vancouver and most of the West Coast begging for rain—while literally drying up hot chocolate sales at the bakery. But the weather had mellowed over the past few weeks into typical late-summer temperatures, simply requiring a light sweater for evening strolls. Though I rarely felt chilly anymore.

Lying there with the chocolate chasing my residual magical buzz, I could simply turn my head to take in the brilliant lights of downtown and the dark swath of Stanley Park across English Bay. The topmost points of the towers of Lions Gate Bridge peeked out just above the hundred-year-old evergreens of the park, leading toward the North Shore Mountains looming over West and North Vancouver.

I was happy in Vancouver. Happy with my bustling bakery, and pleased that I'd been able to help Gran anchor the magical grid that would eventually help her oversee all the new Adepts who'd been filtering into the city and neighboring suburbs. Kandy seemed more than content to enforce rules and regulations over that growing magical population, and I hoped that Kett would return to the city soon as well.

I was about to be married to a man I adored, who was more than my match. My engagement party was less than eighteen hours away. I was healthy...strong, focused.

And yet … and yet …

I stroked my necklace, feeling the power of the instruments of assassination thrumming contentedly underneath my fingers.

Kandy snapped off another piece of chocolate, offering it to me. And I forced my scattered thoughts into the present.

Warner had been gone for three days. And I was likely just feeling off because I needed a workout with someone who matched me blow for blow instead of always needing to hold back. And by 'workout,' I most certainly meant in bed as well as out of it.

Kandy's phone pinged. While she checked her text messages, I stole the second half of the Fleur de Sel bar she'd been hoarding. Rolling to my feet in order to better defend my bounty, I took a second to check the magic of the anchor point and collect my socks and shoes.

I brushed my fingers across the damage I'd done to the path, making a mental note to ask one of the other witches to fix the radiating crack. If I concentrated, I could distinguish the slightly different tenor of each of the other twelve anchor points feeding back and forth in a loop all around Vancouver—from Stanley Park and the West End, through Kitsilano and Shaughnessy to Marpole, South Vancouver, and the East Side. But there was no hint of my blood. That magic had been consumed by the spell.

Which was good, because I occasionally regretted fueling spells with my blood. That included the knife that Warner wielded, which I'd inadvertently made powerful enough to kill an ancient vampire. Though I had no regrets whatsoever over the blood wards that covered the building housing my bakery and apartment. No Adept could feel the power residing in those wards and believe that they had any chance of hurting the people protected within. Except maybe the guardians. But other than my father, Yazi, Vancouver was generally beneath the dragons' collective notice.

"It's coming online at Pearl's," Kandy said, referencing her cellphone. "She can currently see residual from all thirteen points on her map."

After much trial and error, it became apparent that the power creating and supporting Gran's magical grid interacted best with a hand-drawn map etched across all four walls of her otherwise empty recreation room. Thankfully, the Godfrey coven included an oracle who could also draw. But still, getting Rochelle to agree to key her own magic into the grid had taken both my grandmother's and my mother's considerable powers of persuasion.

To be fair, it wasn't that the oracle hadn't wanted to be involved. She usually drew only visions and tattoos—the things her magic specifically moved her to sketch. But apparently, Rochelle's magic had become more receptive to direction after she'd spent some time with the witches. Moreover, Gran and Scarlett had set up extensive wards around the property that Rochelle and her husband, Beau, had bought in Southlands six months before, after Gran had purchased the downtown apartment that the oracle inherited from her birth mother. The map was the result.

According to Rochelle and Chi Wen the far seer—who acted as the young oracle's mentor—oracle magic tended to key in on the most powerful Adepts within its sphere. And I was blissfully overjoyed that Rochelle hadn't had any visions involving me since I'd collected the final instrument of assassination. Keeping it that way was completely out of my control, of course, but the time since had been seriously heavenly. Slightly boring but fairly peaceful. And I had managed to add a bunch of new cupcakes to the bakery menu.

"Hey!" Kandy cried, belatedly noticing that I'd absconded with the second bar. "Where do you think you're going with that?"

I tossed the final piece of delectable chocolate back to the werewolf, double-checking that all the chalked runes had disappeared as the water dried. Then I turned, slowly wandering west along the seawall.

"Home?" Kandy asked, a little mournfully. She fell into step beside me, though.

"I've got to bake in less than six hours." I smiled. "You did well tonight. Gran will be delighted."

Kandy huffed, though she seemed secretly pleased. "It was mostly witch work."

"Please. You brought the idea to Gran. You scouted the grid points, and you're the one who's going to be on call to investigate any incidents."

"We're taking shifts."

"With you leading it all."

Kandy shrugged, but her lips were curled in the slightest of smiles. The green-haired werewolf liked to be useful. More than once over the uneventful course of the previous year and a half, I'd grown concerned that she was going to become bored and return to the heart of the pack in Portland. But the magical grid and the fairly rapid influx of Adepts to Vancouver had kept her in town. Happily, I thought.

Vancouver, once a magical backwater, had seen a steady stream of relocating Adepts. Starting with Beau and Rochelle over a year before, followed by more shapeshifters putting some distance between themselves and various packs. We had also seen a number of witches arriving, some half-blood or less, drawn to the city to study under Gran and Scarlett.

Then there was Kett, who had tried to buy Rochelle's apartment—a five-thousand-square-foot penthouse suite overlooking False Creek—after Gran acquired it. Gran had only allowed the vampire to lease it, though. The chair of the witches Convocation and head of the Godfrey coven was rather controlling when it came to real estate, Adepts, and Vancouver. And though she tolerated his presence, it was a safe bet that the executioner of the Conclave was going to remain barred from officially establishing any sort of residence in witch territory.

Kandy and Warner were of the opinion that my claiming the instruments of assassination—and pretty much telling the guardian dragons to screw off in the process—had created unintended consequences. In the aftermath, Adepts who were uncomfortable with or ill-suited to fitting into the structure imposed by the pack or other covens were being drawn to Vancouver. Magical misfits, as Kandy called them. Those who might not magically conform, or who might have been seeking haven with others—namely me—who bucked the traditional and often prejudiced restrictions of Adept society.

And the fact that no one but a select few should have known what had transpired with the instruments, the guardians, and me didn't seem to shake Warner or Kandy of their belief that I'd somehow effectively claimed Vancouver as an independent city.

Whatever the true reason for the influx, Gran had actually implemented an application process for the newcomers, though I didn't think she'd turned anyone down as of yet. Housing in Vancouver and the surrounding areas was pricey, and most of the Adepts seeking a new home base didn't come from families who'd spent generations accumulating assets—like the Godfreys or

MEGHAN CIANA DOIDGE

the Fairchilds. So occasionally, Gran would organize temporary housing as well.

Walking the seawall, rather than cutting through the streets of Kits Point, we rounded a wide corner as the sandy stretch of Kits Beach came into view. The ocean was to our right, with a stretch of sparsely spaced evergreen trees interspersed with picnic tables to our left.

The taste of peppermint tickled my senses. My step hitched.

"What?" Kandy whispered, immediately alert.

I glanced around. The moon was still a tiny sliver overhead. The buildings ahead of us were dark. I could see a pair of joggers in the distance, lights clipped to their wrists.

But no magic.

No vampires.

Specifically, no Kett.

"Kett," I murmured. "I thought I tasted Kett's magic."

Kandy grumbled under her breath. The werewolf was seriously peeved at the executioner and elder of the Conclave, who hadn't been in Vancouver for longer than a day or two since the previous October. And who had barely communicated with either of us since late April.

"He's coming for the engagement party, isn't he?" I asked, slightly annoyed at the needy note that twisted its way into my question.

"He RSVPed," Kandy said with a shrug. Her attention was glued to her phone. Still texting with Gran about the grid, presumably.

We continued along the seawall, our naturally swift strides quickly taking us past the empty volleyball courts along the beach and then the Boathouse Restaurant. Disappointingly, I didn't pick up any other traces of peppermint magic.

I missed my vampire BFF. Before he'd seemingly gone to ground in the spring, we were still texting fairly often. But even then, he'd had duties that kept him elsewhere. Secrets, maybe, based on his infrequent texts over the last few months. They felt veiled, even for him. Though I knew that when Kett wanted to share, when it became important, he would tell me.

As we neared the fork in the path at Kits Pool, Kandy glanced up. "I'm just going to jog ahead to Pearl's. I'll meet you back at the apartment."

"Hopefully I'll be asleep by then."

Kandy flashed a grin my way. "Unless your dragon is waiting for you. He'll like all the extra-tasty magic you're carrying from the grid casting."

I shook my head, grinning.

Kandy slipped the second strap of the backpack over her other shoulder. Then, continuing along the seawall, she took off in a loping jog without another word.

I veered left with a sigh. Truthfully, I wouldn't have minded getting a look at the magic running through Rochelle's map in Gran's rec room. But I'd be cranky without at least a few hours of sleep before baking. And no one liked a crabby baker, least of all me.

I paused at the crosswalk at Cornwall, waiting for the light traffic to clear without bothering to press the walk button. And as I did, the shadows in the weeping birch tree to my right shifted, transforming into a nebulous figure that only I could sense or see.

The taste of burnt cinnamon toast teased my senses.

A shadow leech.

A being created through the melding of some sort of demon and multiple human sorcerers—or, more specifically, the souls of those sorcerers. The leeches were all but immortal, which was vaguely appropriate, since they were fueled by the life essence of immortality seekers. All of them led and sacrificed willingly by Shailaja.

There was only one shadow leech left now. Specifically, the dark cloud of malcontent roosting in the fork of the lowest tree limb. Its clawed wings were folded tightly against its body as it watched me warily with slitted blood-red eyes. Soon it would flash its needle-like teeth and chitter at me demandingly.

And I couldn't bring myself to kill it.

I was already pretty certain that the stark restrictions I had placed on the leech's diet had forced it to somehow absorb the only other two that had survived our siege of the tomb of the phoenix. I hadn't seen the other leeches in months, and the magic of the sole survivor had intensified enough to manifest a unique taste—as well as the blood-red eyes and the ability to hold a physical, though still shady, form.

The creature was drawn to me. Bound to my will—or, more specifically, to the power I'd stolen from Shailaja after taking her head. Taking her life.

A year and a half had passed since then, and I was still pending trial for the blood alchemy that I'd performed at the far seer's behest. Chi Wen had made it impossible for me to refuse the collection of the power that had flowed in Shailaja's veins—counting on the fact that I had wanted to keep on living myself.

But the murder? I had to take responsibility for that on my own, along with the repercussions.

I reached down, lightly stroking my jade knife in its invisible sheath to draw the leech's attention.

The shadow demon froze. It knew what I could do with that knife—and it wasn't simply about vanquishing the creature. After consulting with a witch versed in summoning and a necromancer, I had ascertained that the leech couldn't actually be vanquished or banished back into whatever dimension the demon-sourced part of it had originally been pulled from. Its demonic makeup was too intertwined with the life essence of the sorcerer who'd been willingly sacrificed in order to allow the demon entry into this world. Or multiple sorcerers, as might have been the case with the leech currently perched in the branches of the birch tree.

Though the shadow leeches were practically indestructible and capable of replenishing their magic almost instantly, that wasn't the same as true immortality.

Because I could kill them. Shred them, separate and absorb their magic into my knife, necklace, or katana. Or, if I was feeling especially insane, I could take their power for myself, as I had done with Shailaja. As I wanted to swear I would never do again. Except I'd learned the hard way exactly what I was capable of doing when those I loved, those who were under my protection, were threatened.

Lines had been crossed. 'Never' wasn't a concept I could fully embrace anymore. At least not if I didn't want to be a complete hypocrite.

Perhaps there was nothing that couldn't be destroyed given the right circumstances…or the right weapon. I touched my necklace, currently wound only once around my neck so that it hung to just above my belly button. Besides the wedding rings that I had diligently collected over years for the traces of residual magic they held, the heavy gold chain was now home to the instruments of assassination. And I was the wielder. Capable of killing creatures that were otherwise immortal.

The leech slid back into the deep shadows of the tree, slinking away from me as though it could feel the shift in my mood. And I didn't doubt that it could. The dreadful magic that had called it forth and bound it to a human soul resided in me now...completely absorbed until it had become indistinguishable from my own power. The magic of a rogue dragon, daughter of the former treasure keeper.

Brushing away the useless guilt that had intruded on my otherwise lovely evening, I loosened my hold on my necklace. I dug into my jeans for the three flat pieces of sea glass that I'd taken to carrying with me since the leeches had followed me to Vancouver. They were always in my pocket, along with any gold coins I pilfered from Warner's stash. Roughly the size of a misshapen quarter, each of the blue, green, and brown shards had been smoothed by the sea, then imbued with my magic. Yes, by simply being in my pocket.

I stepped to the side of the path, carefully balancing the pieces of sea glass on the top rail of the chain-link fence that ran between the park and the busy street.

The shadow leech shifted forward, peering eagerly through the hanging branches over my shoulder at my offering.

"Stay away from the grid magic, leech," I murmured. Then I jogged across the road, leaving the sea glass and the residual it contained behind. Feeding the leech as I would a feral cat.

I had murdered its former master, after all. It was my responsibility now.

# Chapter Two

*I* continued jogging up the steep hill, running all the way up to West Fourth Avenue in the hopes of burning off the rest of the tasty residual energy I was still carrying with me. So I could sleep. By the time I turned left into the alley off Vine Street and caught sight of the bakery door, a light sweat was beading my forehead. I slowed as I approached, already anticipating the comforting weight of the blood wards slipping across my skin as I stepped into my nirvana—

A thick parchment envelope appeared before me with a burst of smoky dragon magic, slapping against my chest before I could duck out of the way.

Oh, crappity crap.

The other shoe had just dropped.

I snatched the envelope, not wanting anyone who might have been looking out of the apartment building backing onto the alley to notice me staring at it—while it hung suspended in midair.

I immediately recognized the handwriting scrawled across the front of what I was fairly certain was a summons to appear before the Guardian Council.

*Jade Godfrey.*
*Wielder of the Instruments of Assassination.*

Pulou. The treasure keeper. My former boss and general asshole. Well, at least he had been since I'd retrieved my knife, necklace, and katana without his permission, and had inadvertently claimed the instruments of assassination at the same time. He didn't trust me, believing that I'd colluded with Chi Wen, the far seer, to kill Shailaja and take her power along with the magical artifacts.

To be fair, when Pulou had locked me up in one of the magical dampening cells he housed in his territory of Antarctica, his brain might still have been scrambled by the centipedes that Shailaja had unleashed against him.

But mitigating circumstances or not, I was holding firmly to my grudge. I didn't like my loyalty being questioned. Kandy, Kett, Warner, and Drake had almost died collecting the instruments—all at the treasure keeper's behest.

The envelope started to vibrate in my hand. I knew that if I didn't open it voluntarily, it would explode all over me. Then I'd be stuck baking with the taste of Pulou's black-tea-and-heavy-cream magic choking me all morning.

I glanced mournfully at the back door of the bakery.

I'd been so close.

I pressed my finger to the golden seal, noting the dragon image within the wax. It was reminiscent of the tattoo that had once bound Warner to the instruments.

The envelope unfurled. The message contained within was deceptively simple.

*You are summoned.*
*Council Chambers of the Guardian Nine.*

Damn it all to hell.

I needed sleep. I was supposed to bake. And my Gran was hosting a freaking engagement party for Warner and me that night. A trip to the nexus—where time had its own way of doing things—and being questioned by the nine most powerful Adepts in the world wasn't going to fit into my tight schedule.

I refolded the envelope, tucking it into my back pocket and reaching for the door handle. The welcoming magic of the wards slid across my hand. Stepping into the dark kitchen, I almost missed the three pieces of sea glass carefully placed on the threshold.

I collected the glass fragments, which were now devoid of magic, and tucked them into my front pocket. The shadow leech had siphoned off the magic, then had left the glass for me to find. The exchange was a game we played every couple of days.

Shutting the door behind me, I almost turned right up the stairs and retreated into my apartment. Almost gave into the impulse to bury myself beneath my goose-down duvet and ignore the summons.

Instead, I stepped forward in the dark, placing my hand on the cool steel of my workstation. With my other hand, I wound my necklace around my neck twice more so that it lay tightly across my collarbone. Then I reached out with my dowser senses, first scanning the footprint of the bakery, then upward into the apartments above, and finding all that space empty of magical signatures.

Warner wasn't waiting for me.

Sigh.

I stepped into my office, unable to justify delaying the inevitable—and pissy enough that I had no intention of changing out of my printed T-shirt and jeans and into more appropriate attire for an audience with the guardian nine. Whatever that appropriate attire might have been. Not bothering with the lights, I opened the large standing safe tucked behind the door. Then I retrieved my katana from its magically fortified depths.

Strapping the weapon with which I'd decapitated a dragon over my back, I locked the safe, then crossed back through the kitchen and into my pantry.

The delectable scents of cocoa, vanilla, and spices clung to me as I passed through, opening the door to the basement and descending the open-tread stairs. Standing on the dirt floor before the portal, I reached out to the magic slumbering in the brick-and-concrete wall underneath my kitchen. It responded eagerly, twirling around my raised hand.

After I had claimed the instruments of assassination and left the nexus in the throes of a childish temper tantrum, I'd realized that the portal magic felt different. I had absorbed the magic of the daughter of the former treasure keeper, and that magic—now embodied within the current treasure keeper—had originally created the portal I was standing before.

I could have closed the gateway to the guardian nexus then, but I didn't. And though I hadn't crossed through it myself for over a year and a half, Warner and Drake used the portal often. As far as I was aware, they were the only dragons who knew the portal existed at all, in addition to Pulou himself. I had never caught anyone else, not even my father, using it.

Done contemplating the past and incapable of doing anything about the immediate future, I stepped through the portal magic. My right foot fell upon the white marble of the nexus without any pause or shift in transition. The passage was seamless, almost instantaneous.

Nine pillars of gold, nine ornately carved doors, and all the overwhelming magic that came with the nexus assaulted all my senses. For a moment, I was blinded by it. Then, buffered by my necklace and my own acquired immunity, the intense magic settled and my sight cleared.

A broad-shouldered figure swathed in black leather waited for me at the very center of the round room. He lifted his dark-blond head, pinning me with his fierce gaze. Surrounded by the garish gold of the nexus, his eyes were more blue than green. A half-healed wound marred the right side of his face and neck. A deep slash, most likely inflicted by a demon of some power. Because anything else would have healed almost instantly.

My heart skipped a beat.

The taste of deeply dark chocolate, sweet-stewed cherries, and dense whipped cream—delectable black forest cake—flooded my mouth, almost as though he had reached out and grabbed me with his magic.

My knees weakened.

Then I was in his arms, stretched up on my toes, wrapped around his shoulders and neck, and pressing my lips against his fervently.

Warner.

Mine.

He wrapped his hands around my face, tucking his long fingers into the thick curls at my temples and softening the kiss enough to whisper, "Jade …"

I opened my eyes, meeting his heated gaze. Then I hovered my hand over the vicious, practically-still-bleeding gouge across his cheek and neck. "You're hurt."

Warner shrugged, pressing his lips lightly against mine. Loving touches, full of promise. "The blade was unusual."

"A knife cut you like this? How is that possible?"

"Magic I hadn't confronted before. Wielded by an elf."

"An elf …" That was something I hadn't expected to hear. "As in 'worse than vampires?'" I remembered the exchange I'd had with Warner when we first met, in which I joked about elves, having believed up to that point that they were harmless mythical creatures.

Apparently they weren't either of those things.

"It was nothing your father and I couldn't handle. A few dimensional interlopers at a rift that Pulou had previously sealed. I will not be caught so off guard next time."

I closed my eyes, kissing him lingeringly. My desire to wring every last bit of information from him warred with my determination to keep my distance from anything having to do with the guardians. Focusing instead on the heat of his skin and the press of his lips, I tangled my fingers in the hair at the back of his neck—and realized that it was longer than it should have been. I'd seen him only three days before.

Unable to let the idea of the elves and the wound completely go, I broke the kiss but not the embrace. "How long have you been gone?"

Warner shook his head. "Feels like weeks. But it's not important now. Not when I've got you in my arms." He kissed me again, somehow searing everything he didn't want to talk about into my lips.

I wasn't completely surprised at the discrepancy in the passage of time. He had been with my father, and time moved oddly around all of the nine guardians. I opened my mouth, flicking my tongue against his playfully. But Warner didn't want to tease. He slipped his hand underneath the back of my T-shirt, seeking skin-to-skin contact. His tasty magic followed in the wake of his touch, and I melted into the moment.

"Wait," he murmured. "I didn't miss Pearl's party, did I?"

"It's tonight. Hours away."

"Ah, good. That's good." He slipped a hand down to cup my ass and press me against him. Unfortunately, he got a handful of the parchment in my back pocket, which suddenly reminded me that we were groping each other in the middle of the nexus.

I sighed. "I've been summoned."

"I know." Warner groaned lightly, then forced himself to step away.

I allowed my fingers to traverse the muscled steel of his arms, then tangled them with his. When I met his gaze, he was looking at me steadily.

"I won't let them keep you, Jade."

I nodded, trying to ignore the doubts that flared up to nag at me.

He pressed a kiss to my hand, then to my palm. "They'll rule in your favor."

I nodded, more vigorously this time. "Where is this damn council chamber, then?"

Warner nodded toward the archway that led to the residential wing of the nexus. If you could call it a wing. The architecture of the guardian headquarters was entirely capricious.

"Really?"

"You have to present yourself and it will open."

"What, really?" I groaned. "Stand in front of the archway and beg for entry?"

Warner stifled a laugh. "And you won't be able to bring the weapons."

"I'm the wielder of the instruments of assassination," I said indignantly. Then I touched the hilt of my sword over my right shoulder. "And the dragon slayer."

"Exactly." Warner sounded far too amused. "I think the T-shirt makes that pretty clear, though. Don't you?"

I glanced down at the printing emblazoned across my chest. *Never mind the cupcakes. I can totally kick your ass.* Then I looked up at Warner.

He wagged his eyebrows at me, leering.

"Fine. But this is the second freaking time tonight." As if summoned by my acquiescence, a rough-hewn wooden sideboard with carved legs appeared a few feet in front of the archway.

"Second time?"

"I had to take them off to help raise the grid." Eyeing the table distrustfully, I caught a whiff of lemon verbena-scented magic. Blossom's magic—the brownie who had pretty much declared the bakery and my apartment her territory, along with Gran's house and Warner's family home in Stockholm, though he didn't live there full-time.

"Were the witches successful in the casting?"

"Yep. It was quite the high."

"I'm sorry I missed it," he murmured, letting me know with another lusty look that he meant seeing me surrounded by the magic, rather than observing the actual process.

I laughed, pressing myself against him and darting my tongue just through his lips. But before he could close the embrace, I slipped away, already pulling the katana off over my head and shoulders.

There were very few people I would trust to guard my weapons, but Blossom easily made the short list. Mostly because the brownie was crazy possessive, and the only Adept I knew who could move around me without my knowledge. And if she could do that to me, with my ability to taste magic, I had no doubt that anyone who wanted to lay hands on my necklace or my knife wouldn't be able to track her either.

So, dutifully disengaged from my delectable fiance, I shed my artifacts one at a time, laying them across the pockmarked table.

Warner set his curved knife—another artifact of my own construction, which could cut through any magic—next to my jade blade. As he did, he paused to brush his fingers across two of the rune-scribed, age-darkened gold wedding rings attached to my necklace. Dragon magic stirred beneath his touch. Guardian magic, actually. One of the two rings had belonged to his mother, who had been the guardian of Northern Europe when she had Warner and was married to his father.

"Blossom won't let anyone take it," I said.

Warner raised the same two fingers, brushing the magic that he'd stirred against my lips. Desire shot through me so intensely that I had to struggle to contain a groan.

"Who could possibly take anything from you, Jade? Who could claim anything you didn't want to give?"

Feeling as though the only thing that held me upright was the featherlight touch of his fingers on my bottom lip, all I could do was stare deeply into Warner's eyes. The gold of his dragon magic simmered at the edges of the starburst of blue around his pupils.

No matter the pending trial, no matter the very public location, I wanted him more than I had ever wanted him before. The feeling was so acute that it held me frozen in place. Forcing myself to act, I nipped playfully at his fingertips, claiming the magic still dancing on his skin.

He laughed huskily.

Then a large double door appeared in the archway on the other side of the table. An Asian-inspired dragon motif stood out in gold relief from the dark wood—nine dragons set within what appeared to be fire, water, earth, and air, and with different gemstones denoting each of their eyes.

Warner dropped his hand, stepping behind me as I crossed around the table without another word. I was ready to face the guardians. I was ready to answer their questions. And I was certainly prepared to stand my ground.

Yes, I had killed Shailaja.

Yes, I had taken her magic and had avoided dying myself.

Yes, I was the dragon slayer. The wielder of the instruments of assassination. I had claimed my destiny. I'd been presented with a choice. And I'd chosen.

The door before me opened of its own accord. My step faltered as the room beyond came into view.

The decor of the chamber of the Guardian Council echoed the gaudy gold-and-white marble of the nexus. The room was so vast that I felt quite certain its outer edges didn't actually exist in this reality…or dimension…or wherever the hell the nexus existed at all.

But oddly, for all its size, the room was empty except for the nine ornate chairs sitting on a three-foot-high rectangular platform. I had the weirdest feeling that there should have been an altar standing before the chairs. But why, or what purpose it would have served, I didn't know.

Each high-backed throne was ornately carved of what appeared to be solid gold, and covered in velvet fabric of various shades. I felt certain that if I could compare each chair to the nine doors of the nexus, I'd find that they matched, one pair each. Fleur de lis for the portal that led to the territories of Suanmi the fire breather in Western Europe. First Nations engraving, matching the door through which I'd just arrived, for the territory of Haoxin the guardian of North America. An Incan or Mayan design for Qiuniu's territory of South America, and so forth.

I also had a sinking, sickening feeling that I'd seen this room, this chamber, before. Not that I'd been there exactly, but that I had seen something terrible take place there. Something that floated in the back of my mind like a memory that wasn't entirely my own.

A future unmade …

The vision Chi Wen had shared with me in the phoenix's tomb …

That vision was the reason the far seer had manipulated events—or, as he'd put it, simply tightened the timeline in which I was fated to claim the instruments of assassination and become the dragon slayer.

Feeling a little unsteady without my necklace and knife, I reached back and brushed my fingers against Warner's forearm. He caught my hand and squeezed reassuringly, leaning forward to whisper in my ear, "We don't have to wait here—"

"Hello!" A perky voice sounded out from behind us. "What are you looking at?"

Haoxin, dressed head to toe in black flexible body armor, shouldered past us to peer across the chamber before I could turn around. Finding the room empty, the petite blond guardian turned back and grinned at me. "Dowser! I didn't recognize you without …" She waved a hand in a gesture that encompassed me from head to toe instead of finishing her sentence.

"Guardian," I said politely, despite the fact that she had somehow managed to sneak up on me, and that her mere presence was oddly increasing the nauseating sense of deja vu I was fighting. "I've been summoned to trial."

"What? When? Yesterday?"

I fished the summons from my back pocket.

But Haoxin shook her head at my offering. "How long have you been in the nexus? Pulou sent you another notice. We've exonerated you, though I still really don't see why there was a trial set at all. But then, I'm only one voice among nine."

My brain stuttered over the information the guardian had just casually dropped on me. "Exonerated?"

"Then why the summons?" Warner's tone was pissy, but he quickly softened it. "Guardian?"

"There's no need to growl at me, sentinel. Wires must have been crossed. The far seer spoke. Showed us the vision he'd been concerned about. We voted."

Haoxin stepped closer to me. But she was eyeing my necklace on the table behind me, staring as if it might have been a poisonous viper. Which, from the perspective of a guardian, it was. Her hair was braided tightly against her head, and the hilt of her sword protruded over her left shoulder. The guardian of North America was prepared to kick ass.

I struggled to quash an immediate and intense need to ask her about what she was preparing to face, to offer my own sword, to run into battle at her side.

A wicked smile spread across her face, revealing slightly turned-in eye teeth. A tiny imperfection that somehow only highlighted her otherworldliness. She raised her blue-eyed gaze to meet mine, and the taste of spicy tomato and basil magic flooded my mouth.

I steeled myself for whatever request was about to accompany her look, reminding myself that Haoxin's secondary title was 'reckless and adventurous.' Reminding myself that I had no idea what powers—above and beyond practically being a demigod—accompanied that designation.

"I like the T-shirt," she said, nodding down toward it.

I stared at her dumbly, completely thrown.

"I want one. Except sub espresso for the cupcakes … or something along those lines."

"Oh, ah … my friend Kandy designs them. I'll let her know you'd like one."

"The werewolf? With the Herakles cuffs?"

I nodded, not certain that Haoxin had ever spoken to Kandy—other than the time the guardian had found her, Warner, and me all floating in the ocean off the Abaco Islands before we collected the first instrument of assassination. Just hours before Kandy almost drowned … for the second time.

Haoxin's smile waned as her gaze once again fell upon my necklace laid across the table. "Take up your weapons, Jade."

Something terrible lurked underneath her command, but I eagerly stepped forward. I made a show of lifting each artifact from the table, rather than showing off and simply calling them to me.

The guardian's shoulders settled as I twined the necklace around my neck three times. "Better. It was making me itchy." She reached up and touched her neck.

And then seeing her framed there in the doorway, the nine throne chairs behind her, the sense of having been in this moment or a moment just like it hit me so hard that it took every other thought with it.

"I … I … I've been here before …"

I wove my fingers through the wedding rings on my necklace, feeling the magic of the braids writhe underneath my hand as I did so. Blinking, I forced myself back to the present. Trying to recall the vision Chi Wen had shown me was somehow warping my actual sight.

Haoxin was watching me too closely.

The magic of the instruments of assassination subsided, melding with the general tenor of the necklace's power.

I inhaled, realizing that I'd been holding my breath.

Haoxin nodded. "Chi Wen said he'd shown you, but that you might not remember. He had to bring a oracle from my territory into the chamber to relay the vision himself."

The guardian's words sank in like a body blow. "From your territory…Rochelle?" A fierce wave of anger rushed through me. "The far seer snatched up Rochelle, who is under my protection, and dragged her here…to be…used as a …"

Hearing what I was saying, I clamped my mouth shut. A little too late.

Haoxin narrowed her eyes. "Snatched up? While in service to the guardian dragons? How is that possible?"

I shook my head, not at all certain how to mitigate my blunder. Any of the guardians would have thought that Chi Wen had bestowed a great honor upon Rochelle, not realizing how terrifying being brought before the nine of them might be.

Though since I'd heard nothing about it, apparently Rochelle hadn't been terribly upset. And the far seer acting as the oracle's mentor was actually a relationship formed at my behest—though I was pretty sure that Chi Wen would never do anything that didn't ultimately benefit the guardian nine.

In any case, I had to get my protective instincts under control. Vancouver was witch territory, though ultimately within Haoxin's purview, of course. But either way, it wasn't for me to take exception to guardian business. I wasn't interested in going toe-to-toe with any of them.

Haoxin stepped closer. "I'm not certain how the far seer held on to the vision after … the future shifted." The something terrible that had lurked beneath her words before was now reflected in her expression.

Calling my knife to me, I clenched the hilt of the weapon, unable to stop myself from doing so.

Haoxin reached out as if to brush her fingers along my necklace. But then she paused.

The taste of Warner's magic intensified, as though he had tensed, ready to move.

I felt trapped, suspended on the edge of chaos. My mind was warring with memories that weren't my own. Images of Drake, looking not much older than he was now. Standing over Haoxin, who was arrayed on the altar that I remembered having seen set down before the nine ornate chairs. The thrones that currently stood framed in the doorway of the chamber behind the guardian, who was standing before me alive and well.

In the shared vision, I had seen one of the instruments of assassination—the five-colored silk braids—coiled around Haoxin's neck. Except she couldn't have been a guardian anymore, not if her death had manifested in Chi Wen's vision. Not if Drake was set to take the mantel of Haoxin, though he was the far seer's apprentice.

The recollection was hazy and disconcerting, though. Something I wasn't meant to remember but could never really forget. A future unmade.

"You hold my death, dragon slayer," Haoxin whispered. "Twined there, around your neck …"

I swallowed, moistening my lips in order to speak. "Like a pretty trinket."

"Yes," she hissed.

Warner shifted in my peripheral vision. His knife was in his hand, his hooded gaze on Haoxin.

I raised my hand to the side, releasing my grip on my knife and holding him off with a gesture.

"That's a future the far seer thwarted, guardian. Isn't it?" My voice wasn't as steady as I would have liked.

"For Drake, perhaps." She dropped her hand, raising her fierce gaze to meet mine. "But we may still meet, wielder. I will not be as easy to kill as a deranged, power-hungry dragon."

"There was nothing easy about killing Shailaja." My tone edged closer to steely than was likely advisable when dealing with a guardian dragon.

"But you've been training since, haven't you? With the instruments? You didn't have them at your disposal then."

I didn't answer. Haoxin's gaze flicked to my katana where it rested on the table.

Then she stepped back.

"It would be foolish not to train to wield what is yours to command. Wouldn't it, sentinel?" Haoxin threw the question at Warner without looking at him.

"It would," he said calmly, slipping his knife into the sheath built into the right thigh of his dragon leathers. The deep slash that had marred his face just a few minutes before had almost completely healed.

I knew that I should have kept my mouth shut, but I couldn't let Haoxin's veiled accusation go unanswered. "I have no reason to want you dead, guardian."

"Your ability to absorb magic might yet turn into a need, Jade Godfrey."

Warner opened his mouth angrily, but I cut him off. "We don't know each other very well, guardian."

Surprise flashed across Haoxin's face. "Do you hope to woo me with cupcakes, dowser? As you have Drake, Suanmi, and Qiuniu?"

"I don't think it's the cupcakes that interest the healer," Warner said snidely.

Haoxin threw her head back and laughed.

And just like that, the tension that had been constricting my chest and weighing down my shoulders eased.

"The healer flirts with danger. We all do," the guardian said, still chuckling. "First you were the warrior's daughter, then you were the beloved of the sentinel, and now you are the wielder of the instruments of assassination. To flirt with you is to flirt with our own mortality."

"Plus the cupcakes," Warner said dryly.

"Exactly. You owe me an espresso, Jade. And now a T-shirt, if your werewolf provides. I shall come to collect."

"Fantastic," I said, trying for honest exuberance and completely failing.

Haoxin chuckled. "We'll agree to leave the future where it lies. For now, the sentinel and I have some incursions to clean up."

Warner inclined his head dutifully. "The warrior has given me leave for a few hours. A reprieve."

Haoxin glanced between the two of us, smirking. "Fine. Have Pulou open a portal for you when you are ready to join me. After your reprieve." She hit the last word with all the snark she could muster. "I'm certain the cupcakes will be invigorating."

"I believe we've already decided I'm more than simply a treat," I said.

That gave the guardian pause.

I kept my gaze locked to hers.

"I apologize, Jade," she said, nodding thoughtfully. "I'm apparently still disconcerted by the vision the far seer shared. I should be thanking you. Even if the future is only forestalled, your claiming of Shailaja's magic at Chi Wen's behest has only benefited me." She smiled tightly. "We are dragons of an age. You, Drake, the sentinel, and me. We are the future of the guardians."

Haoxin stepped around me, suddenly appearing before, then opening, the door to North America without another word.

As the guardian disappeared into the portal magic, I glanced over at Warner, letting out a relieved sigh.

"An apology from a guardian," he said. "Unprecedented."

"We are dragons of an age," I murmured. "Suanmi said the same thing, though she didn't include Haoxin in the group."

"When you were wooing the fire breather with cupcakes." The sentinel curled his lips, amused.

I snorted. "Yeah, I'm pretty sure I was the one being seduced."

"And yet it was me you fell into bed with," he said huskily.

I smiled. Warner had skillfully skipped over the arguments, the tears, and the declarations that had come between those two points, and I had no need to recall them either. "Take me there now?"

He had me up over his shoulder with his hand firmly planted on my ass before I could finish the question. I was laughing madly, my curls brushing the back of his knees as he carried me effortlessly through the portal to the bakery.

There would be time to analyze the conversation with Haoxin and the exoneration of the charges Pulou had brought against me later. Hopefully after a couple of hours of mindless pleasure with a man, a dragon, who adored me—cupcakes, deadly magic, and all.

Warner set me down on the dirt floor of the bakery basement. The portal magic snapped shut behind us, leaving us in the dark. But before I could turn away, climb the stairs to the pantry, and pull my dragon into bed, he cupped my face in his hands and kissed me softly.

"Jade …" He kissed me a second time, and a shudder of relief ran through him.

A sharp pinpoint of pain shot through my chest. He'd been worried about the trial—and then the possibility of having to protect me from Haoxin.

Mimicking him, I pressed my hands to his face, brushing my thumbs across his cheeks. Smiling with my heart so full that it actually felt heavy in my chest, I kissed him back. "I don't make it easy for you, sixteenth century."

Warner let out a shuddering laugh, his fingers slipping back through my hair in a slow caress.

I nibbled on his ear teasingly—but once again, my dragon didn't want to be playful. He ran his hands up my back, slipping my katana off and dropping it to the floor. Then his right hand was up under my T-shirt, opening my bra and flicking my nipple while he unhooked my belt and unzipped my jeans with his left hand.

I moaned at his sudden escalation, but I had no time to get my breath back as his mouth crashed over mine and his touches grew more intense.

He took a half step back, loosening the closures on his leather pants. But when he tried to remove my jeans, they got caught up on the sheath strapped to my right hip. So instead of fiddling with the strap and removing my knife, he simply tore my left pant leg off, leaving the right in place.

I started to protest, teasingly. But then he did the same to my underwear, had me up against the brick wall, and was buried deeply within me before I could find the words.

"Warner …" I groaned.

As if satisfied by being as close as humanly possible to me, his grip on my hips eased. He pressed another soft kiss to my swollen lips. "I'll replace the jeans. And the pretty panties."

"You'd better believe you will."

"I've missed you."

Again, I stopped myself from asking where exactly he'd been. Or what he'd been doing. Or why his hair was longer than it should have been after the three days that had passed for me. Instead, I tightened my legs around his waist.

"You have me, Warner. You're back, and you have me."

"Jade," he whispered, slowly picking up the pace of his thrusts. "My Jade."

I laughed breathlessly. "I guess we aren't going to make it to the bed?"

"That's next."

"After cupcakes, yes?"

"Oh, yes," he groaned.

I smiled into the heated skin of his neck, then just hung on for the ride. Even if it meant I didn't get a wink of sleep before my baking shift, I most certainly didn't mind letting Warner steer on occasion.

Normally, I didn't believe that cupcakes belonged in bed, with the risk of crumbs and all. But for Warner, I made an exception. Or maybe it was him making the exception to my own appetites. And satisfying those appetites.

Multiple times.

With snacks in between.

Whatever the case, I found a half-dozen of my newest creations in the fridge in the bakery on our way up to the apartment—*Elation in a Cup*, a dense but moist peanut butter cake with a swirl of chocolate buttercream, and *Delirium in a Cup*, a chocolate-peanut butter cake generously topped with creamy chocolate-peanut butter icing. I then proceeded to tear each cupcake in half, eating the top half myself while feeding the bottom cake half to Warner.

Sixteenth century didn't utter one word of protest over my hogging all the buttercream to myself.

Of course, the fact that we'd switched positions—with me on top and moving achingly slowly—might have been slightly distracting for him.

And it wasn't like I was a total monster. When I halved the final cupcake, I went top to bottom.

When Warner finally succumbed to the exhaustion that I was fairly certain had slowed his healing, falling into a deep sleep sprawled across my bed, I took a moment to simply watch him. Then I dozed, curled up against his warmth.

I was woken abruptly about an hour later by a strange tickling sensation on the bottoms of my feet.

I sat up, carefully lifting Warner's hand off my hip. Whatever had disturbed me hadn't affected the sentinel. He continued to breathe deeply beside me.

Stirring my hand in the pile of ripped jeans and leather beside the bed, I called forth my knife. I stepped into the center of the dark room, naked except for my necklace.

Then I waited.

Magic tickled the bottoms of my feet again. I curled my toes on the worn hardwood of my bedroom floor as I tried to identify the power touching me. But it tasted of nothing. Almost as if …

… it was my own magic.

"The grid," I whispered.

Warner slid out of bed. One moment, he'd been deeply asleep. The next, he was standing beside me in the dark with his wicked knife in hand. Also naked.

I took a moment to leer at this display of manly prowess. "Nice look, sentinel."

He chuckled quietly. "You are wanton, woman."

"For you."

He scanned the bedroom, serious again. "What woke you? I felt …" He trailed off.

He meant the instruments. He would have felt my magic shift and the instruments responding. Though Pulou had removed the spell that had once tied Warner to the map that revealed the instruments of assassination, he was still the sentinel of the instruments. And since the magical artifacts and I were one, Warner was therefore my sentinel. The sentinel of the wielder of the instruments of assassination.

It might have been an ungainly title, but thankfully it wasn't a sore subject between us. I was, however, terribly glad that he had proposed and that I had accepted—eventually—before any question could have formed in my mind as to whether Warner was interested in me. That he was in love with me, and me alone. And that he wasn't with me, or in my bed, out of any sense of duty.

"I believe I've inadvertently tied myself to the grid," I said with a sigh.

He chuckled. "Of course you have."

"Hey!" I reached down and retrieved my bra and T-shirt from the pile of clothing at our feet. "Maybe it happened to all the witches. Maybe I'm not the only one with itchy feet."

"Itchy feet?"

"Yep. You'd better get dressed, sentinel. I'm fairly certain I need to go for a walk."

He tugged on his leather pants without protest, and I took a moment to slowly steal a full-body caress—from his shoulder to his groin—before he got them done up. A girl could only stand so close to such majesty without touching for so long.

He grinned at me.

"I'd like to spend some time fortifying your weapon," I said, changing the subject. "Before you head out to help Haoxin."

"I assume you mean my knife. Since you just had a handful of my other so-called weapon, and it is thus well fortified."

I laughed. Apparently, my dragon was feeling playful again. A warmth spread through my chest at the thought that just by being with each other, we could affect our moods so positively. Maybe that was part of being in love.

Still grinning, he slipped the aforementioned blade into its built-in sheath while I attempted to find a clean pair of jeans. The itchy feet were intensifying, and I was becoming antsy about where the feeling might be leading me.

# Chapter Three

Slipping out of the shadows of the concrete stairs that led to both of our apartments, Kandy joined Warner and me as we hit the sidewalk on West Fourth Avenue. Though it was just after 3:00 A.M., I'd texted, expecting her to be sleeping. But if she had been in bed, she dressed a lot quicker than I did. Her attention was currently riveted to her phone. Texting. Again.

She was also wearing the purple dinosaur backpack cinched tightly over both shoulders.

Warner eyed the bag. "Interesting fashion statement, wolf."

Kandy lifted her lip in a snarl but didn't otherwise rise to the bait.

Compelled by the magic that was now heating the undersides of my feet—even through my shoes—I jogged across the empty but well-lit street, darted south along Vine Street, then turned left on West Fifth Avenue. Warner and Kandy followed at my heels without question.

Just a block to either side of West Fourth, the shopping district gave way to walk-up apartment buildings, converted triplexes, and the occasional stand-alone Craftsman. The narrow lots were teeming with rhododendrons, cherry trees, and laurel hedges. Both sides of the street were lined with vehicles of all shapes and sizes, mostly permit parking only.

"Jade," Kandy said, clicking the remote locks on a hulking SUV I was about to pass on my left. The headlights flashed, momentarily destroying my night vision.

"It might not work like that," I said over my shoulder, continuing to jog. "My feet might need to be in contact with the ground."

Ignoring me, Kandy climbed into the SUV while Warner stayed at my shoulder. We could jog two abreast without issue. Dark homes blurred past us as we silently and swiftly crossed Yew Street, continuing east. Then the hulking SUV roared up beside us, Kandy at the wheel.

The werewolf matched our pace, hissing through the open passenger window. "Mountain View Cemetery, you twit."

"What?"

"Itchy feet is just a weird side effect. Only affecting you, as far as we've figured. Pearl says the map is lit up at the cemetery."

"Lovely," I grumbled, darting between parked cars and hopping into the SUV before Kandy had pulled to a stop. "I love weird side effects and unknown magic lighting up cemeteries with equal fervor."

Warner climbed into the back, stretching across the seats and closing his eyes.

Kandy glanced over her shoulder at him, then picked up speed along the dark, narrow street. "Nice to have you back, dragon."

Warner responded with a grunt. "Wolf."

Kandy grinned at me toothily. "Wore him out, did you?"

"I wish it was just me," I murmured.

"Oh? Something up in guardian land?"

"You know I'm not interested enough to ask questions."

Kandy snorted doubtfully.

"Oh, and they dropped the charges … or maybe voted in my favor. Anyway, the guardians exonerated me of Shailaja's beheading. Though you know it was the magic absorption that really pissed off Pulou. Plus Haoxin wants a T-shirt. Something about espresso."

"What?" Kandy cried, turning right onto Arbutus, then speeding through the blocks up to Broadway far too quickly. "A T-shirt?" Then she grinned at me happily, in a way that had nothing to do with the guardian of North America's demand and everything to do with me being free and clear. According to the guardians, at least.

"Yeah," I said softly. "I'm pretty pleased about not being locked away in that magic-dampening cube room again."

Warner grumbled from the back seat as Kandy ignored the red light and veered left onto Broadway. "That was never going to happen, dowser."

My itchy feet seriously disagreed with Kandy's choice of route. "Wouldn't Sixteenth Avenue be better?"

Kandy snarled pissily, executing a sharp U-turn in the middle of the four-lane street. My forehead glanced against the side window, but my feet were pleased when we turned back onto Arbutus, heading south again.

"So far, this grid thing is utterly delightful," I said.

"It always is with you, Jade," Kandy snarked. Then she tilted her head thoughtfully as she murmured, "Something with espresso …"

Warner chuckled to himself in the back seat.

I grinned, gazing out the window at the mixture of apartment buildings, businesses, and restaurants that populated this revitalized section of Kitsilano. Being compelled to speed off in the deep dark of the early morning to investigate unknown magic with my BFF and my fiance at my side?

Well, it didn't get any better than that, did it?

Though I did miss Kett.

A zombie was blocking the almost-hidden side entrance to Mountain View Cemetery. No gate between it and me. Just a short set of concrete stairs and a path that cut through the unruly cedar hedges. Directly across from dozens of residential homes in the middle of the Riley Park neighborhood, about a fifteen-minute drive south of Kitsilano.

The memory of Hudson, the only other zombie I'd ever come face-to-face with—and the heartbreaking results of that confrontation—rushed back on me like a wave. Momentarily disconcerted, I paused to contemplate the rotting corpse, uncertain as to whether or not I should stab it in the head. It was wearing the remnants of a dark suit, a tie still tight at its neck, though the collar of its shirt had rotted away. I could see its teeth where its cheeks should have been, and it appeared to have lost its nose somewhere. Perhaps while crawling from the grave?

If you had asked me a moment earlier, I would have guessed that a grave-risen zombie would stink. But this one didn't.

Mountain View Cemetery occupied a huge amount of property west of Fraser Street and north of West Forty-First Avenue—two exceedingly busy streets, even at this early hour. Stretching easily ten city blocks north to south and four residential blocks east to west, the vast graveyard was surrounded by tightly packed homes on all sides.

Homes currently filled with slumbering, vulnerable people.

The zombie's jaw hinged open, and the taste of toasted-marshmallow magic rolled across my tongue. Then the voice of a sullen junior necromancer emanated from that rotting maw.

"I've got it under control, Jade."

Mory.

Morana Novak, to be specific. Pain in my ass, to be explicit.

I saw the junior necromancer every Friday at the bakery during a scheduled meeting with Gran, who was mentoring Mory in some fashion. At a casual glance, that mentoring appeared to be more about knitting than magic. But I fed Mory as many cupcakes as she would tolerate, occasionally adding the antique coins I'd collected from Warner to the necklace she always wore—after carrying them in my own pocket for a while to imbue them with my magic.

"Well," I said casually, "since I'm talking to a corpse, that appears to be in some doubt."

The zombie huffed indignantly, lurched into motion, and began to shamble deeper into the graveyard.

"That's all creepy as hell," Kandy muttered to my right.

Coming from a werewolf who could transform into a seven-foot-tall, three-inch-clawed monster, that was saying something. But I didn't disagree.

Warner appeared to be trying to choke back laughter that would normally be completely inappropriate. Except he was laughing at me rather than the zombie situation.

"Maybe you want to take another nap, sentinel," I said pertly.

He stifled the smile, nodding seriously. "I'll check the outer perimeter. To ascertain that the apocalypse isn't upon us. Despite your necromancer's insistence to the contrary."

I shot him a look for the sarcasm and the 'your necromancer' comment. "You do that."

He nodded curtly, dour faced now, then jogged off silently down the street. Almost instantly, he disappeared within the deep shadows next to the six-foot-tall cedar hedge that defined the edge of the property. Once there—and out of retaliation range—he started chuckling again.

I shook my head. "It's a complicated relationship, all right?"

"With the dragon?" Kandy asked, frowning.

I sighed. "No. The necromancer."

The green-haired werewolf snorted. "You don't have to tell me."

Glancing around for other walking dead, I entered the graveyard—completely begrudgingly. Mory shouldn't have been playing with corpses, even beyond the fact that it was seriously creepy. Because middle of the night or not, we were surrounded by family homes.

The zombie had shambled off toward the eastern side of the cemetery. Not that I needed to follow it closely. The taste of Mory's necromancy and the individual tenor of the magic embedded in her necklace intensified in that direction.

The fact that I had originally crafted Mory's necklace as a way to bar the ghost of her brother, Rusty, from draining his sister of her life essence was where the 'complicated' part of our interactions began.

Or actually, no.

The wedge that would always be stuck firmly between us went further back than that, by about three months. Three long, annoyingly eye-opening months, during which I had figured out—far too slowly and exceedingly late—that my foster sister, Sienna, and Mory's brother had teamed up to murder werewolves and drain them of their magic. They had used the trinkets I'd made as some sort of conduit.

Hudson had been one of those werewolves. And someone who I'd thought I might be able to truly care about.

Sienna had ultimately screwed over her partner in crime, sacrificing Rusty to fuel a blood-magic spell with the intent of foiling the investigation into the murders. Utilizing Rusty's latent necromancy powers, she had also raised Hudson as a zombie, nearly killing Kett in the process. Because magic had a twisted sense of humor, and apparently zombies trumped vampires.

Rusty's ghost had returned—or perhaps it had never left this plane of existence—in order to exact revenge. He'd tried to use Mory to get to Sienna. Nearly killing his own sister in the process.

And as if all that wasn't messy or guilt-riddled enough, Sienna had then kidnapped Mory, holding her for three months and siphoning off enough of her necromancy magic to raise three demons in London.

No matter that Sienna had died for her crimes. No matter that Rusty had been complicit, or that Mory ultimately came through it all—I still harbored the idea that the original kidnapping had been aimed at me. Even in retreat, and despite how Sienna had ultimately used Mory, my sister had wanted to prove that I couldn't protect anyone. Or at least not everyone. That I was never going to be quite strong enough. That I was always going to have to choose when it came down to it. Vanquish a demon but lose Mory ... rescue Mory but almost lose Kett ... and so forth.

Kandy, Drake, Kett, and I had saved Mory from being sacrificed that evening in London. But I couldn't give her back her brother, or the three months my sister had stolen from her. And that wasn't even getting into what she must have seen and experienced as she was dragged through Sienna's ongoing murder spree across Europe.

So yeah, I still wore the guilt. And feeding Mory while I continually fortified her necklace were the only things that eased it. The necromancer was a symbol of the hole in my heart. Damage that could only be shored up, never fully mended.

Something grabbed my ankle. I went down, managing to fling my arms out to break my fall but ending up with my forehead barely an inch from slamming into a gravestone. Teeth scored my leg, trying to gnaw through my last pair of clean jeans.

Served me right for wallowing in the past instead of focusing on the present.

I glanced back to see that a second zombie had crawled through the dark night between the tightly spaced headstones. It was crawling because apparently—reduced to bones and hanging bits of leathery skin—it had left its bottom half behind somewhere.

"Jesus Christ ..." I muttered.

Kandy started chortling. "All right there, dowser?"

I glared at her, snapping a kick with my free leg to the zombie's head that easily decapitated it. Its white skull spun off into the night.

Kandy lost it. She was full-on laughing, with her hands on her knees and everything.

I scrambled to my feet, brushing off my jeans as best I could. The toasted-marshmallow magic animating the corpse intensified. Then the zombie skeleton started crawling away, patting the ground frantically as if it were looking for a lost contact lens. Except, of course, it was looking for its head.

"Jesus freaking Christ," I muttered. "Now I'm going to have to find a freaking severed skull."

Kandy gave up the pretense of standing, falling to the ground and gasping for air between guffaws.

I shook my head at the werewolf, attempting and mostly failing to maintain a stern, adult demeanor myself. I was in charge. Well, technically, Kandy was in charge. But I couldn't let Mory walk all over me. No matter how much fun it would have been to kick the heads off more corpses, it was just wrong.

Scanning the graveyard for more grabby zombies and one decapitated head, I slowly moved toward the epicenter of Mory's necromancy. The legless corpse slithered ahead out of my sight, suddenly and disconcertingly mobile.

Even in the filtered moonlight, the landscape of the cemetery was exceedingly inconsistent. Large, low buildings occupied an eastern section of the property near Fraser Street. Rows upon rows of eclectic headstones, including some sporadic statuary, were interspersed with wide sections of flush-mounted grave markers. Many huge trees were planted throughout—cherry, maple, and various cedars, some trimmed, some not.

I rounded a massive chestnut tree, spotting the petite necromancer perched on top of a light-gray gravestone, which appeared to be backed by a three-foot-tall white concrete statue depicting a woman holding an urn. Mory was wearing a deep-red poncho and—as near as I could determine in the low light—had dyed her hair since I'd seen her the previous afternoon, in shades of blue ranging from aquamarine to navy. She was also knitting.

The zombie that had greeted us at the gate appeared to be crawling its way back into the grave underneath her dangling feet. The second corpse was crawling toward a disturbed grave three headstones away. Its decapitated head was tucked underneath its arm.

Well, that was one blessing.

I paused, trying and failing to gather together words for the lecture that the situation obviously called for. Normally, I didn't have to work at being pissy when opportunity knocked. But as with all my earlier soul-searching, the dynamic with Mory always felt … strained.

The necromancer looked up, tucking a lock of hair that had fallen across her dark-brown eyes behind her ear. She leveled a scowl my way, even as her hands steadily and efficiently churned through stitches on what appeared to be a knitted tube. A sock, probably. Her colorless magic—at least to my eyes—was coiled tightly around her, concentrated in her hands and at the center of her forehead. The last time I'd seen her casting full force had been in Tofino. She had tried and failed to kill Sienna with what felt like a death curse. The power she now appeared to be wielding effortlessly was much, much stronger.

But that was the way with magic. It grew with age. And with use.

"See? Taken care of," Mory said snottily.

I bit back a retort about raising the corpses in the first place.

Kandy, who had apparently gotten the chuckles out of her system, appeared silently at my side. Thankfully, she had no apparent compunction when it came to chastising Mory. "Unacceptable, fledgling. Not only did you get us all out of bed, but that was probably someone's uncle! And … well, I couldn't really tell with the second one."

Mory jutted her chin out. "It wasn't intentional."

"How many more are running around?" Kandy asked.

"None."

Kandy looked pointedly at a grave with a flush-mounted dark-gray headstone just a few feet away. The sod and dirt to one side of it had been churned up.

Mory grimaced.

Kandy then jabbed a finger toward a fourth grave, this one topped with a concrete cross. Again, it appeared as though a corpse had crawled up from underneath it.

"I took care of them both," Mory said. "That one didn't even get fully out."

"Ah, Mory." I sighed, disappointed.

The necromancer dropped her gaze to her knitting.

Kandy glanced at me. "Do I need to be hunting zombies or not?"

I shook my head. I could taste how Mory's magic was confined to our immediate vicinity. And even that was slowly fading as the final zombie disappeared from view. "We'll need a witch, though. Unless we want the caretaker to find the graves messed up like this."

"Burgundy is on her way back," Mory said quietly. "She dropped me. We were at Tony's playing board games."

I didn't know who Burgundy or Tony were. But I was much less interested in anybody playing board games than I was in the 'wasn't intentional' aspect of Mory's necromancy. "This isn't on your way home," I said. The Novaks lived in a Georgian Manor in Shaughnessy.

Mory shrugged. "My magic needed it." But before I could interrogate her further, the necromancer eyed the werewolf through her blue bangs. Her gaze homed in on the purple dinosaur backpack. "So … you teaching kindergarten now?"

I snorted, then immediately quashed my involuntary amusement.

Kandy bared her teeth. Then, somewhat inexplicably, she said, "I shoulder my responsibilities while you sit here knitting and playing with magic beyond your abilities."

Mory twisted her lips belligerently but didn't answer, returning her gaze to her work.

Kandy sneered at the fledgling's bowed head, then looked at me with a dismissive shake of her own head. "I'm going to do a circuit. You deal with the dysfunctional necromancer."

Great. The green-haired werewolf took off before I could protest being left to deal with the nineteen-year-old.

Mory peeked at me through her long bangs. "I know, Jade. I know, okay? I didn't do it intentionally."

"But your magic … needed it?"

"Not like that. Not after I got here … I thought it had settled."

I resisted the impulse to start pacing or to raise my voice. Such reactions would have been irrational. But when it came to Mory, my protective instincts were already heightened. Add the itchy feet, the race to get to the cemetery, and the zombies, and well …

I took a deep breath. "Can I look at your necklace?"

Mory huffed. But she untangled one hand from her knitting and tugged her necklace from the collar of her poncho without further protest.

I had stripped the artifact back over the previous two years, removing and replacing elements bit by bit.

The only original piece was the thin gold chain, which was now woven through a thick-linked white gold chain. Silver didn't take to my alchemy as well as gold did. I'd also repurposed the gold bangles and the single wedding ring that had once been part of it, so that the necklace was sleeker—just the chains and the coins. Something Mory could keep tucked away underneath the knit scarves she wore year round.

I took a moment to contemplate Mory's current fashion choice—a chunky knit with a thickly striped fringe of orange, purple, and electric blue, which likely fell to the necromancer's calves when she was standing. Various-sized beads were knotted within the fringe, which I expected meant that Mory clattered while she walked.

Apparently, necromancers had no need for stealth, or for blending into their surroundings. At least not this particular necromancer.

Still, the poncho looked gloriously comfy. Though I'd have had to drop twenty pounds and shrink five inches to pull it off.

I stepped forward. But even before I touched it, I could tell something was odd about the magic of Mory's necklace. First of all, it was ... churning.

"Did you recently access the power held in the necklace?" I asked.

"You know I can't use it like that." Mory enjoyed reminding me that she wasn't a witch. Constantly.

"So, no?"

"No." Then she added, "Not knowingly."

"Did someone hit you with a spell? Something malicious?"

"I think I would have noticed."

I brushed my fingers along the woven chain and the drilled coins, calming the magic within them. "The necklace might have simply deflected it without you noticing."

Mory didn't answer. I lifted my gaze to hers. Though she'd been watching me intently, she dropped her eyes back to her knitting.

"What are you making?" I asked. "Socks?"

"Arm warmers." Then she hesitated. "I thought … you might like them."

Surprised, I glanced down at the thin metal needles she was using. They were purple. Mory continued clicking away, working stitch after stitch. The magic that had accumulated around her hands had faded.

"Cashmere and a little bit of silk." The fiber content was offered up with a kind of reverence, and an attempt at enticement. "I harvested the yarn myself. Reclaimed from two separate sweaters. Then I Kool-Aid-dyed it lime green. With blue and darker green speckles. Speckles are super hot right now."

I grinned, only really understanding that Mory was voluntarily knitting me something green that I could wear on my arms. "Who'd say no to that?"

A smile flitted across the junior necromancer's face. "Is my necklace okay, then?"

I returned my attention to the magical artifact in question. "What did it feel like? When your magic 'needed' you to come to the cemetery? Like a compulsion?"

Mory shrugged. "It's like that sometimes. If I haven't cast in a while. Usually carrying Ed helps."

Oh, God. I really didn't want to know. "Who is Ed?"

"My red-eared slider. My pet turtle."

I really, really didn't want to know. "And … you … carry him in your bag? Like … dead?"

Mory narrowed her eyes at me.

I raised my hands, palms out. "No judgement."

"You are totally judging me, Jade."

I really was. "I'm not. Carrying Ed is like … using your magic casually, passively?"

"Yeah, like almost subconsciously. So it doesn't … leak."

I waved my hand toward the grave Mory was still perched over. I'd been careful to step to one side of the churned earth when examining the necklace. "So things like this don't happen."

"Well … this is my first time with people, you know. Usually it's birds, snakes, rats—"

"Jesus, Mory!"

"You asked."

"So the corpses were just a … leak?"

Mory shook her head. "No. That was … an uncontrollable urge to raise the dead."

"Like a compulsion?" I asked for the second time.

Mory locked her dark-eyed gaze to mine. "You know what it takes to get past the necklace," she whispered. "I would have felt it if someone spelled me. I know what that feels like."

I nodded. Mory didn't need to remind me of the exact circumstances in which she'd been hit with so much magic that the protective barrier of her necklace had been breached. And I didn't bring Sienna up either. Not out loud, at least.

"Plus," the necromancer continued, "you've strengthened it. Many times. Since."

I nodded thoughtfully.

"You want to meet him?"

"Who?"

"Ed."

"Jesus, no!"

Mory cackled, delighted at her own joke.

Then the taste of peppermint drew my attention away from the necromancer. I stepped back from her and the magic of the necklace to reach out with my dowser senses, certain for the second time in just a few hours that Kett was nearby.

I could sense Kandy about a block away, and Warner closer to where we'd parked the SUV. But again, no white-blond vampires.

A shadow shifted in a deep crook between the branches of the chestnut tree beside and slightly behind Mory. I frowned, shaking my head at it.

Mory cranked her head, following my gaze. Then she stilled when she laid eyes on the shadow leech watching us from the thick branches of the tree.

"What is that?" she whispered.

"You can see it?"

"Why else would I be asking?"

I stifled a sigh. Heaven forbid that the necromancer could give me a freaking break for one freaking second. "I'm just surprised. Not everyone can." I settled my fingers along Mory's chain, focusing on adding another level of protection into the artifact. "It's drawn to my magic. It won't hurt you."

Mory huffed.

Silence fell between us. I concentrated on interweaving her toasted-marshmallow magic with my own energy, then weaving both into the necklace. She watched the shadow leech over her shoulder.

"It's a demon of some sort, right?"

"Of some sort."

"You can't just give me a plain answer?"

I dropped my hands from her necklace, shoving them in the back pockets of my jeans. Possibly so

I couldn't wring Mory's neck. "It's a shadow leech. A sorcerer obsessed with living forever who willingly sacrificed himself so that demonic energy could be drawn into this dimension. There were dozens of them originally. Warner, Kandy, Kett, Drake, and I killed them all except three. Then, when I murdered their master and absorbed her magic, the leeches were drawn to me. This one absorbed the other two, becoming more substantial, probably because I refused to let it consume the magic from every Adept it wanted to suck dry."

Mory was staring at me, wide-eyed and open-mouthed. She had finally stopped knitting.

"Happy?" I asked pointedly.

She snapped her mouth closed, then started knitting again. "So it can't be vanquished."

"I can kill it. But …"

"It has a soul. Some of the life essence of the sorcerers."

"So it appears," I murmured. I watched as the shadow leech shifted closer along the branch.

"Well … that's one way of living forever."

I didn't have an answer to that. Just an opinion. Immortality wasn't something that appealed to me. In fact, it seemed as though living forever might well be more of a curse than a gift.

"I shall name it Freddie," Mory declared.

"What? The leech?"

She nodded sagely. "Yes. You'll feel better, having accidentally tamed it, if it has a name."

"It isn't tame. Don't think it's tame, Mory. Do not try to befriend it."

Mory shrugged noncommittally.

Jesus. Like I didn't have enough to worry about when it came to the junior necromancer. Zombies, leeches... what was next?

Perhaps sensing my mood, the leech retreated back into the shadow of the chestnut tree, taking its cinnamon-toast-scented magic with it.

"Who's Burgundy?" I asked, seeking to change the subject. Mory had mentioned the name when we'd talked about needing a witch to clean up her mess in the graveyard.

"You know. Burgundy."

"Nope."

"My friend Burgundy. She's been in the bakery like a dozen times."

I shook my head.

"Amy," Mory snarled, as though I had just asked her to skewer her friend through the eyes with hot pokers.

Which was a seriously creepy image. Where the hell had that come from? I blamed the current environment. What with the corpses set to rise out of the ground underneath my feet at the merest thought of a necromancer who delighted in needling me.

Mory was glowering. A huffy, pissy pixie swathed in knitwear and perched on a gravestone. "My friend, Amy," she repeated, clicking her thin metal needles together viciously. "You bought us ice cream. She's Burgundy now, training with Pearl."

"Oh! She's like, what? A quarter-witch?"

The further furrowing of Mory's brow gave me a sense of what fragile ground I was on. Which was fine, really. I was way more comfortable being the instigator of mayhem rather than the person who cleaned it up. I only 'adulted' completely willingly around bakery business.

"She's hoping to focus on medicine at UBC. And on training in healing spells and such."

'And such' covered a hell of a lot of ground when it came to witch magic, but I let it go. "Huh. Okay. So she can …?" I waved my hand at the disturbed grave underneath Mory's dangling feet.

"Yep. At least I think so."

Catching another hint of magic, I asked, "Does her magic taste like … jelly beans?" I smacked my lips thoughtfully. "Sour grape, maybe?"

Mory gave me a withering look.

Right, not a witch. And as far as I knew, I was the only half-witch who could taste magic. So it was a stupid question, which I tried to cover by explaining. "It's an odd taste for a witch …"

But then I caught a hint of a darkly tinted spice that I knew intimately. A flavoring that I still couldn't identify …

It wasn't cardamom or coriander or cumin … I'd come to believe that its root was so ancient that even though the magical blood that carried its taste continued on, the plant itself was extinct.

But in any case, that spice had no business being paired with the taste of sour-grape jelly beans.

I pivoted toward it, peering into the darkness toward Fraser Street. I could hear traffic from that direction and sense Kandy moving toward me. But I couldn't see any intruders.

Mory laid her hand on my arm, her gaze riveted to something near my waist. "It's okay, Jade."

I glanced down. I had called my knife into my hand without even noticing. Not wanting to freak Mory out further, I loosened my hold on the hilt and the blade immediately settled back into its invisible sheath.

"He's okay."

Mory knew the source of the magic I had tasted. Damn it.

"He's a vampire," I spat. "Loitering outside a cemetery."

"Yeah, I know. It's the third evening. I think he's trying to … you know, say hi."

I looked at her incredulously. "A vampire is attempting to open up a dialogue. With a necromancer. In a graveyard."

My tone was nearing 'unbecomingly strident' territory. But what the freaking hell? Vampires weren't friendly with necromancers. The immortal undead didn't take kindly to the fact that some necromancers could control them. Also, for some strange reason, zombies could hurt the fanged. I was fairly certain that few knew that last little tidbit, thanks to the vampires having obliterated many of the necromancer bloodlines. Though even that destruction was more rumor than concrete fact.

Mory herself had informed me of the animosity between the two Adept races. Plus, she had always maintained a careful distance between herself and Kett. And what the hell was a sour-grape-jelly-bean-tasting bloodsucker doing in Vancouver anyway?

"Jade," Mory said soothingly. "His mother is a necromancer."

That gave me pause. Because it forced me to remember that Vancouver now boasted two full-fledged necromancers. Danica Novak, Mory's mother, and Teresa Garrick, who was pending trial with the Convocation. A trial that had something to do with why her son Benjamin was a fledgling vampire without a master.

"Benjamin Garrick?" I said. It wasn't like I hoped he was chained up in a basement somewhere, but I hadn't thought about Benjamin having free rein to wander around Vancouver stalking necromancers under my protection.

"Yeah. I think so, at least. I haven't met him. But he feels like—"

"Be right back."

I took off without another word, darting between gravestones and feeling Kandy immediately chase after me from the parallel edge of the property. Then Warner's black-forest-cake magic was moving with me as well, from where he was likely still on the outer sidewalk.

"Jade!" Mory called after me. "Give him a chance!"

A dark-haired vampire lurked among the thick-leafed branches of a massive chestnut tree at the eastern corner of the expansive cemetery property just inside the gate off Fraser Street. He might have been able to see Mory from his perch, but he didn't see or hear me coming. Though I couldn't blame him. I moved quickly.

He also missed the werewolf and the dragon. But then, Kandy moved through the grass and around the gravestones without a sound, and Warner pretty much became one with the shadows when he wanted to, as a result of his chameleon abilities.

I waited a couple of seconds for the vampire to notice me standing in the dry grass underneath the tree, but he kept his dark-eyed gaze riveted to the pixie necromancer. So I jumped up, grabbed his ankle, and ripped him from the branches.

He spun in midair, losing hold of a worn black-leather satchel as he crashed onto his back. He didn't make a sound, not even a peep of disconcertion.

Bonus points for him.

Of course, he hadn't seen my knife yet.

The slightly built vampire yanked his leg from my grasp, scrambling back and slamming up against the base of the chestnut tree. It was thickly trunked, easily forty years old, but it still shuddered at this mistreatment. So he was strong. Nowhere near as strong as Kett, but way, way stronger physically than the petite necromancer he was apparently stalking.

His pale skin had an olive undertone. His eyes were dark brown, almost black in the filtered moonlight. Appearing to be around nineteen or twenty, he stared up at me, self-consciously tugging at the sleeve of a thin, dark-navy wool sweater that was slightly too large for him, hanging past his wrists. Dark-washed jeans and lace-up ankle boots of black leather completed his outfit. He was about my height, as long as I wasn't wearing heels.

Warner and Kandy appeared at my back, standing to either side like silent, brooding sentries. Not bothering to pull my knife again, I leaned over the fledgling vampire, watching his eyes finally widen with fear. But interestingly, I didn't see even a hint of the red of his magic.

"Hunting necromancers is frowned upon in Vancouver," I said, pointedly but not nastily. I liked to be nice, after all.

His jaw dropped, revealing teeth that were so perfectly straight he must have worn braces at some point. Before he'd been remade into a vampire. As with the eyes, I didn't see any hint of fangs. But as far as I could figure, a young vampire confronted by three unknown and greater predators should have been instinctively fighting back.

"I … I …" the dark-haired vampire stuttered. "I wasn't … hunting."

"Calm, controlled," Warner said. "Interesting."

Kandy huffed in disappointment. "Really, dowser? You got me going, what with the running. And this baby vamp was the threat?"

The vampire's gaze snapped to me, his fear easing into curiosity. Apparently he knew my title when he heard it, even if he didn't recognize me by sight.

Warner chuckled at the wolf's dissatisfaction. Then he turned his head slightly. "Expecting a witch?"

"Mory's friend," I said, having caught the taste of green watermelon over top of the grassy base of witch magic a moment before he spoke. "Amy, now known as Burgundy."

The vampire worried his bottom lip. "Is the necromancer okay, then? I, uh, noticed … the … you know …" He walked two fingers over the palm of his left hand, apparently concerned about naming the zombies out loud.

Warner melted into the shadows, heading off to make sure that the witch we'd both felt approaching was of the helpful, friendly variety.

The vampire muttered excitedly to himself, reaching for the leather satchel that had fallen out of the tree alongside him.

I darted forward, catching his wrist carefully so as to not hurt him. He flinched nonetheless. When he moved, I had tasted a secondary tenor of magic hidden beneath his primary jelly-bean taste. I didn't know if he was reaching for a weapon or not. Though vampires didn't usually carry objects of power, what with their ability to beguile prey, then tear its throat out.

Kandy had darted around behind me to snatch up the satchel, which she unclipped and upended beside the vampire.

Two black notebooks, a fancy pen, a leather-bound book that looked ancient, and a bag of blood tumbled out onto the grass.

Ben moaned quietly. But in embarrassment, not hunger.

Huffing, Kandy tossed the satchel over the bag of blood, stalking around the tree until she stood beside me again.

"You know who I am," I said quietly. Ignoring—for the moment at least—that he carried blood with him.

The dark-haired vampire nodded.

"Do you know the proper way to introduce yourself?"

He nodded again, but this time as though he felt stupid for not having done so earlier. Even though I had just yanked him out of a tree instead of greeting him formally. So some of that was on me.

I blamed Mory. I was overly protective of her.

"Go ahead." I let go of the vampire's wrist, stepping back.

He gained his feet effortlessly, straightening his sweater and brushing off his jeans with hints of the fluid movement that came so naturally to Kett. Then he lifted his chin proudly. "Benjamin Garrick. Son of Teresa Garrick, necromancer. Child of Nigel Farris, vampire, deceased. Ward of Kettil, the executioner and elder of the Conclave."

Kett's ward? Well. Surprise, surprise. Was Benjamin the reason the executioner had been more circumspect than usual lately?

"Invoking the name of the executioner is not to be done lightly, baby vamp," Kandy said with sudden viciousness.

Benjamin wasn't fazed. "I speak it with permission."

Kandy gave me a look, and I nodded. Though I wasn't privy to the fledgling's connection to Kett, it made sense. Gran had negotiated the Garricks' entry into Vancouver, and she normally wouldn't have been all that keen about having Benjamin in what was traditionally witch territory. Except I had some unusual friends.

Vampires were known to be…well, complicated to coexist with. And as such, it wouldn't have surprised me to learn that the bag of blood Benjamin carried was one of the conditions of his admittance into Godfrey coven territory.

"It's a pleasure to meet you, Benjamin," I said.

He smiled. "I go by Garrick."

"Nope," Kandy said. "Too confusing. And contrived."

Benjamin's expression went forlorn at this pronouncement. "A real vampire wouldn't go by Ben. Or Benjamin."

"Not our problem, fledgling." Kandy sniffed.

"Really?" I asked, trying to keep a straight face. "He can't decide what he wants to be called?"

"He can put more thought into it, can't he?"

I cleared my throat, tamping down on my amusement at Kandy exerting her dominance over a fledgling vampire so we could follow through with the formalities. "Kandy, werewolf, enforcer of the West Coast North American Pack."

"The wielder's wolf," Kandy said darkly.

Well, that was new. And not at all intimidating. For me, at least, since I was the wielder in question and Kandy's forthright claiming of the relationship sounded intentional and specific. Still, I had no idea what she meant by it.

Benjamin's fingers flexed as if he was desperate to be holding something. But again, the tenor of his jelly-bean-infused magic remained controlled. Even sedate.

"Jade Godfrey," I said. "Dowser, granddaughter of Pearl Godfrey, chair of the Convocation."

Benjamin bobbed his head, confirming that he already understood full well who I was.

"Alchemist," Kandy added pointedly. "Wielder of the instruments of assassination. Dragon slayer."

I sighed inwardly.

Benjamin's jaw dropped, then stayed down.

Kandy snorted smugly. Werewolves loved to play games, especially with vampires. Apparently, being young didn't gain Benjamin any leeway.

Ignoring Kandy and all the posturing she apparently felt was necessary, I spoke to him. "May I see the magical artifact on your wrist?"

Surprised, the dark-haired vampire wrapped his left hand across the wrist of his right, mortification flushing his face. The sleeves of his sweater hung to the knuckles of his long, almost-delicate fingers.

"I'm sorry," I murmured. "It's rude to ask after another Adept's magic, but it's pretty much my job now."

"How did you know I had … a magical artifact?"

"I'm a dowser. That means, for me at least, that I taste magic."

His gaze fixed on me. A smile slowly spread across his face, becoming practically all encompassing. The expression of wonderment transformed the young vampire from completely average in the looks department into heartthrob territory. Like, instantly. "You … taste … magic."

Kandy leaned in, eyeing Benjamin with renewed interest.

Oh, yes. It was a good thing I was seriously attached to my fiance. But I was going to have to keep an eye on Mory. I wasn't at all certain that the necromancer could stand up to that smile or the irresistible magic that backed it.

"And me? Do I…taste like anything?" His question ended in a hushed whisper, filled with a tense neediness paired with gleeful anticipation.

For other young adults his age—if my loose understanding of Benjamin's recent transformation was accurate—the world revolved around sex and food. But the fledgling vampire was obviously fueled by knowledge. Specifically, knowledge about the magical universe he'd just been reborn into, and the Adepts he shared that world with.

I laughed quietly. "You taste like a vampire, of course. Some kind of intense spice that I haven't quite figured out yet. But mostly like jelly beans. Sour grape, I think."

He frowned thoughtfully. "I taste like super sweet, sugary…sour…grapes?"

"Yes. Except the artifact on your wrist is necromancer magic, which I can feel more than taste. It's not Mory's, though, or her mother, Danica's. Your mother's?"

He nodded, then dropped his gaze. "To help keep me…in check."

Ah. That was why he'd been upset in response to my mentioning it. And that also made a likely explanation for the sedate tenor of his magic. I'd heard that young vampires were driven by bloodlust, but Kett's own control was rather epic in contrast. I'd seen him surrounded by bleeding, mortally wounded shapeshifters and witches—including myself—and he hadn't shown a hint of fang. Magic was the one thing that seemed to put the executioner over the edge, but even then, I'd never seen him bite anyone simply because he was out of control.

Benjamin started to roll up the sleeve of his sweater.

"Never mind," I said. "I get it."

He shook his head. "No. I understand rules. You've got them, and I'll follow. It took me almost a year to convince my mother I could leave the house. I like Vancouver. I'd like to stay."

He uncovered what appeared to be a cross between a two-inch-thick cuff and a torture device. Constructed out of the woven bones of a small animal or bird, the bracelet was embedded into his flesh, just above his wrist. And because of his vampire magic, his skin had healed, half-absorbing the bone cuff. It seethed with necromancy, and not the tasty toasted-marshmallow kind that Mory wielded.

It looked, tasted, and felt as though the casting and the wearing of the device had to be painful. As in, continually. This wasn't a magical artifact. It was a necromancy spell—a perpetual working, probably fueled by Benjamin's own magic—designed specifically to keep his vampire nature from rising.

I grimaced, clamping down on my sudden need to tear the magic-laced bones from his flesh.

Beside me, Kandy folded her fingers into fists, clenching her teeth. Then she stalked away, pacing a few steps before coming back again.

Yeah, I wasn't the only softhearted one.

"Um …" Benjamin said, watching the werewolf warily. "Do you mind if I make notes?"

"Excuse me?"

"Notes. You know? I'm starting a chronicle."

"A chronicle?" Kandy asked mockingly. "'Dear Diary, today I saw the necromancer again. I desperately want to bite her, but I just can't bring myself to confess it to her.'"

Frustration-fueled emotion flitted across Benjamin's face. The magic of the torture device he wore on his wrist flared, and he covered it with his hand. Attempting to hide it, and the pain it caused, from our sight.

"Take it off him, dowser," Kandy snapped.

"What?" Benjamin cried. "No!" He tugged the sleeve of his sweater down so it covered the woven bone bracelet, blinking at me. "You could, though? Remove it?"

"She's an alchemist, isn't she?" Kandy snarled, starting to pace again.

"I thought…that's not about turning lead into gold?"

"What?" Kandy cried. She indignantly threw her arms up in the air.

"That would be a pretty cool power," Benjamin said enthusiastically. "Useful, you know?"

Kandy looked at me, shaking her head.

"What?" I asked. "How's he supposed to know?"

"Kett's supposedly mentoring him."

"Well, that explains everything," I said sarcastically. "The executioner is just so verbose."

"He brings me books," Benjamin said defensively, crouching down to grab the leather tome Kandy had tossed in the grass among his notebooks and the bag of blood. He waved the book as though it were supporting evidence. "Other chronicles. But they're really old. So…I thought…you know."

"That you'd write your own."

Benjamin nodded, swiftly repacking his bag.

"Industrious," Kandy said.

"Everyone needs a place," I murmured.

"It's dangerous," Kandy countered. "Writing about magic, maybe about Adepts who don't want to be chronicled." She waved her hand at me, as though suggesting I was liable to murder anyone who jotted down facts about me.

Benjamin straightened, dropping his satchel over one shoulder but keeping a pen and a black Moleskine in hand.

Kandy rounded on him. Again. "Have you mentioned your little project to Kett?"

The dark-haired vampire became still, which made me realize he was breathing, slowly and surely. I wondered how long he'd keep that habit up, other than to speak.

He was also scared of his so-called mentor.

But then, who wasn't, really? At least a little bit? The executioner carried a lot of magic—and carried it uneasily, according to him. Even Warner kept tabs on Kett. They were currently engaged in playing some remote chess game they had started months before.

Benjamin swallowed. "Are you going to tell him?"

"Are you going to ask permission?" Kandy asked pointedly.

The young vampire bobbed his head.

"Fine," the werewolf huffed. "We won't say anything. Yet." She nodded toward the notebook in his hand. "A tablet would be smarter. More useful."

"I've got one. And a laptop. But I prefer the feel of pen on paper. You know?"

"Paper," Kandy sneered, crossing her arms. "Well, go ahead. We've got things to do."

The dark-haired vampire flipped open the Moleskine, uncapping what appeared to be a snazzy fountain pen that carried a hint of residual magic. Vampire magic.

I watched as Benjamin flipped to a blank page and carefully wrote Kandy's name and titles across the top of it.

"Did Kett give you the pen?" I asked.

Benjamin nodded, not looking up from his notes.

"And the notebook?"

"A box of them," he said, almost absentmindedly.

I nodded at Kandy knowingly, and she tipped her head in acknowledgment. There was very little that the executioner missed, and very little that he did unintentionally. Apparently, Benjamin already had Kett's permission to chronicle whatever he wanted. Which, of course, raised the question of why. Perhaps Kett simply wanted the young vampire to have some focus—something other than the bloodlust that I was guessing the bone bracelet on his wrist helped hold at bay.

"I ain't standing around all day," Kandy snapped. "You get two questions."

"Each?" Ben asked hopefully.

I laughed quietly.

Kandy glowered at me. I wasn't particularly helpful at keeping fledgling Adepts in line—or at least not keeping them toeing the line the exacting werewolf wanted them on. For their own protection, of course and always. But no matter how gruff and blunt Kandy preferred to appear, she had taken on the duty of enforcing the magical grid seriously. Embracing the opportunity almost gleefully, in fact.

"I really should check in on Mory," I said. "And the witch."

"Burgundy … UBC … healing spells …" Benjamin muttered under his breath, reminding himself—and at the same time, inadvertently letting me know how sharp his hearing was. "Formerly Amy."

"Also off limits," I said. "For biting."

Benjamin looked affronted. "It would be difficult to make friends, and, you know, write a chronicle about the modern age of the Adept if I went around trying to bite everyone."

"You'd be surprised," Kandy muttered.

I shot her a look. She didn't need to be giving the fledgling vampire any ideas about his potential ability to beguile anyone and everyone with a mere bite. I was already worried about the enthralling magic that backed his smile.

Kandy flashed me one of her patented nonsmiles in return, tugging her phone out of her pocket and scanning her messages. "Pearl texted earlier to say the bloom had faded from the grid. Nothing since."

"The grid?" Benjamin asked hopefully.

"Is that your first question?" Kandy snapped back.

The dark-haired vampire tilted his head. Apparently, he needed to think it over.

I quashed another smile, leaving Benjamin to Kandy and swiftly crossing back into the graveyard.

# Chapter Four

I veered toward the side entrance of the cemetery, hidden in the cedar hedge where I felt Warner loitering in the shadows and Mory and Burgundy on the street beyond. As I stepped onto the sidewalk, I saw Mory climbing into the passenger side of an older Honda Civic. The car was already running.

"Everything all right, then?" I asked, speaking to my dragon where he had appeared at my shoulder.

"The witch, if you can call her that, used a masking spell," Warner said with a sneer. "Premade."

"Careful, sixteenth century," I teased. "You're letting your prejudice show."

Warner grunted, crossing his arms and continuing to glower as the Honda backed up until it was even with me. The twenty-year-old witch at the wheel had streaks of blue threaded through her wavy brown hair. It was an easy guess that it had come from the same dye application as Mory's. Rolling down the automatic window, she leaned across Mory in the passenger seat, waving at me. "Hi, Jade!"

Now that I laid eyes on the curvy and cute hazel-eyed witch, I recognized her, of course. But the taste of her green-watermelon magic was so muted that it was unlikely I ever would have tasted it over Gran, or any of the other Adepts who might have been in the bakery at the same time as Burgundy. Also, I wasn't entirely certain I'd been reintroduced to her by her chosen witch name.

"Thanks for coming by, Burgundy."

"Oh, yeah, no problem. I'll ask Pearl for a reversal spell in the morning." She was still grinning widely. "I think she can key it on an exact window of time, so I had Mory make a note. I don't have classes on Saturdays, so I can do it right away."

"Yes, I would think it would be a priority," Warner grumbled.

The junior witch's smile faltered around the edges. "Um, right."

I stepped up to the car, placing my hand on the open window edge next to Mory's shoulder. "You'll call me."

"I'll text," Mory snapped, not looking at me. "If it happens again."

"No," I said, attempting to be patient. "You'll call me if it feels like it might happen again."

Mory turned her dark eyes up to meet mine, trying and failing to pin me with the look. "And what would you do, Jade? You aren't a necromancer."

I held her gaze steadily, tamping down on the need to threaten or frighten her with a full list of everything I was capable of doing if her necromancy got out of control. Zombies would not, could not, be yanked from their graves to go free range in Vancouver. Above and beyond the panic and the extensive cover-up, Mory would be tried and convicted of exposing the Adept world to those without magic—a massive population that easily and extensively outnumbered magic users. I wasn't sure what the punishment would be, but it wouldn't be light.

Mory looked away, wrapping her hand around her necklace. "I'm not Rusty," she muttered. "I'm not Sienna."

I sighed. "I know."

"You don't."

"Be reasonable, necromancer." My voice hardened. "You raised four zombies tonight and you can't explain why. Either you're lying and I'm an idiot for letting you walk away, or someone spelled you. Whether you want to be or not, you're mine to protect. From yourself, if necessary."

"Fine. And I suppose you'll be talking to my mother? And Pearl?"

"No. Because those are your next conversations."

"Fine."

"Fine."

"Great!" Burgundy said, overly brightly. "Maybe we'll see you at the bakery later?"

I nodded, straightening away from the car. Burgundy took her foot off the brake and it rolled back slightly. "And stay away from the vampire, Garrick," I said, using Benjamin's preferred name.

Mory narrowed her eyes belligerently, but she didn't answer.

Burgundy pulled away. But even over the purr of the engine, I caught her thrilled tone as she asked, "Vampire? What vampire?"

I sighed heavily, watching the Honda drive away on the narrow street, sliding past dark homes and parked cars. After the vehicle turned the corner, I shifted my gaze to Warner, who'd been watching me.

He raised an eyebrow sardonically. "Warning her off the fledgling vampire is simply asking her to seek him out."

Jesus. He was right. I shook my head helplessly.

"I'm just an idiot around her. Give me demons or death-defying magic any day. I might be impulsive, but I just … I don't know …"

Warner unfolded his arms, stepping closer to brush his fingers lightly through my curls. "Would you blame her brother's actions on Mory?"

"Of course not."

"Yet the same rule doesn't apply to you?"

I narrowed my eyes at him. Life lessons from the sentinel, who had been living in the modern world for only three years, weren't high on my list of likes.

He grinned. Sometimes I thought Warner preferred me a little pissy, a little crazy. Riled up. His smile widened. "Let's collect the wolf. I wouldn't mind some more time in your bed before I must return to duty."

I nodded, ignoring the way my stomach squelched with fear rather than desire. Danger permeated every mission Warner undertook each time he walked through the portal. But he wasn't mine to wrap up and tuck away from the world. Just as I wasn't his to shelter. Officially married or not, we made—and would continue to make—our own choices. Together if there was time for conversation, but apart if the situation demanded immediate action. I wouldn't have it any other way.

But that didn't mean I couldn't want to lock him away in my pantry with all my other favorite things.

He brushed a kiss across my forehead. "You know I always come back. I can't not return to you."

"I know." Then, shaking off my own irrational reaction, I teased him. "Plus, if I ever really want your attention, all I have to do is take the instruments out for a spin."

Warner grunted. "Hopefully it never comes to that."

Preceded by her red-berry-and-bitter-dark-chocolate magic, Kandy appeared, strolling in from the far corner of the cemetery. Magic glinted off her three-inch cuffs, and I stuffed my hands in my pockets in order to stop myself from reaching out to stroke them as the werewolf closed the space between us. Apparently, working on Mory's necklace hadn't dampened my need to use my alchemy. But then, I'd always been a magpie when it came to pretty magical things.

I might have earned my living baking cupcakes while thwarting evil on the side when it became absolutely necessary. But my mild obsession with anything magical was something I maintained all of the time.

"The fledgling?" Warner asked Kandy.

She shrugged. "He's under control. Which is more than can be said for the necromancer. If the rumors are true about necromancers being able to control vampires, then Mory's the potential threat in this situation, not Ben."

"Not all necromancers carry the same abilities," Warner said mildly.

"But I imagine the necromancy working he already wears would make him especially susceptible," I said.

"Mory isn't going to hurt anyone, dowser," Kandy said. "Not unprovoked. And you wouldn't want her to hold back if she was in any sort of jeopardy."

I nodded, turning toward the SUV.

"Plus, he'd just bore her to death with questions," Kandy grumbled, unlocking the doors and climbing in. "Baby fang kept insisting that my cuffs had to have a name. Said all powerful artifacts should be named. Then he completely rejected me naming them 'the cuffs of might.'"

"Oh! Haoxin called them 'the Herakles cuffs.'"

"Helpful, dowser."

Warner chuckled quietly, climbing into the back seat behind me and immediately stretching out and closing his eyes. "Most magical artifacts are named after their maker," he said. "But occasionally, that gets amended if the wielder is the more powerful or influential figure. The dowser's knife…the dowser's necklace…the dragon slayer …"

"Is that me or my katana?" I clicked my seat belt closed.

"Both."

Kandy started the SUV. "So what do I have to do to get the cuffs renamed, say to 'the Kandy cuffs'? Or 'the cuffs of Kandy?'"

"Immortalize yourself." Warner's pronouncement made it sound as though doing it was as easy as saying it. Then he added with some amusement, "Having a famous chronicler write about your exploits would do. And I'd call them 'the wolf's bracers.' Not cuffs."

Kandy sniffed, flicking her bangs in the rearview mirror while reversing away from the curb. "Shows what you know, dragon."

"True," Warner admitted with a smile. "Being infamous might be enough." Then his breathing deepened as he dropped off to sleep without another word.

Silence filled the dark interior of the SUV. Kandy drove smoothly through the neighborhood, heading in the direction of the bakery much more slowly than she'd raced to get to the cemetery.

"So…you going to make baby vamp a T-shirt?" I whispered teasingly.

"Don't you start on me, dowser." Kandy's voice carried a warning tone. "Benjamin is under our protection, you know? Right up to the moment he tries to bite someone without permission."

"Even after that, I suppose ..." I gazed out at the dark city slipping past my window, wondering whether I should mention that I'd tasted peppermint-laced magic again. I had no idea why Kett would have been stalking me. The vampire liked to play games, of course. Maybe he wanted to be chased? Kandy would have liked that.

But if the peppermint power I kept tasting wasn't Kett's? Well, then I was seriously flummoxed.

"What color shirt do you think would look good on Ben?" Kandy asked musingly. "A deep green or brown, maybe."

I laughed quietly, then pulled out my phone and texted.

*I met Benjamin Garrick tonight.*

"Kett?" Kandy asked.

I nodded, changing the subject as I waited to see if the vampire would text me back right away. "Do you think raising the grid could have affected Mory's magic somehow?"

Kandy snorted doubtfully. "How could it? There isn't even an anchor point near the cemetery. Plus, it's witch magic, not necromancy."

"True."

Turning back onto Sixteenth Avenue heading west, the werewolf fell quietly thoughtful. "What about the shadow leech? It feeds on magic. I'm just waiting for that sucker to step out of line."

"No," I murmured. "Also, Mory can see it. She named the little freak 'Freddie.'"

"Great," Kandy groused.

My cellphone vibrated in my hand and I glanced down at the screen, swiping to read the incoming text from Kett.

*>Did he survive the encounter?*

"Kett wants to know if I slaughtered Ben Garrick."

"Makes sense."

"What? I don't just go around killing people."

Kandy just gave me another of her nonsmiles in response. "Ask him when he's getting his ass into town."

I applied my thumbs to my phone.

*I didn't murder him.*

>*Pity.*

I angled my screen so Kandy could glance at it. She snorted and started to cackle, then checked herself with a look in the rearview mirror at Warner still sleeping in the back seat.

*Seriously?*

>*No.*

>*You'd be all upset. And that's dreadfully boring.*

"The vampire is a joker tonight," I muttered as I texted back.

*Are you in Vancouver? Are you going to make it to the party?*

>*Yes.*

Concise as always. Maybe he just wanted to avoid interfering with the casting of the grid when I had tasted his magic earlier, just as he would not have wanted to tangle with Mory's zombies. Though it wasn't like the executioner to not wade in.

I sent him a smiley face emoticon, but he didn't reciprocate.

"You're baking now, yes?" Kandy pulled my attention away from my phone.

"In a couple of hours, if I push it."

"I'll talk to Pearl about the grid possibly malfunctioning then."

"Mory will think we're tattling on her."

Kandy grunted. "The grid already did the talking. I'll just be filling in the details."

"True."

A comfortable silence filled the dark interior of the vehicle. The sound of Warner's steady breathing and the SUV's tires on the asphalt lulled me into a light doze. Then a sharp right-hand turn woke me from my slumber. Kandy skillfully wove through a couple of side streets, then actually parked in the exact same spot she'd vacated over an hour before.

The werewolf shut off the engine. But before I could open my door, she reached over and brushed her fingers across my forearm. "I'm pleased I won't be needing to break your ass out of guardian jail."

Warmth flushed through my chest. "Me too," I said simply, squeezing my best friend's hand. "Though … if someone decapitated me, draining my magic …"

"Have you been trying to murder guardian dragons in this scenario?"

I laughed, but with no humor. I was the dragon slayer, after all. "I guess so."

"Well, then. You'd deserve it, wouldn't you?"

"Right …"

"But that doesn't mean that whoever came for you wouldn't still have to go through me … and Warner … and Kett, Scarlett, Pearl, your father. Drake. Probably that damn leech, and the creepy necromancer. Hopefully the oracle wouldn't get involved, though. Everything would go all to hell, then."

I grinned goofily at Kandy in the dark, knowing she could see me better than I could see her. "You say the sweetest things, wolf."

"All the better to woo you, dowser." She snapped her teeth at me.

Warner spoke up from the back seat. "Get in line, werewolf."

"I was here first, dragon. Plus…you can join in anytime. Just leave the sentinel's blade out of it."

Warner laughed, surprised enough to practically bark.

"What?" Kandy asked, batting her eyelashes at me. "I was talking about his knife."

"Right," I drawled.

Laughing, we piled out of the SUV, making our way to and through the bakery, then into our respective beds.

Scarlett had vacated the second apartment upstairs when Kandy returned to Vancouver. Unbeknownst to Gran, my mother had bought a house a half-dozen blocks from the bakery, over on Fifth Avenue and Stephens. Then she'd had it renovated into a triplex, selling all but the top floor and making a killing in Vancouver's crazy housing market. Since Pearl was the real estate mogul in the family, this hadn't gone over well.

Though it wasn't like I could tell the difference, really. Mother and daughter still practiced their daily routine of outward politeness strained by silence.

Once home, Warner fell onto my bed without another word, making me realize that it was soon to be officially our bed.

Stripping down to a tank top and panties, I curled up next to him and tried to not fret over what had exhausted him. Or how an elf-wielded weapon had cut him so badly. Or even what he'd be doing in another couple of hours. But in truth, we both drove each other a little crazy that way, making it completely fair play.

Still, I'd been safely tucked away in the bakery for over a year now without a major incident. Until that night. But the blip with Mory, as unresolved as it felt, was oddly unsatisfying.

I hadn't had a chance to stab anyone with my knife, so maybe that was all that was bothering me. Putting up with all the annoying itch but none of the satisfying scratching.

Warner had vacated the bed by the time my alarm went off an hour later at 6:00 A.M. He'd left a chocolate bar on his pillow, which combined with the lack of black-forest-cake magic in the apartment to let me know he'd already left the building. And the country, for that matter.

Knowing that I'd be bouncing off the walls by noon if I ate it, I examined the blue-and-gold-printed bar from Marou—a 74 percent single-origin dark chocolate from Vietnam. Then, tearing the inner gold foil even though I'd tried to be gentle, I snapped a generous piece from the bar, allowing it to slowly melt across my tongue. I savored the hints of prune and raisin that mellowed into mild espresso, with a lingering cacao aftertaste.

Consuming the chocolate piece by piece, I tugged on jeans, a navy blue-and-pink-printed Cake in a Cup T-shirt, socks, and sneakers. Then I gathered my unruly curls into a messy bun and made my way down to the bakery.

My pristinely clean kitchen smelled like lemon verbena, and the cupcakes I'd left in the antique glass cake stand I'd bought specifically for Blossom had disappeared. As such, I surmised that the brownie had made a pass through while I was asleep.

Cutting it a little tight before I needed to open at 10:00 A.M., I checked the fridges for leftover batter, finding none. That meant I'd be baking through opening in order to have at least two dozen of everything on the current menu. Bryn was usually early for her 9:00 A.M. shift, though, and her frosting technique was much more refined than mine. So I might just make it.

After setting out butter and eggs to let them come to room temperature, I liberated a glorious vat of freshly roasted peanut butter from the fridge. I'd begun to expand my peanut butter offerings, and was testing similar recipes with cashew butter from the same local roasters. Even if I found a combination I was happy with, though, the cashew butter would make for rather pricey cupcakes, and I never knew ahead of time whether the market would bear the increase or not.

Still, the *Clarity in a Cup* I made with eggs from Rochelle's Westphalian deathlayer flock—marketed as local and organic, and marked up a dollar each—usually sold out moments after opening every Tuesday. The oracle, who was still slowly expanding her flock, dropped off at least a dozen eggs every Monday afternoon.

I slipped into the pantry for cocoa, sugar, and flour. Then I put my head down and fell into the peaceful rhythm of measuring and mixing. Only in my kitchen could I just allow myself to be, with no worries of magical grids and itchy feet, or of wherever Warner had been dragged off to, and whoever he might be fighting or vanquishing.

In these few hours five mornings a week, it was just me, my magic, and all the tastiness I got to play with.

Half of the cupcakes I needed for a Saturday were either out of or in the oven, and half of those had cooled enough to be slathered with icing. I had just slipped a tray of *Happiness in a Cup*—a dense peanut butter cake with a subtly sweet honey buttercream—onto a holding rack when the magic of the wards shifted, indicating that someone had just grasped the handle of the back alley door.

Already smiling, I spun around, tasting his magic moments before he opened the exterior door. The early-morning sun shone through his white-blond hair, briefly kissing his skin with a golden wash before he stepped through into the kitchen.

Kett.

Dressed in his typical combo of cashmere sweater and designer jeans, all in hues of grey this time, he shifted his ice-blue gaze, scanning the kitchen for me. My smile widened, spreading across my face. And an answering smile tugged at the corner of his mouth. Two steps later, I was in his arms.

He lifted me, twirling me around. His grip was bruising—or at least it would have been to anyone else. I threw my head back, laughing.

Kett set me on my feet. Curls tumbled down around my face, loosened from their clip. Barely making contact, he brushed my hair back, then pressed a kiss to my forehead.

But before I had more than a moment to marvel at that rare, intimate gesture, I noticed the tenor of his magic. It wasn't muted, exactly. Just less intense. And though its peppermint overtones were similar, the underlying base—the dark-tinted spice I hadn't yet identified, which Benjamin Garrick also shared—was less pungent. Less present.

"What's wrong?" I murmured, setting my hand on his shoulder. "Are you hurt?"

He stepped away, keeping his gaze on me but breaking physical contact.

My hand fell to my side. And I waited. I waited for him to tell me where he'd been since late April. I waited for him to explain why he'd been in town hours earlier—based on the magic I'd tasted twice—but was only coming now to say hello.

"I am entirely as expected," Kett said.

"Your magic is … back in its box."

He nodded, just a dip of his chin to acknowledge and accept my assessment.

"I've missed you," I said, stepping back to finish frosting a tray of *Enchantment in a Cup*—decadent chocolate-peanut butter cake with creamy peanut butter icing. I wanted to hit him with a barrage of questions—why he'd been away since the spring, why he hadn't mentioned mentoring Benjamin, and what was going on with his magic. But I knew that he'd be more likely to share if I gave him space.

He stayed by the door, as if rooted to that spot.

But when the silence had stretched too far between us, I glanced over at him and he offered me a hint of a smile. So he hadn't slipped into one of his fugue states.

I went back to my work. Kett finally moved, crossing into my office and coming back with a stool. Then he settled on it on the other side of my stainless steel workstation, simply watching me bake. It was another thing he'd never done before, though Kandy, Gran, and Scarlett often joined me in the bakery kitchen.

I felt like offering him something as a way to soften the silence—a cupcake, or coffee, or a piece of the chocolate bar I'd slipped into the pocket of my apron. But vampires drank blood. And I couldn't offer him mine—not even if I'd wanted to. I was poison to the executioner, though he'd never held that against me.

"What are you smiling about?" Kett whispered the words, as though he didn't want to disturb me.

I shook my head, laughing quietly. But before I could explain it to him, the timer went off for the batches of cupcakes in the ovens. I reached for my oven mitts, but Kett had already stepped in to pull out the scalding-hot muffin tins, placing them on the cooling racks set on the counter next to the ovens.

I almost laughed. Almost teased him about being domesticated, about being tamed. But then his hair fell forward across his brow in a terribly human, terribly vulnerable way, and my heart squelched.

Something was wrong.

Something he didn't want to tell me, or didn't know how to tell me.

Kett closed the oven, glancing down at his hand as if he'd burned himself and was surprised at that. He looked over at me.

I offered him a strained smile, showing him the oven mitts.

"Ah," he said. "And how do I know they are done?"

I swallowed past the worry stopping up my throat. "You press down on the center, just lightly. If the cake bounces back, it's done."

He bowed his head over the trays, carefully testing a cupcake near the center, and nodding when he seemed assured it was ready. "And these next?" He gestured toward the muffin tins I'd filled with batter and set to the side of my workstation.

I nodded, feeling apprehension prickling the skin of my arms. "Ten minutes. Then rotate."

Kett carefully placed the filled tins into the oven, positioning them exactly in the center of each rack. Then he set the timer.

"Are you looking for a job, executioner?" I tried to be playful as I said it, though the question came out strained.

"Am I not allowed to simply spend time with you, dowser?" he asked coolly.

I nodded, letting the subject drop. Working for a long while in silence, I systematically piped creamy peanut butter icing onto the tray of *Glee in a Cup*, trying to smile pleasantly as I iced the fourth of my new peanut butter cake bases. I failed spectacularly.

"I don't want to interrupt you," Kett murmured finally. "Perhaps I should come back later."

"Just tell me," I said without looking up from my work. "Just tell me what you need to tell me, and we'll move forward."

When I glanced up, he smiled. A sad, terrible smile.

Tears sprang to my eyes. I blinked them away. I told myself I was overreacting, reading far too much into his actions. He had simply missed me. I'd missed him.

"I don't want to lose you."

Ah, God. I wasn't wrong.

"How could that ever be possible?"

He looked down, watching my hands. I placed the piping bag down.

"Is this about Benjamin Garrick?"

"No."

"Did you drain Warner, Kandy, Gran, or Scarlett on the way over here?"

He laughed involuntarily. "No."

"Well, then." I wiped my hands on a tea towel printed with tiny cupcakes. "There's nothing else you could do to lose me, is there?"

He met my gaze. "I suspect you don't know yourself as well as you think, dowser."

A spike of anger broke through my anxiety. "Oh? Are you here to school me, vampire? Think you're up for it?"

The red of Kett's magic rolled across his eyes, and the taste of peppermint flooded my mouth. I raised an eyebrow at him, challenging him further. Because apparently, me being all soft and mushy wasn't helping him tell me whatever it was he needed to tell me.

"Are you going to stab me, Jade? Again?" He was amused. Which at least was better than whatever else he'd had going on a moment before.

"If you're lucky, all I'll do is skewer you. Unless that's what you want? Because I'm not into that whole S & M thing."

He frowned as though he didn't get the reference. But then he laughed quietly. "If I ever feel the need to be spanked, I'll ask the werewolf."

I chuckled. "With the cuffs on, I imagine she could make it worth your while."

He threw his head back and laughed.

Something tight loosened in my chest. Kett was all right. We were going to be able to get past whatever was haunting him.

The oven timer went off.

Kett glanced at me questioningly.

"Rotate," I said, tossing the oven mitts at him. "Then set it for another ten minutes. And take the baked cupcakes out of their tins now so they can cool further."

He opened the oven, following my instructions to the letter. I finished icing the last tray of already-cooled cupcakes.

"Jade," Kett said, abruptly appearing beside me. "Something has … something that was planned to occur has happened under unforeseen circumstances—"

A knock sounded at the back door. The magic of the wards shifted, bringing an earthy base and a hint of butter.

"Sorcerer. Unknown," I murmured for Kett's sake. I turned toward the door.

He nodded, then appeared in front of me, beside the back door but out of direct sight. Pissed at having our conversation interrupted before he'd had a chance to broach whatever was worrying him, I wasn't in as much of a hurry.

The unknown sorcerer knocked on the door again, sounding impatient as well as rather stubborn. I'd been informed on more than one occasion that the blood wards I'd coated the entire building with were fairly intimidating to newcomers. But my visitor was unfazed enough to have reached into those protections twice.

I opened the door halfway, so I didn't squeeze Kett against the wall.

A sorcerer stood at the back door to my bakery. Her dark hair, dark eyes, and earthy undertone of magic were typical of every sorcerer I'd ever encountered. The twist of a smile she offered as she met my gaze was different, though. Sorcerers rarely smiled at me.

I knew that she wouldn't be able to feel my magic while I was standing behind the bakery wards. That probably helped.

The fact that she was female was also unusual. Logically, I knew that female sorcerers existed. Rumor said that Rochelle's sorcerer grandmother had held the entire territory of Hong Kong to herself for over fifty years. But like male witches, female sorcerers were unusual enough that I'd never met one.

"Jade Godfrey?" she asked—instead of introducing herself properly.

And for some reason, that put me off. That, the double knock, interrupting me while I was baking, and intruding on my conversation with Kett. Not that she could have possibly guessed at the importance of the last point.

"Adepts usually visit the bakery during opening hours," I said.

She frowned. A few strands of silver were laced through the part in her hair, putting her possibly in her midforties. Though among those of the magical persuasion, true age was often hard to judge. She was wearing a long floral-print skirt. Gold toe rings glinted on her feet, though it had really been far too chilly in recent mornings to still be wearing sandals.

"I wasn't told," she finally said, after doing her own once-over of me that turned her expression dour.

I couldn't place her accent. Latin American of some sort, by best guess.

"I'm simply following the protocol that was laid out," she added.

"You really aren't," I said, even more peeved now that I was being forced to insist on any sort of etiquette, whether it was formal introductions or when it was appropriate to drop by the bakery. And for the second time in less than twenty-four hours.

Kett chuckled quietly from behind the door. I was pretty sure the sound wouldn't carry through the wards.

Frowning, the woman raised her chin defiantly. What was it with sorcerers and their freaking attitudes? Unless maybe she thought I was just a witch?

Well, it was going to be fun stepping past the wards and proving her wrong. "I'll be right out."

Her frown deepened as she glanced around the alley, lingering on the dumpsters with a subtle sneer of distaste.

I closed the door in her face, covering my childish smile.

Kett closed the space between us, brushing his fingers across my wrist. "I'll take the cupcakes out of the oven before I go."

"You're leaving?"

He didn't answer. Because, of course, he'd already told me as much.

"I'll tell her to come back," I said stubbornly. "You're more important to me."

"I know," he said. Then he added with mocking sternness, "Do your duty, Jade Godfrey."

I stuck my tongue out at him. Then I opened the door and stepped out into the alley.

# Chapter Five

A gust of wind stirred the loose curls around my face as I stepped out into the back alley. It was a bright morning, but I knew that if I shifted my gaze from the sorcerer waiting for me, I'd see the North Shore Mountains still shrouded in smoke from the endless forest fires that had plagued British Columbia all summer. It needed to rain. Soon, and in volume.

Standing with the wards of the bakery still brushing my back, I took a moment to get a good look at the Adept who'd interrupted my baking. The dark-haired sorcerer was tall but curvy. If I'd been guessing, I would have said she was of Spanish descent, though growing up and living full time in Vancouver didn't provide me much context for that. And I might have just been jumping to conclusions based on her multicolored tiered skirt and the strands of beaded necklaces layered around her neck. The dozens of gold bangles on each of her arms could have played into the image as well—except by the way they teemed with magic, they weren't simply accessories.

I wasn't a huge fan of cataloging and assessing every new Adept who came to the bakery, but apparently that was my thing now. Whatever magic they wielded or whatever reasons had brought them to Vancouver, the newcomers flocking to the city all eventually came to the bakery, often bearing tiny gifts of magic for me ... the Dowser. As if my favor needed to be ... not bought, but at least requested. Assured. As if they needed to make certain I knew them.

Even though I was a huge fan of magical trinkets, this behavior made me uncomfortable. And not just because I'd already had a hint of how Haoxin would react if she thought a half-dragon was attempting to un-officially annex a section of her territory. But because I didn't see myself that way. As someone whose favor needed to be curried.

During business hours, I'd simply wave a new Adept through the door, chat, give them a cupcake, and invite them to talk to whoever else—Gran, Scarlett, or Kandy—was in the bakery. But whether or not it was just my own prejudice rearing its very ugly head, I wasn't interested in inviting an unknown sorcerer into my kitchen. My haven.

The only sorcerer I'd ever met who seemed to consistently place others before himself was Henry Calhoun. But the charming US Marshal had been bitten by Kandy, so I might have been predisposed to like him. Not to mention that he'd let me play with his nifty magical handcuffs.

Yeah, I was pretty easy to woo overall. Good chocolate or magic usually did it for me.

I stepped farther into the alley, feeling the wards slide across me as though they were reluctant to let me go. Since they'd been created and powered by the magic in my own blood, that sensation wasn't unexpected, though personifying magic usually put one on shaky ground. As such, I always tried to ignore it when certain magical artifacts felt moody, or eager, or protective.

The taste of brown-sugar shortbread flooded my mouth. The sorcerer's magic was dense yet buttery. A deadly combination when it came to baked goods—though I hoped the deadly part didn't extend to the meeting I was about to have in the back alley. Mostly because, despite the magical artifacts she wore, the sorcerer wasn't even remotely a match for me. Notwithstanding how few Adepts were a match for me anymore.

I ignored the pinch of disappointment that came with that observation, just as I'd ignored the late-season mosquitos that had plagued me after the sun set the previous night. Teeming with power and armed to the teeth, I was still no match for the bloodsucking bugs. That was everyday life.

"I'm sorry if I've come at a bad time," the sorcerer said.

I still couldn't place her accent, but her conciliatory tone was obvious. As was the increased magic swirling around her wrists. I'd been staring at her for too long.

"The bakery isn't just a front for the Adept," I said, trying for teasing but coming up waspish instead.

I closed the space between us but didn't offer her my hand. She would hesitate to touch me, and I didn't want to bully her with the gesture.

She smiled by rote, not out of joy. Up close, her eyes were a dark hazel, and the dozens of thin gold bangles she wore on each wrist teemed with power that wasn't completely her own. Perhaps she'd inherited the artifacts from an ancestor.

"Angelica Talbot," she said, flicking her gaze momentarily around the alley as if expecting to find someone hiding behind the dumpsters. She lowered her voice. "Sorcerer. Mother of Liam, Tony, Gabrielle, Margaret, and Rebecca."

I couldn't contain my surprise at the long list of offspring. Adepts rarely had more than one child, if any. And then I couldn't help but wonder why a sorcerer would choose to relocate her five children to witch territory. That would have been a pretty big shake-up of their lives. Gran would no doubt know, but she kept her paperwork confidential.

Angelica shifted her gaze to focus on my left shoulder, rather than continuing to look me in the eye. Or to stare at my necklace, perhaps. Yeah, sorcerers had a real thing for magical objects—even more so than most Adepts.

"I was told to present myself to you."

"By Gran?" I asked, surprised. Then I corrected myself. "My grandmother, Pearl Godfrey?"

"No. Henry Calhoun."

A sudden smile spread across my face at the mention of the werewolf-bitten sorcerer. "Henry! I haven't seen him in about three months. I'm sure he was just being funny."

Henry visited Vancouver as often as his job as a US Marshal allowed, spending time with Kandy, of course, but also with Rochelle and Beau. The oracle had created a tattoo that allowed Henry to control his involuntary transformations—a tasty piece of tart-apple magic etched directly into the sorcerer's skin.

Angelica shook her head. "I don't believe so. He was very specific."

"All right, then," I said. "Hello. I'm Jade Godfrey. Dowser." I left off all the other titles. The conversation was awkward enough already. "So now you can let Henry know we've met."

Angelica nodded absentmindedly, glancing behind me toward the bakery. "The wards … are … very …"

Sorcerers felt magic, perhaps even more intensely than many witches. They had to in order to harness it, which was how they wielded power—often aided by magical objects. But witches typically sourced their power from the earth and the energy continually surrounding us. Henry Calhoun had his brilliant handcuffs. Blackwell, evil sorcerer extraordinaire and someone I hadn't laid eyes on since he'd abandoned us on a mountaintop in China, had his amulet, along with numerous objects of power that his family had collected for centuries. Angelica apparently had her bracelets, and perhaps the necklaces as well.

I waved my hand offishly. "The wards are of my construction. They won't harm you."

Angelica gave me a look. Yeah, now that I was standing on the other side of the beguiling wards, my big blue eyes, blond curls, and pink-frilled apron didn't fool her in the least.

"You and your family are welcome to come into the bakery, during operating hours, whenever you wish. I'll simply need to invite you inside the first time. Through the front door."

Angelica nodded. "Thank you, dowser." Then she turned and marched out of the alley without another word.

Completely thrown by the abrupt end to the conversation, I watched her until she turned left onto Yew Street and stepped out of sight. I pondered the awkward meeting that had apparently been about nothing at all as I tracked the taste of her magic. She continued to walk down the hill toward the water instead of getting into a vehicle. The Talbots were probably living in Kitsilano, then. Perhaps in one of Gran's houses.

Then I realized what had put me off about her—besides the fact that it was apparent, even to me, that I was bigoted when it came to unknown sorcerers. That was definitely something to work on. Or, even better, to just let go of. But beyond that, it was the fact that Angelica Talbot didn't find me charming. Not in the least. Meeting me was an annoying duty, apparently imposed upon her by Henry.

Next time, I'd woo her with cupcakes. That always worked. Unless she was gluten or dairy intolerant. Or vegan. Then every conversation would just be a strained mess.

Yeah, needing to be considered charming all the time was awfully shallow of me. But admitting it was half the problem, right? Or was that half the solution?

The influx of Adepts to Vancouver was the prime reason that Gran had gathered twelve witches, plus me, to erect a magical grid system covering the entire city. When Kandy had hatched the plan with Gran almost a year before, I'd thought it was overkill. But as I stopped tracking Angelica's brown-sugar-shortbread magic and headed back into the bakery kitchen, I found myself wondering if Kandy and Gran had foreseen issues that I was still willfully blind to.

Vancouver was my haven, after all. So why shouldn't it be that for others as well?

Kett had left the building by the time I got back to the kitchen. He had pulled the muffin tins before going, as promised. Unfortunately, he hadn't also frosted the rest of the cupcakes, and I was now seriously behind schedule. Being able to move quickly, or even to run full out for miles, was in no way helpful when it came to baking. Or trinket making, for that matter. Both activities were slow and considered work. Slapped-on icing might taste exactly the same, but it wouldn't be the least bit appealing to my customers.

Plus, Bryn would seriously lose it if I tried to stuff the display cases with shoddy cupcakes.

Running my conversations with Kett, then Angelica, through my head in an annoyingly endless loop, I dropped butter into my standing mixer, adding a heaping half-cup of cocoa powder. Then I mixed the two ingredients slightly too vigorously.

Kandy would be delighted that the vampire had arrived in town with a secret, though I wasn't so much a fan of gossip and hidden agendas. Still, the werewolf wouldn't let Kett dodge her questions for very long. Ironically, Kandy was as circumspect about anything personal as the vampire was, but she wouldn't put up with being out of the loop.

I added powdered sugar to the mixer. And as I did, I stuffed my concern over whatever Kett was worried about telling me, along with the weird meeting with the sorcerer, deep down underneath the small mountain of cupcakes that still needed to be baked and frosted.

After adding *Exultation in a Cup*—smooth dark-chocolate buttercream on an insanely tasty chocolate-peanut butter cake—to my ready-for-the-bakery rack, I paired the rest of the delectable buttercream with the last of my fluffy, super-light white cake bases, resulting in a bonus dozen *Wonder in a Cup*. I might have also licked the spatula. After I'd finished scraping the bowl, of course.

Halfway through baking the chocolate cake base I used for *Lust in a Cup*, *Love in a Cup*, and *Hug in a Cup*, keys scraping in the alley door lock heralded one of the only three people who needed to use mundane means by which to enter the bakery kitchen. Specifically, because they lacked the magic needed to be keyed to the door lock spell. The blood wards posed no issues to them for exactly the same reason.

I glanced over my shoulder as Todd practically stumbled through the door. Dark, silver-rimmed sunglasses shielded his eyes. But based on the way he held his head, they did nothing to mute his hangover. He lost hold of his backpack one step over the threshold, then shuffled past me toward the storefront without a word.

He had cut his brown hair so short that it no longer curled. His brown Cake in a Cup T-shirt appeared pristinely pressed. But the rest of him wasn't remotely ready to be out of bed.

"I was expecting Bryn." I picked up a *Buzz in a Cup*, placing it on the far corner of the stainless steel workstation a moment before Todd walked by.

He didn't even pause, scooping up the mocha-fudge cupcake as he passed and cramming it into his mouth. He chewed, swallowed, then cleared his throat. Rather disgustingly, actually.

"She texted last night."

Delightful. "She's still in Whistler?"

Todd nodded, then winced as if he regretted that movement.

"Ah, crap." I surveyed my exceedingly full workstation, then the only-half-full rack of ready-for-sale cupcakes. "I'm behind."

Todd pushed through the swing doors that led into the storefront. "I'll help. Just let me wash down the aspirin with a quad."

I snorted doubtfully, fairly certain that Todd's frosting skills were even sloppier than mine. But I wasn't in any position to turn down another set of hands.

I heard the steamer of the espresso machine, knowing that no matter how hungover he was, Todd would always meticulously clean and prime the pricey piece of equipment—which he'd insisted was worth every penny. He considered coffee his domain at Cake in a Cup, going so far as to have sneered condescendingly when I'd asked him to train Tima, my other part-timer, to make it.

Todd was a graphic artist, specializing in online comics. A couple of his newer titles were doing well enough that I kept expecting him to give notice. He hadn't yet.

I finished swirling thickly whipped buttercream onto the tray of moist banana-cake bases for *Comfort in a Cup*. After the chocolate cake had cooled, I would use the rest of the buttercream for a dozen *Hug in a Cup*.

Todd, still sporting his sunglasses, appeared in the storefront doorway, leaning into it and cupping a mug as if it held the nectar of life. And maybe for him, it did. I enjoyed coffee flavoring on occasion, but not the drink on its own.

"Problems with the renovation?" I asked.

He looked at me as though I'd just spoken utter nonsense.

"In Whistler?" I prompted. "For Bryn?"

Bryn had finally persuaded me to open a second bakery in the well-heeled ski resort about an hour-and-a-half's drive from Vancouver. I'd agreed only because she had asked to be co-owner, literally shoving the business plan she'd created in my face. Her half had already been fully financed.

Of course, a tiny pouch of the gold just lying around in the treasure keeper's chamber would have paid for everything outright, including multiple years of operating expenses. But I wasn't interested in asking guardians for favors, or in owing them anything. Pulou especially.

"Tile delivery," Todd said.

"On a Saturday?"

He shrugged, taking a generous sip of his espresso. "It's Whistler."

Unfortunately, 'It's Whistler' had become a common expression around Cake in a Cup recently. No matter that we had the finances, finding a location for a new bakery had been a serious challenge. In the end, Bryn had gotten Gran involved—and the two of them had actually leveraged the purchase of an entire building in the village by agreeing to sell the previous owner two of Gran's ski-in-and-ski-out rental properties. I was almost surprised that my grandmother would have done anything as painful as selling, except I knew Bryn could be very persuasive when she wanted to be. So much so that someone might think she wielded a degree of compulsion, though she didn't carry a hint of magic.

As the deal had come together, I also realized that Gran didn't mind having a more public presence in Whistler herself, because some of Bryn's investors turned out to be members of the local First Nations band. Specifically, the members that could also take on the forms of animals they had magically bonded with. Yep, the skinwalkers were interested in cupcakes, and in the jobs that came with opening a bakery.

So while tradespeople had been hard to come by and a renovation that would have taken three months in Vancouver looked as though it was going to stretch beyond the six-month mark, apparently Bryn already had employees lined up. Plus she was renting one of the six apartments that came with the building.

"It'll be great, Jade," Todd said earnestly, misreading my reflective mood as concern about the new bakery.

"Oh, I know. Bryn has everything under control."

"Yeah, she's good like that." He downed the last of his espresso, placed his cup in the industrial dishwasher, and then sauntered over to retrieve his backpack with a bit more pep.

I eyed the dishwasher, which I hadn't tested yet that morning, even though I often washed mixing bowls as I used them so as to not create an impossibly large pile. The brownie, Blossom, was actively jealous of the machine. Sometimes I thought it was only professional pride that kept her from sabotaging it.

Todd hung his backpack up in the office, then started filling the front display cases with the cupcakes I'd already finished.

I glanced up at the clock, which indicated it was 9:16 A.M. It was going to be close.

And I was going to have to seriously look into getting a part-time baker to replace Bryn sooner rather than later. Having her run from Whistler to Vancouver for weekend shifts had made sense early on. But apparently, the closer the renovation was to being finished, the more impossible that schedule was going to become.

In the end, Todd got us set up and open without my help, and I managed to get a dozen of each type of cupcake baked and iced in time to help him deal with the opening rush. Then, letting him deal with the fifth pumpkin-spice cupcake request of the morning, I slipped back into the kitchen to fill the gaps already appearing in the display case.

Every bowl, tray, and dish had been cleaned and returned to its permanent location—including the few that had been in the dishwasher. The scent of lemon verbena lingered on almost every surface. I shook my head, laughing to myself. Blossom liked to lie in wait. Thankfully, none of my nonmagical employees had so far noticed my uncanny ability to clean the kitchen even as I was in the bakery serving customers. Apparently, the treasure keeper and the far seer didn't make enough of a mess to keep the brownie occupied. Either that or she just liked the sweeter messes I made.

I felt the wards shift as Gran entered the storefront, tasting intensely of her lilac witch magic. She must have already been casting that morning. Perhaps Burgundy had requested the reversal spell for the cemetery early.

I was expecting her to check in with me, but Gran took a seat out front instead. Then the aforementioned junior witch with her green-watermelon magic arrived moments later. Now that I'd recognized the taste of Burgundy's magic, I was less likely to miss it, even though Gran's magic alone was enough to overwhelm it.

I finished baking a second round of my bestselling *Cozy in a Cup*, *Serenity in a Cup*, and *Bliss in a Cup* right before the taste of red berries and bitter dark chocolate announced Kandy's arrival at the back door. Without a word, the sweaty, green-haired werewolf darted past me and into the bakery, then returned with a *Tart in a Cup*. I doubted that Todd had even noticed the stealthy thievery.

"Just because there's blackberries in the cake doesn't make it breakfast," I said, referencing the cupcake she'd already eaten half of.

"They're in the frosting too," Kandy said, hunkering down on the stool Kett had vacated on the other side of my workstation. "That counts as two servings of fruit. Plus, you're one to talk."

I laughed. "You've been jogging?"

Kandy huffed. "Checking the anchor points for Pearl."

"Every one?"

"Yup."

Meaning Kandy had just come from jogging around the entire perimeter of Vancouver. I spent a moment trying to calculate how many miles the werewolf had covered … and then abandoned the attempt just as quickly. "That's a lot of ground."

Kandy shrugged, accepting the *Cozy in a Cup* I slid toward her.

"Banana," I said. "Potassium. Plus dark chocolate. Both good for you."

She grunted in acknowledgement, barely getting the paper wrapper off the cupcake before destroying the banana-chocolate-chip cake topped with chocolate buttercream.

My tummy rumbled. But before I could indulge in a cupcake for breakfast myself, my mother strode through the back door as if on a mission.

Clad in a curve-hugging royal-blue wrap dress that fell to her calves, Scarlett was carrying herself stiffly, but the tightness in her shoulders softened as her gaze settled on me. Though who else she might have been expecting to find in the kitchen, I didn't know. She smiled, reaching for me, then squeezing my elbow. My gloved hands were covered in various frostings. "Jade."

"Morning, Mom."

Scarlett's strawberry-scented magic, perfectly matching the cascade of her strawberry-blond hair in volume and intensity, brushed against me. I instinctively stole a lick of residual she left behind, secreting it in my necklace.

Yeah, I blamed my dragon half. Except I hoarded magic, not gold.

Scarlett laughed as though I'd just done something delightful. If I'd been tense, I would have relaxed. That was my mother's power—or at least that was how I reacted to the charm and charisma she wielded so effortlessly.

"Good morning, Kandy," Scarlett said. "How did the grid check out?"

"Smells okay," Kandy said, swallowing the remnants of what I was pretty sure was a third cupcake, based on the chocolate crumbs. "Each point slightly different. For each witch, I guess."

"And Jade's anchor?"

My mother's question sounded entirely casual. But even as she said it, I could tell that it was front-loaded with some sort of importance—though pertaining to what, I had no idea.

"Strong," Kandy said.

"Off-balancing the rest?"

Kandy shrugged. "That's not for me to say, is it?"

Okay, something was going on that I wasn't privy to.

Scarlett frowned at the green-haired werewolf. Kandy avoided her displeased gaze by reaching toward the tray of unfrosted fudge cakes, which were waiting to be topped with peanut butter icing and thusly transformed into *Bliss in a Cup*.

"What's up?" I asked.

Scarlett's shoulders stiffened again. "We'll wait for your grandmother to discuss it." She eyed Kandy. "I'd rather not go unheard. For the second time."

Ah, delightful. And here I'd thought everyone was just dropping by for a friendly visit. But battle lines had obviously been drawn sometime in the night. Possibly after the incident in the graveyard.

"Gran is in the bakery," I said.

"It's a conversation best had out of earshot," Scarlett said.

"Okay. Great." I picked up two trays of frosted cupcakes. "I'll finish these up and have Todd make you a cappuccino. Then I'll get Gran."

"Thank you, darling."

Kandy flashed a toothy grin at me. "I'll take a pumpkin-spice latte. Triple shot."

I curled my lip, playfully affronted. "I'm sure Starbucks would be happy to take your order. You'll find one right across the street."

She chortled.

Ironically, despite all my protests, Todd had been testing a recipe for the ubiquitous seasonal beverage. But there was no freaking way I was adding a pumpkin cupcake to my menu. Honestly, I'd never been a fan of pumpkin pie either.

Two witches were standing hand in hand on the sidewalk beyond the French-paned front door of the bakery. Teeming with power, they were a study in complete opposites—light and dark, poised and untamed. Ice and fire. One of them could have walked through the wards without issue, but the other… well, if it wasn't for the tenor of his magic, I would have taken him for a dark sorcerer on sight, interested in magical mayhem, not delectable cupcakes.

I had tasted her magic when casting the grid the previous night.

Nutmeg.

Wisteria Fairchild. The reconstructionist.

But I had yet to meet her forbidding companion in the long leather jacket and tinted sunglasses.

I slid another tray of cupcakes into the display case, checked to confirm that Todd wasn't frazzled by the short line at the cash, then smiled welcomingly at the witches.

The ward magic shifted in response, and Wisteria tugged her reluctant, dark-haired companion forward and into the bakery. The taste of their magic intensified as they crossed the threshold.

The reconstructionist's nutmeg overtone almost overwhelmed the grassy base that all witches shared, which was unusual. But since I'd seen her last October, something must have occurred to intensify her magic—including the magical artifact she wore on her wrist. A platinum charm bracelet imbued by me with Kett's power in order to give the witch some peace of mind when she had been obliged to work with the vampire. It was now resplendent with her own power … and more.

I stepped around the glass display, accepting the hand she was already holding out to me. "Wisteria."

"Jade."

I stepped to the side so as not to block the doorway, though the morning rush had died down. "I felt you last night. In the casting. I'm pleased you dropped by."

"Ah," her imposing companion said. "So that was you."

I glanced at him questioningly, but he didn't clarify. His accent was odd. Well, odd to my Canadian ear. Like a mixture of Southern-US drawl with a French undertone.

Wisteria smoothed over the comment with introductions. "Declan Benoit, my …"

"Fiance," Declan said. He smirked at the reconstructionist's hesitation.

Wisteria laughed quietly. "Yes. Also … ah …"

"Of the Fairchild coven." Declan's smirk disappeared, a little too quickly.

"Congratulations." Ignoring whatever was transpiring between them, I reached out to him, offering my hand. And kudos to him, he didn't hesitate to shake it. His grip was firm but not too hard. Though it was doubtful I would have felt the difference.

"Caramelized sugar … and fresh-baked, doughy bread straight from the oven," I said. "What's that? Bread pudding?"

Wisteria laughed, quietly delighted. "And what cupcake would you recommend?"

A true grin spread across my face. "If it was December, I'd say *Vixen in a Cup*. For the salted caramel icing."

"I don't follow," Declan said, dropping my hand.

"Jade tastes magic," Wisteria said. "And she believes that the Adepts who eat her cupcakes are … comforted by certain pairings that reflect that taste. Though I think there might be magic involved."

I shrugged carelessly. Whether or not the cupcakes I baked retained any magic was debatable. And since giving any sort of magic to the nonmagical was seriously frowned upon, we of the Godfrey coven made a point of not discussing it. By unspoken agreement.

"Thank you for helping to anchor Gran's grid," I said.

"We were honored to be asked." Wisteria's tone turned formal once again. "And to help celebrate your engagement."

They glanced at each other, again communicating something I was missing. Then I remembered.

The Fairchild coven had lost three of its members fairly recently, including a highly skilled tech witch. Wisteria's cousin, Jasmine Fairchild. She had died along with Wisteria's aunt Rose, whose seat on the Convocation was still empty. It was an appointment that Gran not-so-secretly hoped an elder of the coven, rather than Wisteria herself, would fill. Apparently even my mother, at the tender age of forty-four, was considered a youthful rabble-rouser by the majority of the Convocation's members. Gran's words, not mine. So the reconstructionist, who was still in her late twenties, would probably be a shock to the strict—and honestly, antiquated—governing body.

"I'm sorry," I said quietly. "Gran mentioned that you … had … some …" Then I faltered. Because though Gran had informed me of the sudden deaths—as head of the Convocation, she'd been officially notified in writing by someone within the Fairchild coven—I actually didn't know whether they'd been accidental or not.

"Wisteria!" Gran called out from a high bistro table in the far corner of the seating area. "Declan. Please join me."

Wisteria smiled, politely nodding toward my grandmother over her shoulder. Then she glanced back at me, concerned. "Jade …"

"No worries," I said. I smiled, though apparently there were more mysteries to unravel, and I really didn't have the patience for puzzles. "I'm on shift." I turned to Declan. "I'll get you a couple of cupcakes. Maybe two *Clarity in a Cup*? Apple spice cake with honey buttercream. Wisteria's favorite."

"Who could say no to that?" He grinned, cracking his hard exterior. "But I'm happy to stand in line."

"Ah, but my grandmother won't be happy if you do."

Wisteria laughed.

Declan eyed her. A surprised but delighted curl of his lips softened all the stony edges of his face.

I turned away to help Todd get through the line that had formed while I'd been chatting—and, if I was completely honest, while I'd been attempting to avoid the confrontation I was certain was brewing between Gran and Scarlett. With Gran suddenly occupied, I found myself hoping that if I fussed about, ferrying cupcakes and hot drinks to and fro, maybe my mother would get tired of waiting.

But unfortunately for me, I got my short attention span from my father.

"You clearly added this extra arm," Scarlett said, jabbing her finger at a crumpled piece of paper smoothed out on my workstation between her and Gran. "Even after I threw away the entire thing. Even after we'd agreed Jade shouldn't use runes at all. I didn't even want her at an anchor point in the first place."

Ah, lovely. I paused where I'd stopped in the swing doors between the kitchen and storefront, still holding one of them open—and contemplating retreating before anyone noticed me.

Gran, dressed in charcoal wool pants and a loosely buttoned lightweight blue cardigan, wore her long hair braided down her back. Not a hair out of place, as always. I hadn't even noticed when she'd broken off talking to Wisteria and Declan, let alone when she'd slipped past me and into the kitchen.

Scarlett was a bright beacon next to her mother, not a hint of gray in her hair. Both of them were petite, beautiful women. But they wielded their powerful magic very differently.

Kandy had pretty much crammed her stool and herself into the far back corner of the kitchen, practically hiding behind the dishwasher. When she glanced over at me, I saw that her green shapeshifter magic ringed her eyes.

Doubly lovely. My mother and grandmother were terrifying a werewolf.

"You may be a proficient witch, Scarlett," Gran said stiffly. "But you are no expert in using runes as anchors."

Scarlett straightened her shoulders. A soft smile spread across her face, deceptively sweet and completely deadly. "Well, Pearl, your expertise has tied Jade too tightly to the magical grid."

"It's done nothing of the sort," Gran snapped.

I let go of the swing door but didn't step forward swiftly enough. It hit the heel of my sneaker as it closed, drawing Scarlett's and Gran's attention to me. Both of their eyes were alive with the blue of their witch magic, a power display that combined with Kandy's anxiety, so that the magic threading through the room was suddenly on the edge of stifling. Or at least it would have been two years earlier. Now, the magic of my necklace simply shifted to compensate.

I tried a smile, falling into the role of peacemaker even though my mother and grandmother rarely needed me to intercede. They kept their issues with each other hidden under icy layers of silence.

Scarlett's smile was tempered by my own. But Gran didn't bother, simply waving me forward impatiently as if I was the one invading their space, not the other way around.

"We were just discussing the grid, Jade," Scarlett said. "To figure out how to fix it."

"It doesn't need fixing," Gran said. "It worked perfectly last night, alerting Jade and Kandy to the issue with Mory, and allowing Burgundy time to clean up."

I strolled forward, not thinking before I spoke. "Sure. As long as it didn't cause the issue in the first place."

Gran looked at me as though I'd just stabbed her in the heart. A curl of a smirk flitted across Scarlett's face.

The magic pooling between them intensified.

Kandy muttered uncomfortably, crossing her arms so that her hands were tight around her cuffs.

"Witch magic would not have affected a necromancer," Gran said frostily, crossing her own arms. "Whatever happened to Mory was of her own doing."

"The grid contains more than witch magic." Scarlett was beaming sunnily, yet she still managed to clip her words. "As I cautioned against in the first place."

"Jade is powerful—"

"Jade is too powerful for this casting." Scarlett jabbed her finger at the piece of paper again. From my new vantage point, I could see it was the same paper that I'd copied the runes off the night before. Kandy must have given it to my mother. "And far, far too powerful for this extra leg …"—she traced the swirl at the top of the final rune that I'd used to close the circle—"… which you added. Behind my back."

"Behind your back," Gran scoffed. "Since when are you interested in anything having to do with the coven?"

"I am interested, and always have been, in anything having to do with Jade."

Gran laughed, but she wasn't amused. "Again, since when?"

Blue magic sparked underneath Scarlett's hand, briefly reflecting against the stainless steel of the freestanding counter. She wasn't smiling anymore. "Shall we discuss that now, Pearl? In front of Jade?"

Tension flitted across my grandmother's face as she flicked her gaze to me.

"What's going on?" I whispered.

Neither of them answered me.

I looked toward Kandy. She shrugged her shoulders, but as if she'd been expecting the confrontation, rather than being confused by it.

"Jade." Scarlett chose her words carefully. "Your gran has always had very specific guidelines for you to follow. We disagreed."

"And I suppose you're going to claim you could have raised your daughter by yourself." Gran uncrossed her arms, clenching her fists at her sides instead. "At sixteen? With no husband?"

Scarlett glanced at me. Her gaze was soft. "I would have liked to have been more involved."

"You were as involved as you chose to be. Jade isn't an idiot. She can remember as clearly as I do."

"Does she?" Scarlett whispered. "Does she remember the arguments, the tears?"

"You were a child yourself."

"And Jade was the powerful daughter you always thought you should have had."

Gran sneered. "Being jealous of your own daughter is awfully petty, Scarlett."

My mother abruptly stepped into Gran's space, making me realize for the first time that she was actually about an inch taller than her mother. "You won't frighten me off this time, Pearl. Or bully me so much that I have to get away from you just so I can breathe."

Gran scoffed.

My mother stepped back, angling her shoulder to include me in the conversation but not looking at me.

"And you won't continue to use Jade to further expand your power base."

"That's ridiculous."

Scarlett glanced over at me. "I'm sorry, Jade. I should have taken my concerns to you directly. I've been too worried about playing nice."

"You always wanted everyone to like you, Scarlett," Gran said haughtily. "Jade gets that weakness from you."

Scarlett turned back toward her mother. "That's enough!"

Magic flashed between her and Gran.

Pearl stumbled back.

My jaw dropped and stayed down.

"Control yourself, child," Gran said.

Scarlett stalked toward her. "Make me, mother of mine."

Gran glared at her. Despite her gray hair, she and my mother were practically twins in all ways except their magic. But in that moment, I wondered whether Scarlett had simply been politely hiding her strength. Maybe for too many years.

"You will recast the grid tonight." My mother put on a smooth, practiced tone. "You will have another witch stand in for Jade."

"I will not."

"Then I will, Pearl."

"You think the witches will gather at your behest?"

Scarlett laughed. "Yes, Pearl. I believe they would. Because they all felt Jade's magic in the grid last night. Just as you did. That power thrilled you. Emboldened you. But the rest of us aren't looking to build a weapon."

Kandy straightened suddenly, catching all our attention. Her gaze was fiercely glued to Gran. "The grid is simply a detection system."

Scarlett nodded. "That was the plan."

"We needed thirteen witches in their prime," Gran said. But in her tone, even I could hear that she was suddenly scrambling to cobble together a justification. "Jade is more than capable—"

"Much, much more than capable." Scarlett smiled at me. "But not necessary for a simple detection system. 'Overkill' is an apt expression. But even simply 'off-balancing.' Just ask Kandy what she scented this morning."

Gran jutted her chin out, but she didn't respond.

Kandy shifted, looking thoughtful. But she also remained silent.

"We're in agreement, then." Scarlett offered her mother another blistering smile. "You will gather the witches. Or I will."

She turned away without waiting for Gran's reply, sauntering over to me.

I realized in that moment that I'd been standing immobile, staring at Gran and Scarlett. Shocked to silence. All this magic I channeled, all this strength at my disposal—and still, I would apparently unravel in response to even a hint of familial conflict.

Scarlett touched my shoulder lightly. "Simply reversing the casting will likely be enough, but your grandmother and I will consult on the particulars through the day."

I nodded, even though I wasn't completely sure what I was agreeing to. Or if I was taking sides...assuming sides had to be taken.

Scarlett glanced back at her mother.

Gran's face hardened. Her magic churned around her clenched fists in miniature blue whirlwinds, suddenly reminding me of her fierce anger when I had first opened the portal. Her vehemence.

It seemed that she didn't have any issues with using the power I'd had to uncover for myself. Power that had been carefully mitigated, and therefore easily downplayed, through baking and trinket making. At Gran's suggestion.

"I understand Wisteria and Declan are in the bakery?" Scarlett asked lightly. "Certainly you shouldn't let the opportunity to cement your relationship with the new head of the Fairchild coven languish, Pearl? Especially since the reconstructionist no longer jumps at your command."

"Wisteria Fairchild is entirely mindful of where her loyalties lie, Scarlett."

My mother laughed quietly. "I dare say she is." Then she patted my arm. "Kandy says you made some *Love in a Cup*."

"And *Charm*," I said, speaking by rote. "Same strawberry buttercream." The taste of both had been inspired by my mother's magic.

"I know, darling."

Scarlett exited through the swing doors. And as she went, I found myself suddenly wondering whether her last words had been a stealthy but overt statement—insinuating that I modeled my idea of what love tasted like after her, and not my grandmother.

I looked over to Gran, who was glaring after her daughter.

"You don't agree?" I said quietly. "That my magic has off-balanced the grid."

"I don't," Gran snapped. She crossed over to the workstation, carefully folding the piece of paper still there.

I glanced over at Kandy. "The itchy feet."

The green-haired werewolf nodded, but she kept her gaze on Gran.

"A side effect I'm sure we can sort out," Gran said offishly.

"The runes weren't enough of an anchor," I said.

Gran stiffened. But she tucked the piece of paper in her pocket without looking at me.

"Magic was flowing into the anchor point. But not out."

"How did you compensate?"

Kandy closed the space between us, leaning against the counter. Deceptively casual, her hooded gaze was pinned to Gran. "I already mentioned that, Pearl."

Gran looked at Kandy witheringly. "What you observed might not be the same thing that Jade felt, werewolf."

I didn't like my grandmother's tone. I didn't like her calling Kandy 'werewolf' as though it were derogatory.

"It seems like we have a problem, Gran," I said, deliberately settling my own tone. "What did Scarlett mean...about building a weapon?"

"I had you remove your knife and necklace, didn't I?" Gran said. Not really answering my question.

"Jade and the artifacts are one," Kandy said darkly.

"It should have worked," Gran said in a huff.

"What should have worked?"

"I won't have my words picked apart by you and your mother, Jade." And with that pronouncement, Gran swept through the kitchen and out into the storefront.

Kandy looked at me. "Her words picked apart? Or her intentions?"

"Scarlett and Gran aren't ever going to see eye-to-eye," I said, somewhat lamely. Not addressing any of the things that Kandy or my mother had implied.

Kandy eyed me for a moment. Then she grinned easily. "Are you going to bake the rest of the chocolate-blackberry batter or not?"

I laughed. "Have you been rifling through my fridges?"

"Would you expect anything less?"

Shaking my head, I rounded the workstation and pulled out the mixing bowl with the aforementioned batter. I would let it come to room temperature as I made another round of chocolate-blackberry buttercream for *Sass in a Cup* and *Flirt in a Cup*—two of four seasonal cupcakes originally designed to match my werewolf BFF's magic. So they were, of course, her favorites.

Kandy slid her stool to the edge of the steel counter, placing her chin in her hands and contentedly watching me bake.

Unfortunately, the peace that baking normally provided me was disturbed by my apparent need to run Gran and Scarlett's heated conversation over and over in my head.

"I thought they were going to start throwing magic," I murmured.

Kandy grunted. "Not in front of you. Not deliberately, at least."

Silence fell between us. Then Kandy spoke quietly. "Had Pearl told you that Scarlett abandoned you?"

I shifted my shoulders uncomfortably. "She never used that word."

"No. She wouldn't."

I handed Kandy the beater so she could lick off the buttercream. My best friend let the subject drop. And I made no effort to revive it.

# Chapter Six

I had just slipped the final tray filled with *Harmony in a Cup*—sweet cherry buttercream swirled on an airy white cake—onto the display shelf when magic bloomed underneath my feet.

"Well, that's wonderful timing," I muttered to myself, smiling at a customer who was pointing out the tray of *Sex in a Cup*—a cinnamon-laced cocoa cake with dark-chocolate buttercream—rather enthusiastically to her companion. By the way her friend kept glancing up at the prettily chalked menu over my head, then down at the offerings on display, I gathered it was her first visit to Cake in a Cup.

Tima wasn't on shift for another thirty minutes, and the storefront was devoid of Adepts, who had all wandered off to attend to their own errands and sightseeing. Though Wisteria had talked of her tourist activities being focused around finding the perfect lunch spot.

The magic underneath my feet was tickling me. Then without warning, it cranked right over into itching. Jesus, zombies couldn't walk in the day, could they? I swore inwardly. I was going to have to abandon Todd right before the post-lunch rush.

I stepped past the cash register, whispering to the espresso wizard doing his thing at his machine. "Be right back."

He nodded, then glanced over at the customer waiting on the other side of the coffee counter. The willowy, impeccably dressed brunette turned his head coyly, pretending to not notice Todd's regard.

Right. Everything appeared to be under control.

I hustled back to the kitchen, waving to a few regular customers.

"Quad nonfat no-whip mocha," Todd said with great satisfaction. "May I recommend an *Ecstasy in a Cup* to go with it? The double chocolate cake will compliment the mocha but not overwhelm it. And the lemon buttercream is just an added bonus. On the house."

See?

I wasn't the only one who wooed with tasty baked goods.

I ditched my apron, grabbed my satchel from the office, and hightailed it out the alley door. I texted Kandy as my itchy feet forced me onto, then east along West Fourth Avenue. Quickly zigzagging through the dense foot traffic, I passed my bank, then my yoga studio, and jogged across Yew against the light.

The magic underneath my feet intensified as I traversed the block, heading slightly downhill so that I could see the perpetually long line of customers at Sophie's Cosmic Cafe on the corner of Arbutus. Closer in, I motored past Connie's Cookhouse, wishing I were dropping in for one of their lunch specials.

Then as suddenly as it had come, the magic faded, dispersing more and more with each step.

I paused, stepping over to the curb so as not to block the sidewalk as I glanced around.

No zombies appeared to be ambling along West Fourth. Which was a good thing. But I had just been torn from my bakery by magic I actually didn't want tied to me, so I was kind of spoiling for a fight. Or at least a good rant and rave.

Okay, so I was still carrying an excess of tension from Gran and Scarlett's confrontation, as well as the mounting evidence that I was tied to the magical grid. And in a way that Gran might actually have intended, if she had modified the runes as Scarlett accused her of doing. Of course, I might have done that myself, with—

The magic tugged me back the way I'd come.

"Damn it," I muttered, turning back.

Kandy, freshly showered and outfitted in skinny jeans, a rather low-key, plain green T-shirt, and the still-completely-out-of-character purple backpack, appeared out of the crowd streaming up and down the sidewalk. She paused, peering into the windows of the nail salon we both frequented monthly.

The green-haired werewolf frowned, then looked at me, holding up her phone.

I joined her outside the glass door. "The grid is lighting up?"

"Yep. Itchy feet?"

I nodded. Then I surveyed the interior of the salon.

It was empty.

At noon.

On a Saturday.

"This can't be good," I muttered, trying the door and finding it unlocked.

Kandy grunted in agreement as she followed me in. Then she locked the door behind us. Unfortunately, there weren't any blinds to pull down over the wide front windows.

We stood crammed together in the tiny entrance-way, before a small white-painted desk that held the cash register.

Comfy couches in white faux-leather ran along the wall to our left, adjacent to two matching seats before the front windows. Magazine-strewn side tables sat between them. A couple of still-foamy foot baths, along with manicure tools, had been abandoned at each station. Someone had knocked over a bottle of bright-red nail polish, which had spattered across the white tile floor. Thankfully, the polish had too much orange in it to be mistaken for blood—which I unfortunately knew from experience.

"Got anything, dowser?" Kandy whispered behind me.

I started to shake my head. But then the taste of tart-but-sweet jam—raspberry and blackberry—tickled my senses. It was muted. Perhaps the low intensity was due in part to how tightly I'd been holding my own magic of late. But it might also have been indicating less-than-formidable Adepts.

Or someone who could mask their presence.

Now that would be interesting.

"Two Adepts ahead," I murmured, stifling a smile of grim anticipation. "No underlying base."

Kandy nodded, understanding that I meant I didn't know what type of Adept we were dealing with. She slipped ahead of me, forgetting—perhaps willfully—that I was supposed to take point. We stepped past the reception counter, then through the salon with the high stools at the drying stations to our right. The muted TV was overhead. An old episode of *Charmed* was playing. Appropriate. Except no one in the building was a witch, at least not as far as I could taste.

The open storefront narrowed into a corridor leading to the bathroom, and what I had always assumed was the employee break room.

Two more steps, and I picked up the sound of sobbing. The door to the washroom on the left was closed. Kandy opened it, then glanced inside, shaking her head.

The taste of tart jam increased. We continued on, heading to the back of the salon. The presumably-the-break-room door was closed. And locked when I tried to turn the handle.

I pressed my ear against the hollow-core wood, hearing whispers beyond. "People in here," I said to Kandy. "But the source of the magic is farther back. Maybe in the alley?"

I knocked lightly. The chatter within increased. Then a tiny woman in her midforties opened the door, blinking behind thick-rimmed pink glasses a few times before she recognized me.

"Jade!" Jenny, the salon owner, cried. "You don't have an appointment."

"Um, no," I said, surreptitiously glancing into the room. "Everything okay?"

"Sure, sure," she said, opening the door far enough to reveal seven people crammed into the small space behind her. Four of the shop's estheticians, all in their white uniforms, were attempting to manicure three customers around a tiny table.

Math wasn't my strong suit, but I was fairly certain two customers were missing—the two who'd been getting the side-by-side pedicures. The two who tasted of tart jam—including whoever was almost-silently weeping farther down the hall.

I met the owner's gaze, raising an eyebrow and allowing silence to stretch between us. It was a pointed questioning technique I was trying out. You know, when I didn't have any cupcakes with which to extract information.

Her lips tightened, but she held my gaze without obvious guile. So apparently, the silent treatment only worked when I was on the receiving end. Jenny didn't have a drop of magic in her. So I couldn't actually ask her outright what the hell was going on if she wasn't going to offer it up.

"Okay," I said. "I'm just going to wander into the back. I think I have … I'm meeting friends here."

The owner nodded. "Fine, fine."

Then she shut the door in my face.

I looked at Kandy with disbelief.

She dropped her jaw in silent laughter.

Shaking my head, I slipped to the very back of the salon, pausing at the exit to the alley. But then I turned back, feeling the raspberry-and-blackberry magic emanating from what I assumed was a storage room.

I stepped up to the door, calling my jade knife into my right hand. Kandy set herself just behind and to the side of me, reaching around and placing her hand on the storeroom doorknob. Magic glinted off the rune-carved gold cuff at her wrist.

The slow smile I'd been suppressing before spread across my face. My magic stirred, responding to my completely inappropriate anticipation. I should have been baking, not looking for the chance to knife a dangerous Adept in a storeroom.

I also should have been focused on containing the situation. Not daydreaming about it suddenly escalating into an all-out brawl in the streets.

Kandy nodded.

I shifted my weight forward over the balls of my feet.

The werewolf flung the door open, snapping off the knob in the process. I gathered she assumed it would have been locked.

A wild blast of tart-raspberry magic hit me full in the face, rippling harmlessly around me and bringing with it an inexplicable urge for Pop-Tarts. Kandy slipped behind me for protection, though the weakness of the magic made that completely unnecessary.

Not bothering to absorb whatever spell the Adept in the small storeroom was trying to use against me, I blinked, adjusting my eyes to the low light.

Then I blinked again, certain that I was seeing double. Or, rather, some sort of weird reflection.

A willowy blond, slightly taller than me, stood with her back to the far wall. Boxes of supplies occupied the shelves to the right. Cleaning gear, an industrial sink, and a short counter took up the left wall.

An exact reflection of the svelte blond was curled in the fetal position at her feet.

Problem was, they weren't dressed the same—one wearing shades of cream and the other in dark gray. And the blond who was upright was currently standing against me with only a blue flip-flop for a weapon.

Twins. In their late teens.

Kandy peered around my shoulder.

"The broom would have made a better weapon," I said, nodding toward where it was hanging next to a mop on my left.

"Too far away," the standing blond said.

"You should have armed yourself the second you stepped in here," Kandy snarled. "Then barricaded the door."

The blond curled her lip, almost as if she were a werewolf herself. But by the taste of her magic, I was certain she wasn't.

"Sis … sis …"

The blond on the floor cried out suddenly, clutching her head. Her eyes flooded with blue-white magic as she shuddered.

Then tendrils of her magic reached out for me, flooding my mouth with the taste of blackberry jam. The power slipped past the barrier of my necklace and tried to enter my mind.

I brushed it away effortlessly.

Kandy grunted, shifting to the side as she raised her hands in a boxing pose, placing the cuffs between her and the questing power flooding off the blond on the floor.

A telepath. But not strong enough to invade my mind, or Kandy's. At least not after whatever had left her curled up on the floor.

Reacting to what must have appeared to be an aggressive move from the green-haired werewolf, the standing blond flung herself protectively across her sister.

It was a completely stupid move for two reasons. First, as soon as the first twin touched her sister, the power of the telepathic onslaught tripled. And second, one look at Kandy or me should have let the first twin know that we weren't something as benign as a sprinkle of rain. If we had wished her harm, using her body as cover wouldn't even have been a stopgap measure.

Again, the broom would have been the smarter move. Though also just as useless.

So, to recap.

Twins.

One a telepath, who was almost insensible on the floor. The other an amplifier, who had absolutely no instincts on how to protect herself or her sister effectively.

It was an easy guess that she had at least tried to get the telepath out of the salon through the back door. Though why the employees and other clients had locked themselves in the break room was still a mystery.

"Dowser," Kandy grunted pissily. "The magic?"

The amplifier's head snapped up at the mention of my magical classification.

I slashed my knife before me in a figure eight, cutting through the tart-jam magic with ease. "Stop touching her," I said pointedly.

The amplifier stared at me dumbly.

"Step away from your sister," I said, as patiently as I could, slipping my knife into its sheath. "You're making whatever is going on with her worse."

The amplifier glared at me stubbornly. "I am not."

I looked at Kandy, shaking my head in disbelief.

"Fledglings," the werewolf sneered. Then she darted forward, grabbing the amplifier by the back of the neck and pulling her away from her sister—all before the amplifier had even reacted to her moving in the first place.

The amplifier squeaked, then opened her mouth to launch into what was sure to be an indignant protest. Kandy grabbed a bag of cotton balls off the shelf and stuffed them in her mouth, pinning the amplifier's arms together behind her back.

Suddenly assessing the situation with more clarity—because being abruptly and efficiently handled by Kandy could have that effect—the amplifier stilled, looking at me with wide eyes.

I nodded curtly, stepping forward to hunker down by the telepath. She looked up at me with her blue-white gaze. Trusting. But then, even without actually accessing my mind, it seemed likely that she could pick up on my intentions.

I looked her over, seeking foreign magic that might have indicated she'd been spelled somehow. I found nothing. Flummoxed as to what could have been affecting the telepath so adversely, I glanced back at her twin. "Are you just coming into your magic?"

Kandy loosened her hold on the amplifier, who plucked the bag of cotton balls out of her mouth to offer me a surly, "No."

I returned my gaze to the telepath. The twins appeared to be about eighteen years old, which would have been late for magic to manifest. But not impossibly so.

"Dowser," the telepath murmured, rolling over onto her back.

"That's me," I said, smiling. "I'm going to try to settle your magic for you, okay?"

She nodded.

I glanced back at the amplifier. "I'm not going to hurt either of you."

"Not yet, anyway," Kandy said. Not entirely joking.

The amplifier folded her arms across her chest, taking a step away from Kandy so she had a clearer view of her twin. "We know who you are."

I nodded, calling my knife into my hand and ignoring the way the amplifier flinched at its sudden reappearance. I flipped it so I was holding the blade. Then I carefully placed it on the telepath's chest, the hilt across her breastbone, the blade between her breasts, and the tip ending just above belly-button height.

I stroked my fingers across the honed jade stone, drawing a hint of the telepath's magic toward the blade.

Then I coaxed the knife to settle her power as it naturally did for mine.

The blond at my feet sighed, reaching up and lightly placing her fingers along the hilt of the knife. "Oh, I see," she murmured. Her magic shifted around her, and I squelched the instinct to absorb it into the knife. It wasn't mine to collect.

Pressing the weapon protectively to her chest, the telepath sat up, supported by one hand on the linoleum floor. Her impossibly straight, jealous-worthy hair tumbled down around her face and shoulders. Her magic settled. She blinked her now sky-blue eyes at me. "The blade is wondrous."

"The dowser is the wonder, fledgling," Kandy said.

The telepath nodded agreeably. Then, with some reluctance, she loosened her hold on my knife, allowing it to fall forward from her chest. She paused, waiting to see if her magic raged back. It didn't.

Then she reverently offered it back to me, the blade placed across both her palms. "Thank you."

I took the knife from her, carefully holding her gaze for a moment and waiting to see if her magic surfaced in her eyes again.

"I'm all right now. The knife showed me ..." She bit her lip, darting her eyes to her sister as if suddenly realizing she was discussing magic with a stranger.

I stood, stepping away from her and sheathing the knife. The amplifier darted past me, helping her sister to her feet.

Thankfully, along with the differing color schemes, the amplifier was wearing cropped jeans as opposed to the pretty floral skirt the telepath wore, so I could tell them apart even when they were standing shoulder to shoulder.

"Introduce yourselves," Kandy said, seriously peeved. "Then let us know why the hell you're in a storage room with eight mundanes only one door over."

The amplifier opened her mouth—but then snapped it closed after a look from her sister. They stared at each other for a moment, and a tiny taste of tart jam shifted between them.

"Communicating telepathically," I said for Kandy's benefit.

Kandy snorted. "Don't make me teach you to obey your elders, my pretties."

"We know."

"We understand."

They overlapped each other, nary a pause between one speaking and the other taking over.

"You first, sis," the telepath said.

"I always go first."

"You're the eldest."

"So they said."

"Why would they lie?"

"I'm not having this conversation—"

"You!" Kandy jabbed her finger toward the amplifier.

The telepath flinched. "She's even more growly than Bitsy."

"She's older." The amplifier shrugged, eyeing the pissed-off werewolf at my side.

"I swear to God," Kandy growled. "I'm going to teach them some manners."

I quashed a grin, looking pointedly at the amplifier. She squared her shoulders, intoning with exaggeration. "Gabrielle Talbot. Commonly known as Gabby. Amplifier. Sister of Margaret."

"Talbot?" I asked. "Daughter of Angelica?"

Gabby scowled. "Adopted daughter of the sorcerers Stephan and Angelica Talbot."

"Margaret Talbot," the telepath said, picking up practically on top of her sister's final word. "Known as Peggy. Telepath … truth seeker."

Gabby shot her a look.

"Well, there's no point in lying to a dowser, is there?"

I didn't correct Peggy's assumption that I could wield my skills to distinguish magical abilities that finely.

Gabby looked from me to Kandy belligerently. "We won't be used. The Talbots won't allow it. Never again."

Kandy cackled. "You think two sorcerers could stand against Jade Godfrey, dowser, alchemist, wielder of the instruments of assassination, if she wanted you?"

"Plus, I'm not interested in using anyone," I said mildly.

"Not the point," Kandy said. "It's the principle. They come into your territory and question your authority."

Peggy looked stricken. "We certainly weren't."

"Henry Calhoun said we'd be safe here," Gabby said quietly.

That gave Kandy pause. She glanced over at me.

I nodded.

"Henry sent you to Vancouver?" the werewolf asked.

Gabby and Peggy nodded in perfect unison.

Kandy grumbled under her breath, retrieving her phone from her back pocket and opening her texting app. I had a feeling there would be T-shirts for the amplifier and the telepath in the near future.

Kandy's self-assigned pack was rapidly expanding. First Rochelle and Beau, then Mory—though the necromancer might have nominally been under the werewolf's protection first. Then a fledgling vampire, and now an amplifier and a telepath. If Kandy ever needed to invade a small country, she was collecting the army with which to do so. With at least a dozen more years of training, of course. And that wasn't even including Drake, Warner, and me.

Either that or the US Marshal, Henry Calhoun, who most assuredly belonged to Kandy by way of her bite and the transfer of magic that had come with it, was about to get an earful.

I gestured toward the green-haired werewolf. "Kandy, enforcer of the West Coast North American Pack."

Gabby and Peggy exchanged another look. Then, by seemingly mutual decision, Peggy spoke. "The pack has a presence in Vancouver?"

Kandy paused her texting to growl. "Why do you care?"

Neither Gabby or Peggy answered.

"Can you tell us why your magic went…awry?" I asked.

"It didn't. Not really. It was just intense and out of the blue."

"And you normally have trouble getting it under control? Or mitigating its effects?"

Another glance passed between the twins.

"No. Not for a long time, I guess." Peggy twisted a large moonstone ring on her left index finger. Gabby wore the same ring on her right index finger, making me wonder if that indicated the twins had different dominant hands.

They spoke with American accents, completely different from Angelica Talbot's. Gabby's intonation was more abrupt, while Peggy had a softer, smoother tone.

"I have a brown spot in my left eye," Peggy said. "If you're trying to tell Sis and me apart."

I smiled. "Your magic tastes different."

"Yeah," Kandy said. "You can't fool anyone who can smell magic, fledglings."

They glanced at each other, and this time even I could see the look of disappointment that passed between them. Maybe tricking people into thinking you were your twin was a fun game?

"You haven't been by the bakery yet," I said.

Gabby shifted uncomfortably. "We were going to come …"

"Mory said we should …" Peggy added.

"But we were waiting until everyone was in town, like officially, so we could all come together. As a family. You know? But Stephan is still transitioning his work."

"No one is going to hurt you in Vancouver," I said gently. My odd conversation with Angelica Talbot was suddenly showing itself in a new light.

Peggy nodded. "That's why we're here … Because we were bred for our magic …"

"… and whored out." Gabby twined her fingers through her twin's, but she kept her steady gaze on me.

"Mother … fecker," Kandy snarled, modifying her language at the last moment.

Gabby narrowed her sky-blue gaze at the werewolf. "We aren't seven."

"Yes." Peggy nodded helpfully. "We just look young for our age."

"A bonus for our breeders."

"You mean it would have been a bonus, Gabby. If the Convocation hadn't rescued us."

"Eventually."

"It was a large prostitution ring, difficult to track and crack."

"We agree to disagree."

"Yes, we do. Anyway, we were pretty damaged by then, as you can imagine."

"So no one wanted us."

"Except the Talbots."

"Yeah, except Stephan and Angelica."

The twins looked at each other for a moment, then turned their expectant gazes on us.

I stared at them, processing this new inundation of information—and catching Kandy doing the same thing in my peripheral vision.

"Okay." I shook my head, attempting to get my whirling thoughts back on track. "Okay. So, um, what went on here?"

"We were getting pedicures." Peggy wagged one of her bare feet at me. "And then there was something coming through the dark. Gabby grabbed me. But just to protect me, not hurt me."

"Something coming through the dark?" I didn't try to hide my confusion, given that it was noon on a sunny Saturday.

"Well …" Peggy shook her head, her brow creasing with distress. "Something … someone trapped, angry, frustrated … and so, so strong. But starving, somehow." She turned to her sister. "Just like I felt last night."

Gabby shook her head sadly. "That was a flashback, maybe. A buried memory?"

"No," Peggy said firmly. "For just a moment, I could see a white tile floor. Like through someone else's eyes. Maybe like the floor of the salon? The edging behind the front counter? And I knew something, someone was coming. Something dark was trying to break through. To get to us. Or maybe…maybe it's already here."

"There's nothing in the salon. Or behind the counter," Kandy said, tucking her phone away. "Nothing magical but you two."

I nodded, agreeing. We had passed the white-painted counter on our way into the salon, seeing only rows of nail polish and the cash register behind a rack of colorful flip-flops. I'd bought my own pink pair here only a couple of months before, when I had forgotten mine and was too lazy to walk a block back to my apartment before my pedicure appointment.

"What you saw," I said, "did it have slitted red eyes?" Maybe the leech had been drawn to the salon despite the fact that it was full daylight. "Sucker-like mouth, jagged teeth? Hooked claws on the apex of its shadowy wings?"

Gabby and Peggy both paled. They glanced at each other, now completely freaked.

Kandy chuckled under her breath.

"So…um…that's a no, then?"

"That's…that thing is out there?" Gabby asked. "Like in the city? Somewhere?"

"Why is everyone else in the break room?" I asked instead of answering. "You didn't mention the dark presence you felt, did you?"

"Nope."

"No."

"But they think Peggy is a psychic. You know?"

"No," Kandy growled. "We don't know."

"They believe in psychics," Gabby said patiently. As if we were idiots.

145

Peggy bobbed her head. "And it's a little difficult when someone is touching me. You know."

"No," Kandy said again, more pointedly this time. "We don't, you know."

"So when I saw what I saw, I just said that I had a feeling they'd be … you know, more comfortable in the break room."

I glanced at Kandy. She frowned at me. Jenny, the owner, had completely covered for the twins without blinking an eye.

"You've been here before?" I asked.

"Sure."

"Yes."

"And maybe you've been … helpful in the past?"

Gabby shrugged.

"Someone was skimming …" Peggy mumbled.

I sighed.

Kandy turned and stomped out of the room. I gathered it was either that or she was liable to wring both twins' necks.

"We said nothing, nothing about magic," Peggy said.

"Yeah, we aren't stupid." Gabby crossed her arms defensively, standing with her shoulder against Peggy's.

"Why don't you get them out of the break room … after Kandy and I leave," I said. "Apologize for the misunderstanding. Explain you got a migraine or something."

Peggy shifted her feet, but she nodded.

Denying your magic was difficult. I knew, because I did it reluctantly every day.

"People do sometimes see wonky things with migraines," Gabby said.

"Yeah." I inhaled deeply, letting my breath out with an exasperated rush. "Finish your pedicures, tip well, then come up to the bakery."

"You'll feed us?" Peggy asked hopefully. As if she'd heard things about me, presumably from Mory.

"Yeah, I'll feed you." I turned on my heel and vacated the salon, hoping that the twins pulled off smoothing over the incident with the nonmagicals. Otherwise, Gran was going to have to come back to the salon with a memory spell. And mind-altering magic, even cast by a witch of Gran's stature, was tricky. Especially when used on people without any magic of their own.

And actually, getting Gran involved further given her current mood would probably have been a bad idea all round. Better to get through the engagement party—which she'd been planning for over a year—first. Then I could worry about everything else.

# Chapter Seven

As was my preference, I turned right off West Fourth Avenue on my way back to the bakery, jogging diagonally across Yew Street so I could continue up the back alley. A quick glance at the time on my phone confirmed that Tima would have come on shift while I was bandying words with the twins and soothing their magic, so I slowed my pace and tried to connect the dots.

Usually, I was so focused on whatever I was doing that I had to be slapped in the face to notice that something else was going on. Something hidden just underneath the surface of a situation. And the consequences of my slow uptake were usually dire. So if I had a moment to try to figure out what was happening before the ground caved in or the mountain came crashing down, I knew I should take that moment.

Granted, two magical surges weren't really enough to indicate a pattern. And perhaps similar incidents had occurred regularly before the magical grid was put in place. Again, Gran would have been the right person to ask. Just maybe not today.

Even as a fledgling, I had never personally experienced anything like my magic being out of my control. Of course, Gran had kept me focused by encouraging my baking and trinket making—and thereby unleashing my unknown and untested alchemy skills in a constant trickle.

Magical surges might well have been a common occurrence for other Adepts, then. And it was only because I was tied too tightly to the witches' grid that it seemed like a big deal. Or perhaps the witches had woven an overly sensitive web even without factoring in my participation.

But still … the telepath's dire warning concerned me. What she talked about having seen and felt sounded like more than just a simple magical surge.

Kandy was waiting for me, leaning against the back door of the bakery kitchen. Still texting.

"How's Henry?" I asked. I paused to enjoy some of the hazy sun on my face and the feel of a light breeze as it slipped through the alley. The trees at the exit onto Vine Street were on the verge of turning golden, but it would be a few more weeks until autumn really took hold of Vancouver.

Kandy grunted. "I'm texting with Pearl right now. The twins spiked on the map."

"Hence my itchy feet."

Kandy nodded. "She thinks … now … that we might have to take the grid down while everyone is still in town to get it back up, in order to get rid of that particular side effect."

"So it is only me?"

Kandy flashed me a grin. "Ain't it always, dowser?"

"And my replacement?"

Kandy snorted harshly. "Pearl isn't quite willing to agree to that part of Scarlett's plan yet."

I pursed my lips. "I suppose I'm going to have to take sides."

"I suppose you are. Don't worry, though. Scarlett will get Wisteria and maybe some of the others to weigh in. Pearl will have to cave if the others agree."

"To oust me."

Kandy shook her head. "You need to decide whether you're pissed at possibly being used by your grandmother, or if you want to be a baby about not being witchy enough to play with the others."

"Can't I be peeved about both at the same time?"

"Nope. Because then you're just in a general snit, and that's supremely boring."

I laughed, readying a retort ... but then the taste of peppermint tickled my senses. I glanced over my shoulder, expecting to see Kett in the narrow slice of shadow along the building at the far edge of the alleyway.

But the area around us was empty of white-blond vampires.

Kandy lowered her phone, watching me.

I shook my head. "I thought I tasted Kett."

She snorted. "The ancient one texted me a few hours ago, officially announcing his presence in the city."

"He dropped by earlier this morning."

"How early?"

"Early. We got interrupted by a visit from Angelica Talbot. The twins' adoptive mother."

Frowning, Kandy pushed off the steel door, pacing into the alley and padding silently up toward Vine Street. Then she padded back. "What do you mean interrupted? He's got a reason for being away?"

"You knew he would."

"He could have just been moping around some castle in Europe again."

"What's making you uneasy?" I asked quietly.

She shook her head in quick denial. Then she relented. "The smoke." She waved her hand in the air.

I glanced up at the mostly blue sky and the haze of smoke that had been sitting over the city for what seemed like the entire summer. Some days, it completely obscured the North Shore Mountains. And since the back of my throat always seemed to carry the taste of it, I couldn't imagine what it was doing to Kandy's werewolf senses.

"Also lots of new Adepts in town," I said, carefully suggesting that Kandy might be antsy about something other than the smoke, which wasn't particularly new.

She narrowed her eyes at me. "Don't attempt to baby me, dowser. You're the one who keeps tasting the vampire's magic."

"And he's in town."

"Lurking around the alley?"

"Well, you never know. He might be playing. He might not want to interrupt our conversation."

Kandy gave me a look, informing me with no uncertainty that she thought I was a moron.

I sighed. "I told the twins to come by for cupcakes."

The werewolf nodded, allowing the redirection of the conversation. "Henry was being belligerent about not checking in with me before sending the Talbots to Vancouver. Said he went through proper channels."

That was surprising. Because Henry Calhoun was anything but belligerent. He gave truth to all those fictional portrayals of Southern charm—something that seemed severely lacking in the world most days.

"He was probably flirting," I said.

"Not with me," Kandy snarled. "I'm his maker, not his mate."

"He flirts with everyone."

"Never mind," she said. "I told him off."

I eyed her for a moment, but she refused to meet my gaze. "So you were nasty to him, and now you feel bad."

"Of course not!" Kandy angrily rubbed her arms, one at a time. But then she growled. "Damn it!" She tugged her phone free from her back pocket, placing a call instead of texting.

I reached for the handle of the bakery back door, intending to give my werewolf BFF some privacy while she sorted herself out. The connection between her and the US Marshal was complicated. And though she rarely spoke of it, I think she wished Henry would join her in Vancouver so she could keep him in her sight at all times. Of course, she would never ask him to leave his life and his job. That would be like asking for a favor. Or worse, asking for someone else to live their life for her. But the only thing Kandy ever asked of the Adepts in her life was for them to follow a short list of rules.

Actually, just one rule. Be willing to fight—and to die if necessary—for those you considered to be under your protection. Everything else was just manners and window dressing for the green-haired werewolf. Henry already followed that rule. And so did I.

The taste of peppermint magic drew my attention again, closer than before. And … too sweet.

I moved. Spinning away from the door, I darted across the alley. Vaulting the six-foot-high solid fence that backed the apartment building situated directly behind the bakery, I landed softly behind a huge rhododendron.

The magic I'd tasted shifted, reacting to my movement just slightly slower than I normally would have expected. Except I was almost certain I wasn't being watched by Kett. Not unless his magic had changed—again—since I'd seen him that morning.

Then it became apparent that whatever Adept I was tracking had no inkling of the extent of my dowsing abilities. Because my stalker was now circling back, believing that he or she was moving too quickly for me.

In the alley, Kandy was talking loudly on her phone. By the blatantly obvious chitchat, anyone who knew the green-haired werewolf would have immediately discerned the ruse. But even as she continued to exude peppermint magic, my stalker apparently assumed the werewolf was distracted by her call.

The unknown vampire darted through the yard toward a high gate that led to a couple of exterior parking spots, seemingly intending to escape through the carport and up the alley.

I slipped up behind her—or at least I was assuming it was a her, now fairly certain that I was herding Kett's maker. I had tasted her magic in London. As I'd predicted, she slipped past a parked car. Then she realized far too late that Kandy was standing in front of her, arms folded and a vicious smile in place, blocking her exit through the alley.

The vampire spun back, intending to retreat. Her dark-golden curls caught the sunlight, fanning across her shoulders and back. Her bright-blue eyes widened as I lunged.

She wasn't faster than me.

She wasn't even a match.

I drove her back across the alley and pinned her against the concrete wall, effectively hiding our confrontation behind a large green recycling bin.

As she wrapped her hands around my forearms, her eyes widened further, perhaps realizing that a grip she'd assumed would be crushingly unbearable was barely bruising me. She should have ducked and rolled, taking out my legs. She should have turned her reactionary spin into a kick to my torso.

It wouldn't have helped, of course. But it was obvious that the vampire I was currently pinning against the exterior wall of the bakery had no idea how to even attempt to fight me.

She also wasn't Kett's dark-haired, pale-skinned maker. Rather, dressed in a light-brown silk blouse, a dark-brown skirt, and gorgeous knee-high suede boots, my stalker was golden haired and creamy skinned from tip to toe. She was also curvy in all the right places.

All of that was seriously annoying. Not only because that look was kind of my thing, but also because there were now two too many vampires in Vancouver.

Kandy slipped up beside me, effectively blocking the vampire off from the only route along which she might have tried an escape attempt. Of course, most vampires with the amount of peppermint power in their blood that I could taste in hers would have simply torn through the tall metal recycling bin to our left. But I was betting she didn't know that. Just like she didn't know how to fight. Or, at a minimum, how to defend herself.

Just like she didn't know who I was, or the extent of my abilities, or that I could pick up the tenor of her magic easily. From blocks away on Kits Beach, or in the graveyard the previous night.

But she was right in front of me now. Tasting of Kett's magic and stalking me. Even I wasn't so dense that I couldn't put those two things together. Though what they equaled, I had no idea.

Breaking the silent staring contest I was having with the vampire, Kandy leaned in, taking a deep whiff of her neck where her skin was exposed at the lace edge of her blouse.

The golden-haired vampire flinched.

The werewolf chuckled darkly. "Good catch, dowser."

The vampire struggled against my hold, finally. Then she panicked, realizing she couldn't break free. The red of her magic flooded her eyes.

"Identify yourself," I spat, already peeved about being stalked by a vampire who had come to Vancouver and not presented herself properly.

"You identify yourself." Her tone was heavy on the snark, though she avoided meeting my gaze directly.

Kandy laughed huskily. "I like her. Too bad she's an unaligned bloodsucker."

The blond raised her chin haughtily. "I have more connections than you'd ever manage in a lifetime, werewolf."

"You might be surprised," I murmured.

Kandy snorted, raising her arms to display her cuffs. "I don't need any backing to rip you limb from limb, vampire."

"I'd like to see you try."

"Sure. Let's have at it," Kandy snarled viciously. "You go right ahead and shake off the dowser's hold. I'll be right here waiting. I was actually just thinking it might be a good time for a nap."

"Or," I said, "we could just hand you over to the executioner. You might carry the magic of his bloodline, but you're in Vancouver without permission."

The vampire flicked her red-hued gaze back and forth between each of my eyes, as if trying to verify whether I spoke the truth. Then she looked away, saddened.

That struck me as being a lot of emotion for a vampire. Even though I really only had three from which to judge. Kett, his maker, and Benjamin Garrick.

"Jasmine," the vampire whispered.

Jasmine? Why did that ring a not-so-distant bell?

She cleared her throat, strengthening her voice and her resolve to introduce herself formally. "Child of Kettil, the executioner and elder of the Conclave."

I dropped my hold, taking a step away from the vampire in disbelief. She kept her gaze on the ground and her back against the alley wall. Her bountiful curls obscured her face.

"Bullshit," Kandy snarled.

I glanced at the werewolf.

"Bull-shitting-shit," she said.

"Jasmine … Fairchild," I said, slowly slotting all the clues together. Her name. Her bright-blue eyes. Even something about the shape of her face. I'd never met Wisteria's cousin, but the tech witch had done a lot of work for Gran and the witches Convocation, including warding Gran's laptop for me as a Christmas gift a couple of years earlier.

"Not anymore," she whispered. She raised her gaze to meet mine, then quickly twisted her head so she was looking away down the alley. "I was hoping … that he had mentioned me when he visited you this morning."

"I'm still calling bullshit," Kandy said. "Does her magic actually taste like Kett's?"

"Yes," I said, far calmer than I would have thought myself capable of being at this revelatory moment. This was Kett's secret. This was what … who he'd thought would tear us apart. "But so does his maker's."

That got Jasmine's attention. "Estelle?"

"Is that her name? We didn't exchange pleasantries while she was threatening to rip out my friends' throats and suck their marrow while I watched."

"What … what does my … magic taste like?"

"Peppermint. Sweeter than Kett's, though."

She snorted. "Yeah, I'm just a treat."

I didn't respond. I wasn't interested in whatever trauma she had going on, though that might have been nasty of me. Because even though two incidents didn't make a pattern, something was up in Vancouver, and that was more important.

I could feel it. The shift in the magical atmosphere, like the smoke that had been plaguing the city. And somehow, for me at least, it had just been further exacerbated by Jasmine's appearance. The golden-haired vampire could be a cause, or a symptom, or another victim. Though she appeared to be in control of her magic, even if not her stalking instincts.

Or maybe she wasn't connected to any of it at all. And therefore she was wasting my time. I kept that dark thought to myself, but really, who could have blamed me? My vampire BFF had made himself a vampire companion—possibly murdering Jasmine Fairchild in the process. Then he'd kept it all secret for months. And I had no idea how I felt about any of it.

"Really not bullshit?" Kandy asked, a little forlornly.

"Kett doesn't have to tell us everything he does," I said, chiding myself more than the werewolf. "Or why, Kandy."

"Hell, yeah, he does!" She gestured toward Jasmine. "He turned a witch!"

"You turned a sorcerer," I said mildly.

"Hey! Not by choice. And private business, dowser!"

I gave Kandy a look. "Exactly."

She glowered at me. "Private business from the likes of her." She pointed emphatically at the vampire. "Not … you know … pack."

"Excuse me," Jasmine said snarkily. "Pack? You think the executioner…belongs to you?" Apparently, the tech-witch-turned-vampire recovered from disappointment quickly.

Kandy stepped forward, thrusting her face next to Jasmine's. Her teeth were bared…and a little too long around the canines. "You think differently, fledgling?"

Jasmine shifted her gaze to Kandy's shoulder, proving she wasn't completely stupid. "Perhaps I'm ill informed."

"Yeah," Kandy said. "Perhaps you should keep your mouth shut while the grown-ups chat."

Anger flushed Jasmine's face. Red-tinted magic whirled in her eyes, but she clamped down on whatever she desperately wanted to say.

Kandy sniffed derisively, turning her back on the vampire—and completely insulting Jasmine's predator instincts by doing so.

Jasmine curled her hands into fists, but she didn't otherwise move.

"I can't believe that Kett would turn a moronic blond bimbo," Kandy said casually, meaning to be insulting.

"Hey!" I cried. That scorn cut a little too close to home for comfort.

"Not you, dowser." Kandy eyed Jasmine over her shoulder, curling her lip scathingly. "Though he apparently has a type."

"Hey—hey, again!"

"I'm trying to insult the vampire, Jade," Kandy snapped. "Stop taking it personally."

"Maybe he didn't have a choice," Jasmine murmured.

"Who could force Kettil to do anything?" I asked the question rhetorically, though not unkindly.

Jasmine met my gaze, the red of her magic still ringing the blue of her irises. "You know her."

Kandy looked at me questioningly.

Then the final piece of the puzzle snapped into place. Kett in Seattle three years before, stalking a certain witch while I had hunted for the first instrument of assassination. Then later, asking Gran to assign that same witch to the case he'd been investigating. The connection he shared with Jasmine.

"Wisteria …" I said.

"Wisteria." Jasmine evoked her cousin's name as she brushed her fingers over a necklace she wore tucked into her silk blouse.

I eyed the section of the gold chain I could see across the vampire's collarbone, picking up the faint nutmeg overtones that were layered underneath Jasmine's too-sweet peppermint. Once again, I quashed the need to handle the magical artifact. Personal property wasn't mine to collect.

Yeah, I would just keep telling myself that.

"She didn't want me to die," Jasmine said.

"Well, she gambled badly, didn't she?" Kandy laughed harshly.

I looked toward the mouth of the alley, tasting Kett's cool peppermint magic moments before he appeared beside me.

He met my gaze dispassionately, not even glancing Jasmine's way. "Circumstances don't always justify the action. Do they, Jade?"

His question was so heavily layered that I had no idea how to address everything he was asking all at once. Not in simple terms, anyway.

Still dressed in the light-gray cashmere sweater and dark-gray jeans he'd been wearing that morning, he didn't close the couple of feet between us.

Her gaze glued to her maker, Jasmine shifted away from the wall, but Kett continued to ignore her.

"My apologies." Instead of waiting for me to speak, the executioner filled the silence that was stretching between us. Perhaps for the first time ever. "I was unaware the fledgling had wandered. In the sunlight." He leveled a glance at Jasmine. "She has adapted to her new existence more thoroughly and readily than I … presumed she would."

"Well," Kandy drawled sarcastically, "it's not like you to underestimate someone. Plus, the dowser's magic is tasty."

A hint of amusement flitted across Kett's face, but he instantly quelled the emotion, returning his icy gaze to me.

"Who am I to judge you?" I finally whispered.

"The only one who truly could," he murmured. "The only one whose opinion I would … care about."

Jasmine flinched, then covered the reaction by scowling at her feet.

"I was … concerned," Kett said, summing up a lot of different emotions with the word.

"Am I so fickle?" I asked, though not as playfully as I'd intended.

"Never, Jade." Kett answered me seriously. "Jasmine Fairchild was dying. I was bound by the Conclave to remake a witch from the Fairchild familial line. A punishment for …" He waved his hand, encompassing me, Kandy, and the bakery alley with the gesture.

"For our relationship?"

"For the power I was … unexpectedly bequeathed in London. Then Peru."

I nodded, understanding that he was talking about being brought back by his grandsire after he'd died in London. Died as a result of taking a blow that would have probably killed me. Then in Peru, he had drunk from Shailaja, even though dragon blood was poisonous to vampires. He had survived that consumption, later indicating that he was holding too much power. And uneasily. So making another vampire had been the Conclave's solution. Their so-called punishment. And the reason his magic now felt more subdued.

Turning Jasmine had cost him, in multiple ways.

But he wasn't going to lose me over it.

"He chose Wisteria," Jasmine said. The interjection was made with some heat, but we all ignored her.

"There was an accident?" I asked. "A situation that demanded a choice be made?"

"Yes." Kett offered me a hint of a smile.

I closed the space between us, reaching up and touching his cheek. "And you fulfilled your obligation," I said. "Saving Jasmine's life in the process."

"If you'd like to perceive it that way."

I laughed, dropping my hand and crossing to the bakery back door. "If you want to be broody about it, vampire, I can't stop you."

Affronted, Kett lifted his chin. "I am not broody."

Kandy started to cackle. Then, as I opened the door into the kitchen, she flung herself at the vampire, hitting him like a cannonball to the chest, then attempting to wrestle him into submission.

Kett stumbled back, his shiny oxfords too slippery to help mitigate the initial blow. The werewolf twined her legs and arms around him, cackling with mad glee.

He grunted, but then held his ground stoically.

To an outside observer, it would likely have appeared that Kandy was preparing to rip Kett's head off. She wasn't. The werewolf would, at a minimum, allow a missing adopted pack member to justify his absence before decapitating him in a hissy fit.

Kandy pressed her hands to Kett's face, eliciting what might have been a wince of pain. The cuffs made the werewolf strong—stronger even than her magic had already made her.

I had been studying the magical artifacts over the past year, tying them specifically—and hopefully irrevocably—to Kandy with my alchemy. I thought there might have been a possibility that the artifact had formed a kind of circuit with the werewolf's magic, so that the stronger Kandy became, the more powerful the cuffs grew. While wearing the artifacts, Kandy had healed—twice in as many years—from wounds that would have been mortal to any other shapeshifter. That manner of extreme healing, alongside her burning through her magical reserves in order to survive, often strengthened magic.

So with all that considered, Kandy was probably one of the most powerful werewolves in the world. Powerful enough to head her own small pack, which she appeared to be building from the collection of misfits who now called Vancouver home. Powerful enough that Gran wanted her to enforce the magical grid. And to make the executioner of the Conclave wince.

I glanced over at Jasmine, who was watching the interplay between Kett and Kandy from the shadow of the building with an intense sadness. The former witch was going to have a difficult time transitioning with Kett as her maker, especially if he had actually chosen Wisteria, as Jasmine implied. I loved him, of course. But he wasn't an easy person to get to know. Loyal to few, beholden to none. As far as I knew, anyway. And if their shared magic was any indication, Jasmine was a heavy magical tie for the executioner.

I shook off my concerns. Worrying wasn't going to help either of them. And as I understood it, they had centuries to work it all out. Assuming Kett ever stopped pushing the boundaries of his immortality.

Of course, the same could be said for me...and Kandy and Warner. All of us were always going to do whatever was in our nature. After all, with power came responsibility and all that, yadda yadda.

I had managed to hone my sense of duty down to a small territory, but I still couldn't deny the need to charge in, to use my magic. To try to enforce some sort of harmony. Even if it was just so I could hold that harmony for a little while, and possibly use it as a balm to the wildness that inhabited my soul.

But right now, I had a bakery to check on, an engagement party to get ready for, and a magical grid to sort out. Hopefully without any more itchy-feet surprises.

Kandy smashed a harsh kiss to Kett's lips, then dropped to the ground and smoothed out her T-shirt. All without a word.

I laughed, utterly delighted with both of my BFFs. Then I stepped into the bakery.

"Are you staying?" Kandy asked.

I caught Kett's answer as the door slowly closed behind me.

"If you'll have us."

Us.

Three vampires in Vancouver.

Gran was so going to lose it.

The phone in the office was ringing when I entered the bakery kitchen. I almost let it go to voicemail, knowing that the only calls that came through on the landline were special orders, and Bryn booked those.

Then, impulsively, I dashed into the office on the third ring, picking up the receiver only to hear a dial tone.

I hung up, not recognizing the 604 number on the call display. But feeling oddly as though I had just missed something important.

Blossom appeared, perched on the edge of my desk.

I flinched, then tasted her lemon verbena magic. The brownie was seriously the only Adept who could still sneak up on me.

"Mistress." Her voice was deep and perpetually gravelly. Instead of the Cake in a Cup apron that she usually wore as a dress, she was clothed in what I would have sworn was a black dress made out of a hoodie. The white drawstring ties that would normally be part of the hood had been woven through the hem, then cinched, creating a balloon shape just below the brownie's knees.

Perhaps this was what she wore on her days off? Though as far as I knew, Blossom didn't take any time off, ever. She divided her time between the bakery and attending the far seer and the treasure keeper.

The brownie blinked her large eyes at me.

I had to stop staring at people too long. I was creeping everyone out.

"Blossom," I said with a smile. "You startled me."

A wide, pleased grin spread across the brownie's face. "I know."

"Yeah. Hilarious."

She laughed huskily.

That was when I noticed the folded piece of paper in her large hands. Thick white paper, looking as though it had been ripped out of a sketchbook.

Ah, damn it.

I knew only one person who drew. And who often had occasion to rip her drawings from a spiral-ringed sketchbook.

"Is that for me?" I asked.

Blossom nodded.

"And there's no chance it's from the treasure keeper? Or the far seer?" It said something seriously screwed up about me that I would prefer to be presented with missives from two guardian dragons over one tiny oracle.

Blossom shook her head. "I wouldn't have folded it," she said nervously. "But the oracle did, saying it didn't matter. This way, maybe the magic won't spill out?"

Double freaking damn.

I couldn't just refuse the delivery, if only for the sake of not wanting to piss off the brownie. My apartment had never been so clean. Plus, I just liked having Blossom around. She loved the bakery almost as much as I did.

The brownie held the folded paper out to me, formally and with both hands.

I took it with a stiff nod, eager to not appear as the coward I was. The taste of tart apple tickled my taste buds. Oracle magic. "I didn't know you knew Rochelle," I said, delaying the unveiling of the sure-to-be mind-boggling sketch.

Blossom placed her hands on her knees, hunkering down on her haunches. "I'm loyal to you, mistress."

I looked over at the brownie, surprised. "As I am to you, Blossom."

She nodded knowingly. "But I do also like farm-fresh eggs."

"From deathlayer chickens!" I laughed. Apparently, the brownie had adopted the oracle as well. "Who wouldn't?"

Blossom nodded, dropping her dark-eyed gaze to the folded paper in my hands.

I sighed, then unfolded the sketch.

Rendered in thick black charcoal, an octagon-shaped object occupied the center of the oracle's drawing. It appeared to be cupped in an open palm. Slender wisps of what looked like severed string or ribbon emanated from each sharp edge of the octagon. Or maybe that was just how the oracle drew magic? Or magical ties?

I had no idea what I was looking at. I angled the sketch so Blossom could see it.

The brownie tilted her head, thoughtful. "A diamond brooch?"

"With that large a gemstone? Could it be a tattoo?" Though Rochelle drew both visions of the future and magical tattoos, I'd gotten the idea that the magical part was an ability she was still exploring.

Blossom shook her head. "It looks as though you're holding it."

Damn it. It did look like a three-dimensional object. I fished my phone out of my back pocket, tapping open my messaging app. "What did the oracle say when she gave it to you?"

"Please bring this to Jade," Blossom croaked.

Rochelle could have taken a picture and texted it to me. Or waited and given it to me the next time she saw me. Instead, she'd uncharacteristically asked for a favor, and I had no idea as to the object's relevance. "No warning? No timeline?"

Blossom shook her head.

I texted Rochelle.

*I got your sketch. I have no idea what it is.*

"It could be some sort of rune …" I gazed at the sketch while I waited to see if the oracle would respond to my text immediately.

She didn't.

"I'll have my grandmother look at it. Thank you, Blossom."

"Mistress."

The office phone rang almost at the same time that I felt magic slide across the soles of my sneakered feet. I grabbed the receiver.

"Hello? Shoot, I mean … Cake in a Cup. How can I help you?"

"Jade?" a familiar male voice said.

"This is she."

"Okay, ah." The unknown person cleared his throat, almost as though he didn't want to be talking to me. "I think you'd better come to the shop."

My feet started to tingle. Then itch. Then I recognized his voice. "Dave?"

"Yeah. Use the back door, okay?" Dave's voice became muffled. "I'll be right with you, sir." Then he spoke into the phone again. "Now, Jade. I called you, but I should be calling the police."

"I'm already there."

He hung up.

Ah, triple freaking damn.

Itchy feet and Sienna's high-school boyfriend on the phone. A completely nonmagical boyfriend, whose family had owned the butcher's shop a block east of the bakery for three generations. Dave and I were part of the same small-business group. Whatever he was calling me for, instead of the police, wasn't something he should know about.

I hung up.

Blossom took the sketch from me, carefully refolding it, then tucking it into her pocket. She patted my arm. "I'll take this to your grandmother."

Then the brownie disappeared, leaving only a hint of lemon to mark her teleportation.

I pulled out my cellphone and was texting Kandy as I exited through the bakery kitchen, finding the alley empty of werewolves and vampires. I left my sword in the office safe.

The last thing the Adepts of Vancouver needed was for the police to be involved in whatever the hell was going on. And carrying a katana through the back alleys of Kitsilano wouldn't help with any exposure problem that might have already been in the works.

# Chapter Eight

*A* werewolf was gorging on raw hamburger in the walk-in fridge in the back of Dave's butcher's shop. And that was less concerning to me than the fact that something was really wrong with her magic.

In my experience, a werewolf should have tasted like some sort of chocolate. But at best, this one tasted of raw cocoa nibs. And honestly, I knew they were all the rage lately, but I wasn't a fan. I found them way, way too bitter. And crunchy. I wasn't big on crunchy bits in my treats.

The predator in the fridge hunched her shoulders, sensing my presence a long while after she should have smelled me, even with my magic tightly coiled behind my necklace and knife. She should have heard me come through the back door. She should have heard my sneakers squeak on the recently washed adobe-tiled floor.

Dave, the owner and current operator of the family business, was looking through the round window in the center of a heavy swing door, dividing the kitchen portion of the butcher's from the storefront. Spotting me in the middle of his workspace, he started to push the door open.

Not taking my gaze off the werewolf in the fridge, I raised my hand, cautioning him. He nodded, then retreated. The door swung slightly on its hinges, allowing me a brief glimpse of the otherwise-empty storefront. It looked as though Dave had thankfully cleared out his customers and temporarily closed the shop.

Dave and I had known each other since grade school, simply by virtue of having grown up in the same area. He wasn't magical in any way. But he'd had a fling with Sienna many, many years before. Before he'd met his wife and had two gorgeous baby girls.

Unfortunately, Sienna hadn't been particularly circumspect about our family's secrets. But some things went unsaid between longtime acquaintances. Things best left unspoken and unexamined. It had been far safer—for his own mental well-being—for Dave to think that Sienna and I were just a little crazy, rather than actually believing that a magical world existed in secret alongside the regular everyday world.

Except that him calling me upon discovering a werewolf in his fridge meant that he had obviously seen and understood more than I thought.

Still, no matter the ramifications, I seriously hoped he hadn't called the police after he'd called me.

Apparently—and erroneously—deciding that I wasn't a threat, the werewolf dug back into the vat of ground meat. Her hands were misshapen. She was attempting to hold the large stainless steel container with what appeared to be a furry stub, while the hand she was shoveling meat with was half wolf claw, half human.

I couldn't see her face, but she was easily six feet tall, with short-cropped dark hair and prominent muscles. Though that might have been due to her partial transformation. She appeared to have medium-brown-colored skin, but I had no idea of her heritage. At least not her human roots.

My phone vibrated in my back pocket. Perfect freaking timing. I really couldn't ignore it, but I half-expected that as soon as I looked away, the werewolf in the fridge would try to scratch my eyes out.

I pulled out my phone, glancing quickly at the incoming text. It was from Rochelle.

>*It's you. Holding some sort of magical object.*

I texted back one handed.

*How do you know it's my hand?*

>*I know it's you.*

*I have no freaking idea what it is!*

>*You'll know when you know.*

Fanfreakingtastic.

*Always a pleasure, oracle. Got to go. About to get my throat torn out.*

>*I doubt it. Not today, at least.*

Hilarious. You just knew everything was going to hell when an oracle started cracking wise about your pending future.

Returning my attention to my immediate present, I tucked my phone into my pocket, clearing my throat.

The werewolf in the fridge hesitated, then furtively glanced my way. Her eyes were a shocking topaz color, and completely human. Her nose, chin, and mouth were an awkward amalgamation of her wolf, half-form, and human form. Raw ground beef was mashed into what appeared to be a dark, spotted pelt across her mouth and cheeks. Her jaw was misaligned. The top half was still partially human in form, and the bottom half fully canine.

The botched transformation looked painful.

Where the hell was Kandy?

"So…um …" I said. "You're letting all the cold air out."

The werewolf let out a low-pitched, soft rumble of a growl, reaching for a huge pack of T-bone steaks without taking her hot-eyed gaze from me. She stumbled slightly, catching her balance on the tall wire shelving. Her legs weren't the same length.

Pity rose in me, filling my chest and taking my breath with it. I shoved it away. I didn't know how to help the woman, but I also had to contain the situation.

"Right." I cleared my throat. "My name is Jade. I'm here to … help. You wouldn't be having any trouble with your magic, would you?"

The werewolf chortled, then started choking on the half-chewed meat in her mouth. I fought the urge to grab the T-bone out of her hand before she skewered herself with it.

"Okay," I said. "That…this doesn't look good, you know? I need you to …" I waved my hand helplessly. "Change back … to human."

The werewolf dropped the half-eaten steak, lurching to the side as she spun to face me. "Human?" she roared.

At least I was fairly certain that was what she said. With her mangled jaw, I was surprised that she could form words at all. Either way, though, it had obviously been a bad suggestion, because she launched herself at me, teeth and claws extended toward all my soft parts.

I had time to regret the fact that I was going to have to hurt her. Then I stepped to the side, tripping her.

She went down hard, landing face first with her arms still extended. She seemed unaware that her body wasn't functioning as she expected. Thankfully, she didn't crack the tile.

Before she'd even come to a full stop, I had grabbed her wrists, twisting them behind her back and willing myself to ignore the screech of pain my rough-ness caused.

Kandy came through the back door from the alley, almost taking it off the hinges. Her magic was glowing wildly in her eyes, and for the briefest of moments, as she paused to take me in—kneeling on the back of a werewolf in obvious pain—I worried that she was going to vault over the steel-legged counter dividing us and attack me.

"What the hell is going on?" she snarled.

I loosened my hold on the werewolf, but Kandy seemed to get herself under control. She waved at me to wait while she closed the door.

The half-transformed werewolf underneath my knees started keening. Soft, quiet notes of pain. She didn't fight me any further.

I squeezed my eyes shut, swallowing the guilt of having hurt her.

Kandy padded around the kitchen, halfheartedly tidying up the shelves of the walk-in fridge, then closing its door. She peered briefly through the window to the store. Then, once she had herself fully under control, she hunkered down beside me.

"Look at me, wolf."

The werewolf's sobs increased in volume, but she didn't turn her head.

Kandy nodded to me, and I loosened my grip on the woman. The partially transformed werewolf rolled to her side, still facing away from Kandy. She slowly scooted backward, sliding across the tile until she'd backed herself into the very corner of the room, leaning against a set of steel cabinets.

Kandy glanced over at me. "Her magic? Same as the others?"

"Different," I said, shaking my head. "Muted. At least… I guess I don't know what level it is normally. But she's… not …" I hesitated. I didn't want to suggest that the woman was handicapped or had some kind of disability. I had no idea. But still, that was what her magic tasted like. Not fully expressed. Unresolved.

Kandy nodded. Her expression tight with concern, she turned her attention to the pained werewolf. "Do you know who I am?"

The woman wrapped her arms around her legs, hugging them into her chest. I noticed for the first time that she was wearing well-worn, neon-pink running shoes. She didn't lift her eyes, didn't respond.

Kandy's magic rose. Deep, bittersweet chocolate threaded through with hints of red berries slipped across my tongue, causing my mouth to water. Her eyes blazed brightly green, a hue lighter than her hair. "You will listen to me, werewolf," she snarled.

The magic laced through her command snapped toward the werewolf as if it might be grabbing hold of her.

The woman's head jerked up. More tears flooded her topaz gaze, but her own magic didn't respond to Kandy's. "Please… please …" she pleaded through her mangled mouth. "Don't hurt. Don't bite."

Kandy went very, very still. "Why would I hurt you?" she whispered. "I'm an enforcer of the pack. I'm here to protect you."

The woman shook her head, almost viciously. Then she snarled, "Werewolves… don't… protect."

"You are a werewolf." Kandy's tone turned soothing.

"Am… not."

Kandy scooted closer to the woman, who flinched, banging her head on the metal cupboard behind her.

"Didn't you know?" the green-haired werewolf asked. "Have you been bitten?"

The woman started to shake. Frustrated tears flowed anew as she raised her hands before her. But the gesture was more desperate than defiant.

"Magic?" Kandy asked without looking back at me.

"Still the same."

"You need to transform," Kandy said patiently. "I can help you."

"No! No!" the woman cried out, banging her head back on the steel door again. This time, she dented it.

"Kandy ..."

My BFF sighed heavily—making me wish I'd never heard that sound from her. Then, with a flash of magic, she grabbed the woman by the throat, yanking her forward and pinning her to the floor.

The werewolf didn't fight. She just lay underneath Kandy's grasp, weeping almost silently.

I pressed my hand to my chest, willing myself to remain present. To not look away. To witness.

"Jade," Kandy said. "I need you to try to help."

I stepped around her, settling at the other side of the werewolf, even though I wasn't a healer and had no idea what I could do. I laid my hand over the hand Kandy had wrapped around the werewolf's neck.

"Trace your magic ..." Kandy murmured, speaking to the woman. "The energy that flows through you, that demands the transformation. Buried within that, you will find yourself."

The werewolf squeezed her eyes shut. Nothing else happened.

Kandy's magic shifted again, wrapping around her like a cloak. "Look at me, wolf," she said. "You can do it. Smell my magic. Let it call to you. Follow me." Hair sprouted along Kandy's arms. I heard her bones crunch as they began to shift.

The werewolf underneath our shared grip started breathing heavily. Fast panting. She was panicking.

"Stop," I murmured. "Wait. You're scaring her." I met Kandy's blazing green gaze. "She's scared of other werewolves?"

Anger hardened Kandy's jaw. "Bitten. Maybe."

I nodded, lifting my hand off hers. Kandy also loosened her hold. Then, frowning, she gathered the woman into her arms, so that she was sitting upright, facing me—and looking completely and silently panicked. She dwarfed Kandy, but the shorter and slighter werewolf held her without effort.

Kandy started humming, some soothing tune I couldn't identify. Then she slowly rocked the woman back and forth. Like a baby.

A look of utter confusion replaced the terror on the woman's face.

"Yeah," I said. "We're not the biting kind."

"Not unless you ask nicely." Kandy chuckled.

Trying to ease the general tension further, I grinned at my werewolf BFF. "I see you forgot your backpack."

Kandy offered me her patented nonsmile. "You should think about doing an open mic night at the bakery. Comedy and cupcakes."

Laughing quietly, I offered my hands to the woman. She watched me carefully. "I'm a dowser. Not a healer. But maybe I can feel for your magic. And help it settle?"

The woman nodded slowly. Then she placed her hand in mine. Her skin was hot and sweaty.

"She's running a fever," I said.

"Yeah," Kandy said. "Her human body is fighting the transformation. She doesn't look like a bitten werewolf to me, and it's nowhere near the full moon." When Kandy had bitten Henry Calhoun, the phases of the moon had affected him so much that he'd been forced into a change every month. Before he'd taken on Rochelle's tattoo, that is. "She just looks stuck. But ... yeah."

I closed my eyes, inhaling and exhaling deeply a couple of times until the werewolf subconsciously began to match my breathing. Then I looked for her magic, seeking out that cocoa-nib-flavored power. Without opening my eyes, I couldn't be completely certain, but it felt as though it was gathered around the areas of her body that were partially transformed.

"There you are," I whispered. "I taste your magic."

"Taste?" the woman echoed, confused. "I ... have ... magic?"

"Oh, yes." I opened my eyes and smiled. "Kandy's tastes of dark chocolate and red berries. Yours is cocoa nibs. Have you ever tasted cocoa nibs?"

The werewolf nodded somewhat doubtfully. Though I assumed her uncertainty was about magic tasting like anything, rather than not actually knowing if she'd eaten nibs or not.

"They smell like deep, rich hot chocolate, yes?"

She thought about that.

"But the taste is different."

"Bitter ..." she murmured.

"But sometimes you can pick up notes of bright berry or toasted nuts."

"Yes ..." She breathed in deeply, as though she'd been hit by a revelation. Then her magic rose and gently shifted her back into her human visage.

"Toasted walnuts," I said, catching the deeper taste of the werewolf's magic. Smiling, I met Kandy's gaze over the woman's shoulder.

The green-haired werewolf loosened her hold on the woman, straightening up and pulling her to her feet in the same motion.

The woman reached for the steel counter, steadying herself. Her gaze was on her perfectly human hands. She was still tall, probably six feet, and her topaz eyes were just as brilliant. But she now appeared to be in her early twenties, with tautly muscled medium-brown skin and a dark halo of coiled curls. Also, she was wearing the cutest light-blue, subtly whiskered, flared denim over-alls—a look that only someone so tall and slim could pull off—over a short-sleeve white T-shirt. The overalls and shirt had survived her transformation, but one of her sneakers had been destroyed.

Kandy let her go, stepping back. "Introduce your-self properly."

The woman stiffened, then turned to gaze at us. Her expression was a strange mixture of defiance and wonder. "You first."

Kandy snorted, crossing her arms. "That's not your privilege, is it?"

"I should know my place, should I?" Without the mangled jaw, the werewolf's accent was obviously American. But again, I couldn't place the region. "We didn't come to Vancouver to be bullied."

"Did you come to break into a shop and risk ex-posing all of the Adept?" I asked mildly. My mind was already focused on whether or not memory spells were going to be needed to fix this.

The woman dropped her topaz gaze. "No."

"Then?" Kandy asked pointedly.

The woman straightened to her full height. "Rebecca Talbot."

Another Talbot. This was getting way beyond coincidence. Rather annoyingly, actually.

We waited, but Rebecca didn't offer any further information about herself or her family.

"And?" Kandy asked.

"And what?"

Kandy pointed at herself. "Kandy. Enforcer of the West Coast pack." Then she pointed at me. "Jade. Dowser. Alchemist."

Then Kandy pointed at Rebecca.

She shrugged belligerently.

"Were one or both of your parents werewolves?"

"Maybe."

"Maybe?" Kandy snarled.

"Time to go," I said, interrupting. I caught another glimpse of Dave beyond the swing door. "I still need to do my hair and makeup."

"Yep," Kandy said. "If you won't talk to us, you sure as hell will talk to the witches." Then she grabbed Rebecca by the arm and half-dragged, half-carried her toward the back door.

That really hadn't been my meaning. But Kandy was the enforcer, and certainly knew way more about how to deal with werewolves than I did.

"I'm not trying to be disrespectful," Rebecca muttered.

"Well, you're succeeding magnificently anyway."

Kandy paused by the door, turning the handle. I hesitated, considering darting out front to talk to Dave. Offering to pay for the damages, and trying to smooth it all over with money rather than magic. And all the while, seriously hoping none of the shop's customers had spotted the werewolf in the fridge before he'd closed up.

Rebecca suddenly slumped to one side.

"Shit!" Kandy snarled.

I dashed over to her, grabbing Rebecca's other arm. "Oh, my God. Is she okay?"

"Passed out," Kandy said. "Happens after a werewolf's first few transformations. I thought getting her on her feet right away might help."

"Well … I guess you can't really get the witches to torture her when she's unconscious."

Kandy sighed as if suffering greatly. "True. Pity."

"We'd better take her home," I said, settling Rebecca's arm across my shoulders. Her head lolled harshly to one side. "Do you have the Talbots' address?"

Kandy pulled out her phone, opening the door with her free hand. "Pearl will."

Thinking it was probably better to carry the magically exhausted werewolf rather than drag her down the street, I picked her up under her knees. She was surprisingly heavy. But then, she topped me by at least three inches.

I followed Kandy into the back alley. "Do you want to pull the SUV around?"

A sorcerer leveled his gun at me. Fresh-roasted, creamy peanut butter—the kind that would just suck all the moisture out of your mouth—flooded my senses of taste and smell. Since I'd been on a peanut butter kick for a while, I instantly liked him.

Except for the gun, of course.

That was just annoying.

Especially since I could taste magic embedded within the weapon as well as in him. An echo of his own. So even though guns were notoriously unreliable around magic and magic users, I had a sinking feeling that the sorcerer's weapon would fire and strike true, exactly where he aimed it. And unfortunately, the place he was currently aiming it was the middle of my forehead.

Yep. A dark-haired sorcerer, dressed head to toe in a Vancouver Police Department uniform, had me dead to rights.

And my arms were rather occupied carrying an unconscious werewolf.

Kandy had paused a couple of steps into the narrow alley between the butcher's and a brown-sided, five-storey apartment building that faced West Fifth Avenue. The rear units would have a perfect view of the alley.

"Hello, VPD." The green-haired werewolf bared her teeth in greeting.

"Sorcerer," I murmured.

"I know," Kandy snorted. "I can smell him." She raised her hands, showing off her cuffs rather than declaring peaceful intentions as she stalked forward two steps. "You know who you have your gun pointed at, right? Because even if you managed to shoot one of us without the thing exploding in your hand, a tiny piece of metal ain't slowing either of us down."

"You're standing at the scene of a reported disturbance—"

"Yadda yadda," Kandy said. "We're the good guys, VPD. Don't we look it?"

The sorcerer glanced my way, exceptionally calm under the circumstances. He was around twenty-three, six feet tall, clean-cut, and in excellent shape. A runner's body, from the look of it. Dark hair. Deep-brown eyes.

Kandy took two more quick steps toward him. "I'm thinking of making him bow before you, dowser. Stinky sorcerer playing at being an itty-bitty policeman with an itty-bitty gun. Oh, excuse me, police person."

I coughed back an inappropriate laugh.

VPD swallowed harshly, glancing at me. "You … you …"

"Yeah, yeah," Kandy snarled. "There's a cupcake on her T-shirt, ain't there?"

I cleared my throat, lifting my burden slightly. "He might not be able to see it. What with me holding a werewolf and all."

My comment seemed to remind VPD why he was pointing a gun at me. "You will put the woman down. Carefully. Then step back and place your hands on the wall."

"She really won't." Kandy was starting to sound amused rather than pissed, which wasn't going to be healthy for the sorcerer.

I glanced around. It hadn't rained in weeks, so the alley looked especially nasty. Tidy, of course. It was Vancouver, after all. But definitely gritty and stained. "On the ground? That seems harsh. These are cute overalls. Do you really want me to ruin them for her? She's had a bad afternoon."

"I'm serious, ma'am."

The sorcerer had nerves of steel.

He'd also just 'ma'amed' me.

"Jesus, I'm like maybe three years older than you!"

"Just take the gun," Kandy said, sounding bored. "I'll break it if I do it."

"My arms are a little full."

The werewolf threw her hands up in the air in mock frustration. Then she beckoned for me to hand over my burden.

"No one is going to move…any farther." VPD's calm facade was cracking.

Kandy and I eyed him for a moment.

"You mean, other than to place her down on the ground?" I asked mockingly.

"Right," he said, grinding the word out. "Right."

"The gun, Jade," Kandy said. "Or I'll take it. And then the itty-bitty sorcerer will cry. Who'd you steal the uniform from, anyway?"

"I won't…be crying." VPD kept the gun steady on me, but Kandy was getting under his skin. "And this is my uniform."

I sighed. Kandy was right. The conversation would go more smoothly without the gun in play.

I stepped forward, allowing the unconscious werewolf in my grasp to roll into Kandy's outstretched arms.

VPD started to squeeze the trigger.

But whether the gun would have gone off or not, I'd never know. Because I moved.

Stepping forward and slightly to the side—just in case the gun was triggered by his magic rather than his finger—I took it.

Stepping back, I held the weapon aloft in my open palm, taking a moment to watch as deep-blue sorcerer magic settled back into its polished metal.

VPD grunted, stumbling back a few steps. Reacting too late to my advance. He reached for the other gun still clipped into his holster. Probably his police-issued weapon, because the gun I held was larger. And teeming with power.

"No," I said, backing my command with a push of magic.

He froze in the middle of pulling the second weapon.

I displayed the gun I'd snatched from him for his benefit. "I can destroy this weapon and all the magic contained within it with a mere thought."

"Impossible," he said, struggling to remain calm.

I smiled. "Test me."

His gaze flicked from me to Kandy. Then he lifted his hands away from his service weapon.

Kandy snorted derisively. "These fledglings are so boring."

"I'm no fledgling." The sorcerer squared his shoulders. "And that's my sister you're holding."

Well, surprise, surprise.

"Another Talbot."

"Yes," he said snarkily. "See the name tag?"

Ignoring the sarcasm, I eyed him thoughtfully as I twirled the gun in my hand, playing with its peanut buttery magic.

Kandy flinched, acting as though I was going to accidentally shoot her.

I glared at the green-haired werewolf. But since her reaction was actually prudent, I stopped playing with the weapon.

Kandy chuckled to herself.

"Liam," the sorcerer said, alternating his gaze from his gun to his sister. Actually, adoptive sister, judging by the difference in their magic. "Liam Talbot. Son of Stephan and Angelica, sorcerers." He was obviously deciding to play nice.

"Specializing in guns?" I asked, honestly interested.

He grimaced, then nodded. "Ballistics, weapons, et cetera."

"And your accuracy?" Kandy asked.

He glanced at his sister again, tension running through his jaw.

"You're the one who pointed the weapon at us," I reminded him gently. "That opened you up."

"For interrogation?"

Kandy laughed. "You ain't seen nothing yet, VPD. And your sister is in some shit as well."

"At this distance, 98 percent accuracy," he said stiltedly. "I wouldn't have missed."

"You did miss," I said.

He looked at me, startled. Almost as though he hadn't sorted that out for himself yet. Yeah, I moved faster than he could pull a trigger. Gun-toting sorcerers beware.

Liam nodded begrudgingly. "I...I thought you were hurting Bitsy. That you'd already hurt her."

"Bitsy?" Kandy echoed.

He nodded toward his unconscious sister. "Bitsy. Rebecca."

Kandy laughed sneeringly, presumably in response to how the werewolf in her arms was anything but tiny. "You don't pull a gun unless you're in immediate danger, sorcerer."

"Sometimes it's a deterrent—"

"No," I said. "There are others who walk the streets of Vancouver who wouldn't have been as understanding as we were."

"Understanding?" he sputtered.

"Where's your car?" Kandy said, ignoring him. "We've got a party to get to. And your sister will probably be asleep for hours from her transformation."

"Transformation?" Liam echoed incredulously. "She … transformed?"

"Partial," I said. "Why? Doesn't she usually?"

He shook his head, then looked chagrined. Like he'd given away one of his sister's deep dark secrets.

I glanced at Kandy. "She is bitten, then?"

"Sorcerer?" Kandy demanded.

"She … was born to werewolves, but …" His voice trailed off.

"Didn't transform as expected? When expected?" Kandy filled in the information he'd left hanging.

Liam nodded.

"So …" Kandy looked at me, some dark emotion surfacing. "Her parents bit her?"

He nodded again.

"I don't understand," I said. "To trigger her magic?"

"It's barbaric," Kandy snarled. "Their alpha should have excised them for it."

Liam snorted harshly. "Bitsy would have been killed if her pack leader had discovered she couldn't transform."

Kandy leveled a scathing glare at the sorcerer. "You have no idea what you're talking about."

He clamped his mouth shut. Not really backing down. But willing to remain silent on the matter.

"That's why she's scared of werewolves?" I asked. "But why the sudden transformation? Like you said, it isn't a full moon."

"No," Kandy said, gazing down at the woman in her arms. Then she looked up at me. "Something is definitely triggering the fledglings' magic."

I nodded. "But not just the Talbots, since it started with Mory. And the sorcerer here looks fine. The grid, maybe?"

"Maybe." But Kandy sounded doubtful.

"What grid?" Liam asked.

We ignored him.

I thought about the sketch from Rochelle, wondering again if it represented some sort of rune I was meant to chalk into my circle when we gathered to recast the grid. Or maybe some sort of magical object I needed to find, then use as an anchor. But I didn't want to mention it to Kandy in front of the Talbots.

Rebecca, aka Bitsy, moaned softly in Kandy's arms. Liam dashed forward, instantly forgetting that he was a hard-assed police officer and murmuring to her in soft tones.

"Um … hey, LT …" Rebecca murmured. Then she appeared to suddenly take in the fact that she was being held aloft by a green-haired werewolf. "Oh … hello? Um, why are you holding me like a baby?"

"It isn't by choice, wolf," Kandy groused.

Bitsy slapped her hand over her mouth, staring first at Liam, then at me with horror. "Oh, God … I … I … I was hanging out with Tony …"

"Tony?" I asked sharply. That was the second time the unknown male had been mentioned. Well, unknown to me. Mory and Burgundy had apparently been playing board games with him the night before.

"Our brother," Liam said, not taking his gaze off his sister. Then I remembered Angelica Talbot having said the name too.

Bitsy's chin quivered. "I was just going to try on some sneakers. The store is having a fall sale."

"From Gravity Pope?" I asked, momentarily distracted by the idea of discount shoes. The store was almost directly across the street from the butcher's. "They have the best Converse selection. Vans too."

Bitsy nodded, her eyes welling with tears. "Then I got really hungry."

"It's okay," Liam said.

"It is not okay," Kandy growled at the sorcerer. Then to Rebecca, she said, "Can you stand?"

The unfortunate werewolf nodded. Kandy settled her on her feet and Liam got his arm around her waist. With the inches Bitsy's wild hair added to her height, she was actually taller than her adoptive brother.

"You'll come to train with me," Kandy said. "Starting Monday."

Rebecca looked traumatized.

"She won't," Liam said stiffly.

Kandy instantly got up in his face. "Don't make me throw down on you, sorcerer. I'm standing inches away and you won't see me coming."

He blinked.

"Rebecca transformed in front of humans." Kandy jabbed her thumb toward Bitsy.

"Did I?" she whispered.

"Well, one human," I said. "Dave. And I think he's figured some of this … all out. He called me." I looked at Liam. "Unless you weren't bluffing about that disturbance call."

Liam looked relieved, then embarrassed. "I was … bluffing."

"But …" Bitsy said.

He cleared his throat. "Mom called."

"Mom called?" Bitsy straightened away from her brother, her tone becoming edged. "As in, she was tracking me?"

"You know …" He dropped his voice to a murmur, presumably thinking that Kandy and I wouldn't hear him. "She tracks all of us."

Bitsy bared her teeth at her brother.

"Finally," Kandy said blithely. "So you aren't just a passive pup."

The bronze-skinned werewolf squared her shoulders. "I'm not available Monday during the day. I have school. Then soccer on Tuesdays and Thursdays, with games on Saturdays."

"What are you studying?" Kandy asked.

"Sports medicine," Bitsy said. "I'm a year away from my degree."

"And the soccer team?"

"UBC women's," Bitsy said proudly.

Kandy snorted. "Cheating isn't it? Being a werewolf and all?"

Bitsy's face fell. She looked to her brother.

Liam rubbed his hand over his face. "It wasn't … but …"

"But?" Bitsy whispered.

"You were suppressing your magic …" Liam faltered, but the full consequences of the afternoon hung off the end of his sentence.

"We'll talk about it later," Kandy said abruptly. "Go home. Come by the bakery after your classes on Monday."

"Bakery?" Bitsy echoed. "What bakery?"

Kandy laughed harshly. "What? Does your family just keep you in the dark about everything?" She hit the word 'family' with as much derision as she could muster. Which was a lot.

Liam flushed. "Of course not."

"Maybe I should pay you all a visit at home," Kandy said conversationally, glancing over at me. "Jade and me. Maybe the sentinel would like to join us. Or even better, now that the executioner is back in town, maybe he'd like a snack or two? Nothing settles down a surge of stupid-assed defiance like being fed on by a vampire. Given the venom and all."

Liam's hand flexed, as though he was thinking about pulling his second gun again.

"I think they're already fairly intimidated," I said. "Aren't you, Rebecca?"

The werewolf nodded her head, almost frantically.

"Liam?" I asked.

He jutted out his chin. "I get who you are. Both of you. Henry Calhoun was clear."

"I don't think he was," Kandy said. "I think he was charming and sweet, and concerned about sending you somewhere that your family wouldn't have to constantly be worried about being... what?" She eyed Rebecca for a moment. "Belittled? Scorned? Bullied?"

"All of the above," Bitsy whispered. She looked at her brother sadly. "Except Liam. He just tried to shield the rest of us. And we moved a lot."

"And now you're here," I said. "And anyone who wants you has to go through us first."

"The bullying seems about the same," Liam muttered.

"Does it, sorcerer?" Kandy asked. "Or did you just pull your itty-bitty gun on two Adepts of untold power, and they're about to let you walk away?"

The green-haired werewolf stepped back, standing shoulder to shoulder with me. "Take a good look, asshole."

Liam's gaze flicked between us.

"Use all your senses," Kandy snapped. Then she muttered to me, "I swear the new fledglings are utter morons."

Liam clenched his jaw. Then his sorcerer magic shifted. I sensed the moment he actually saw us—specifically, Kandy's cuffs and my necklace. His face blanched.

Kandy grunted. "Go home. Next time, I crush the gun."

I closed the space between myself and the sorcerer. Kandy had already put him in his place, multiple times. But I needed to add my own bit. I really didn't like being threatened in my own backyard. And Kandy was right, unfortunately. If Liam was prone to pulling his gun when facing unknown Adepts—whether or not he presumptively assumed they were harming his family—he was going to be in for a nasty surprise when he met Warner or Kett, or any guardian who might be visiting Vancouver.

I'd protected many friends, including some I shouldn't have, without ever pulling my knife. At least not as a first reaction.

"Liam Talbot," I murmured, presenting his gun in my open palm.

He met my gaze.

I deliberately allowed my magic to curl over and around the weapon.

"Please," he whispered.

I raised an eyebrow at him and he fell silent. Then I informed the deadly artifact in my hand that it wouldn't fire against me. Its magic shifted, accommodating my own. "Kandy," I said.

The green-haired werewolf placed her hand over the gun without further prompting.

Reaching for a tendril of my BFF's magic, I fed it into the weapon, also informing it that it wouldn't fire against Kandy.

I nodded. The green-haired werewolf stepped back.

I offered the gun to Liam.

He hesitated. "What did you do to it?"

"You won't be able to use it against me or Kandy."

He looked doubtful. And a little too smug about it.

"Give it a try," I said. "And when the backfire takes off your hand, I promise to let Bitsy drive you to the hospital."

Liam swallowed, gingerly taking the gun from me.

"Is it of your own construction?" I asked.

He nodded.

"Do you have others?"

"No."

"While you reside in Vancouver—"

"Under our protection," Kandy interjected.

"You won't make any more of them." I continued as though she hadn't interrupted me. "Do you understand? You make more weapons like this … you try to figure out how to harm me or Kandy or anyone under our protection, and I will crush you. Not just the gun in question."

"I'm an officer of the law," Liam said stiffly. "I don't hurt people. I know my duty."

I leaned into him. He struggled to hold himself in place. "You held me at gunpoint, Liam Talbot. You threatened my friend, the enforcer of this territory. When we were doing our duty."

"I apologize. I was … mistaken."

"I'll be keeping close tabs on you, sorcerer. In fact, I expect to see you in the bakery, often. How about every Thursday afternoon? You take a coffee break, yes?"

He nodded stiffly.

I eyed him for a moment. "Do I need to repeat myself?"

Liam's gaze flicked to me, then to Kandy.

The green-haired werewolf shrugged. "You're in trouble if Jade Godfrey doesn't like you, VPD. The few people she doesn't like usually come to very bloody ends. If it wasn't so, Henry wouldn't have sent your family here for safekeeping, would he?"

Careful to keep his finger nowhere near the trigger, Liam thoughtfully twisted the gun in his hand. Then he nodded. "I understand the rules. Where we fit within them. And who enforces them. Henry was clear. I just didn't …"

"Believe him?" Kandy asked mockingly.

Liam glanced at me, then away. "He wasn't forthcoming about certain aspects."

Kandy laughed harshly. "Yeah, the blond curls and big boobs confuse a lot of people, VPD. But the power is more than clear."

Liam nodded, wrapping his arm around Bitsy's shoulders. "I'll be at the bakery. Thursday afternoon."

I nodded, pretty much dismissing them.

Kandy and I watched them hurry away.

"My new favorite pastime," I said. "Terrifying fledglings."

"The sorcerer isn't a fledgling." Kandy bumped her shoulder against mine. "That gun was impressive."

"It was."

"Come on. We've got nails to paint, makeup to apply. You don't want to be late for your own party."

"It doesn't take me …" I glanced at the time on my phone. "Four hours to get ready."

"I booked us mani-pedis."

I grinned at my BFF. "You are the best."

She shrugged. "It'll be a good way to figure out if the twins smoothed everything over."

"Ah," I groaned. "The twins. And we need to check out this Tony dude."

Kandy nodded, glancing down at her phone. "The brother. Pearl texted the Talbots' address."

I sighed. "Even if this is all somehow tied to the grid, it would be good to check out the house sooner than later, figure out if the Talbots are connected to it all somehow."

"If it weren't for your itchy feet, this would all be my thing." Kandy gave me a pointed look. "As enforcer."

I raised my hands in acquiescence. "Not stepping on your toes, my toothy friend."

She snorted. "I'll pop over while you're closing up the bakery. I'll let you know if I need reinforcements."

"Trying to get rid of me?"

"Nah, I like you tagging along. I get a big kick out of all the double takes." Kandy grinned wolfishly. "But you know Scarlett is totally going to recruit Wisteria and gang up on Pearl, after the twins and now the werewolf. So I figure you're going to be otherwise occupied."

"And how would my mother know about any of that?"

"Reading my text messages, I imagine."

"Kandy … you're not deliberately pitting my mother against my grandmother, are you?"

"How can you even ask that?" Kandy pressed her hand to her chest, mockingly aghast. "I mean, those would be some impressive fireworks—"

"I take back that thing I said earlier. About you being the best."

Kandy chuckled. "You don't like the itchy-feet thing."

"I don't. I don't like being controlled by an external force. My own internal forces are bad enough."

"And I don't like your grandmother weaving other options into the grid."

My heart grew suddenly heavy at the thought of Gran deliberately tying me to the grid. "Possibly weaving. Or possibly my own fault. With the punching of concrete and all."

Kandy grunted in agreement. Then she wrapped her arm around mine. "So the witches will gather tonight, we'll cast the grid again, subbing you out, and everything will sort itself."

I nodded, allowing her to lead me away up the alley.

A gust of wind buffeted us, and for the first time in a long while, I thought I could feel the promise of rain. Rain would dampen the smoke from the forest fires plaguing the province. The haze over the city would lift. Everything would go back to normal.

And normal was good. Normal was great. Normal was exactly what I wanted.

So then why did it feel as though whatever was going on unseen around us was just getting started?

With Tima and Todd perfectly fine to cover the final hour of the day and close up the bakery, I headed upstairs for a shower. I was almost ready to give up on diffusing my hair and moving on to doing my makeup—because perfect curls were great, but losing half an hour of my life in order to obtain them was ridiculously boring—when Kandy popped her head into the bathroom.

"Burgundy is taking your place."

"For the grid casting?" I switched the diffuser to the other side of my head, eyeing Kandy, who looked just a little bit smug. After we'd had our mani-pedis, the werewolf had followed a trail of text messages to Gran's.

"The witches have so ordained."

"And Burgundy is powerful enough? Even as a quarter-witch?"

"Your mother thinks so. Mostly because her magic will be receptive to the others, so they can support her. Plus the fact that she's been specifically training with Pearl for over a year."

I nodded thoughtfully. It wasn't as if I was a full-blood witch either, and I hadn't specifically trained in spellcasting. Not for years, anyway. And even then, I'd been pretty incapable of actually pulling off any and all witch magic. Burgundy might be only a quarter-witch, but since she was actually in training and capable of casting, I could see why my mother would think she was a better choice, even with Gran so adamant that I participate.

"How much magic was thrown around during the discussion?" I asked.

Kandy grinned. "None. But I seriously wouldn't want to have been the one facing off with Scarlett, Wisteria, and her hottie Declan. It was all polite smiles between the women while Declan singed the rug."

"Singed? Like he casts with fire?"

Kandy shrugged. "Pearl held her own through it. Barely batted an eye, then relented. Then they sat down and put together a plan."

"Which is?"

"You redraw the runes, cast, then break the circle while the other witches maintain their anchor points. Burgundy steps into your spot, then she recasts."

"With the same runes?"

"Nope. Those are too complicated for her. Or, as Scarlett kept insisting, too complicated for the main grid spell."

Kandy leaned against the bathroom counter, stirring her fingers through the makeup I'd strewn beside the sink. She plucked a lipstick from the pile, opened it, then rejected the color—a pretty pink—with a curl of her lip.

"And Gran?" I almost hesitated to ask. "Is the engagement party still on?"

Continuing to sort through and check the color of my lipsticks, Kandy snorted. "By the end of the bloody meeting, she had it all turned around like the whole thing was her idea. A great test to see if the grid would hold should one of the anchor points be compromised, yadda yadda."

"Maybe I should have been there," I murmured, tucking my hairdryer back into its drawer.

"Nah. Then the subject would have twisted back on itself, like it did this morning. Wisteria's presence kept everything civil, and Declan's permanent glare made sure the meeting didn't drag on and on. Though I left when they got sidetracked about other tests they were going to take the opportunity to conduct tonight."

"Other tests?"

"Something about a shield. Or a barrier spell. Should the city ever come under siege, I don't know. Witch porn."

"And your misfits? Will they all be at the party?" I asked.

"Your misfits, you mean? I dropped off beer and gave them money for pizza later. They're playing games at the Talbots'."

"You … dropped off beer?"

"Seem young, don't they? But they're all of age … mostly. In Canada, anyway."

"And?" I asked pointedly. Kandy didn't randomly buy beer and pizza for just anyone. "Is Tony an evil wizard secretly spelling the others?"

She barked out a laugh, shaking her head. "Just a geek with a flashy computer." Giving me a surly look, she added, "I took the opportunity to scout the place. As so ordered."

I snorted. "As if. And?"

"Nothing out of the ordinary. No weird magic. Not that I could smell, at least. They're renting from Pearl. Across from the park."

"The house on Ogden?"

"Yep."

"That's close to the anchor point," I said thoughtfully.

"But not even remotely in line with the magic. It runs along the shoreline in both directions. Trust me, Jade. I checked all the points this morning, and I specifically double-checked the one in the park after I left the Talbots. If the fledglings were tapping into it somehow, I would have scented it."

I returned my attention to the mirror, picking up and brushing some powder across my forehead and cheeks while I thought through all the weird occurrences that I'd witnessed since the grid had been raised. "Maybe they screwed around with it last night. After we left."

"We were pretty heavy on them. I don't think they're mastermind manipulators, especially not when interrogated separately. I'm not even sure the Tony kid ever leaves the basement. And you know that Mory wouldn't lie to you. Not for one second."

I nodded my agreement about the necromancer. But I still wasn't so certain about the Talbots. "Gran must have invited them to the party. Mory, at least."

"Sure. But given the choice, you'd have picked the basement with your friends over Pearl's sure-to-be snotty shindig."

"Any day." I grinned at Kandy. "I mean, as long as there were cupcakes."

She snorted. "Please. Any dessert would do for you." She fished a lipstick from my makeup collection—a purple so deep it was practically black. It appeared pristinely new, so it must have been an impulse buy. "I'm borrowing this."

"It's yours."

"And this." She swiped a miniature sampler containing three eye shadows and two blushes. A gift-with-purchase sort of thing, again unused.

"Do you need some brushes to go with your stolen goods?"

"Nah, I'm fine." Kandy flashed me a toothy grin, then twirled around as if intending to flounce dramatically from the bathroom. But instead, she smacked chin first into a thick parchment envelope that had just appeared out of thin air.

Smoky dragon magic filled the room, followed by earl grey tea so black that it was bitter.

Kandy snarled, reached up, and tried to tear the offending envelope out of the air. She couldn't move it. Not an inch, not even wearing the cuffs. Not even when she grabbed hold with both hands, lifting her knees to her chest and putting her full weight behind it.

So she hung there, suspended from a four-inch-by-six-inch piece of paper.

"Well, that's new," I muttered.

Kandy snarled just to underscore her displeasure. Then she let go and stepped back, allowing me to easily pluck the envelope out of the air.

The taste of the treasure keeper's magic intensified underneath my fingertips. I wondered if he would have been immediately aware of the moment I touched it.

"No," Kandy said. Emphatically. "Your grandmother has been planning this party for months. She's moved the date three times. And where the hell is Warner, anyway?"

Nodding to acknowledge her concerns, I eyed the envelope. It was addressed to Jade Godfrey in a handwritten scrawl of black ink. No title. No official seal. Which was most definitely the treasure keeper's way of being a total asshole.

Sighing, I opened the parchment, reading the eleven words contained within.

*You will attend me at the moment*
*you read this summons.*

I laughed nastily, angling the note so Kandy could read it. "At the moment? Seriously? I'm supposed to transport myself to his side while reading his pissy command?"

Kandy folded her arms across her chest. "Go after the party."

"Go after? The asshole was supposed to have sent me a notice letting me know I'd been exonerated. Or that the trial had been canceled. He didn't. He summoned me. Officially. Letting me think I was going to have to plead for my freaking life before a freaking panel of guardian freaking dragons! He can clean up whatever mess he's gotten himself into on his own." I lifted the parchment before me, speaking formally. "Screw you and the horse you rode in on."

Kandy scrunched up her face. "Horse you rode in on? Do you even know what you're quoting?"

"Nope. But then, neither will he."

The parchment disintegrated, leaving a film of soot across my prettily pedicured toes. I'd replaced the coral nail polish with a sparkly pink OPI shade appropriately dubbed *Princesses Rule*.

"Wow," Kandy said, not impressed.

"Yeah. Asshole to the bitter end."

"I doubt that's the end."

I sighed. "You're probably right."

"There's no 'probably' about it, dowser." Kandy thrust her purloined lipstick before her like a knife, grinning madly. "Get on your pretty dress, pretty baby. The caterers were already setting up before I left Pearl's, and I don't want all the good grub to get picked over before we get there."

I laughed as the green-haired werewolf took off to her own apartment to get dressed. I certainly wasn't going to let itchy feet or pissy guardians ruin my evening, either.

I'd seen the menu, and it wasn't to be missed.

# Chapter Nine

*A* chocolate fountain, copious amounts of champagne, and heavenly bites of candied sockeye salmon on garlic crostini filled the long, linen-swathed tables that occupied the top tier of the patio, closest to the house. Strings of lights powered by bright-blue witch magic flickered along the eaves, swooping across and along the tall fences edging the yard, twining through the branches of a maple tree just beginning to change color, then criss-crossing over the aqua-blue-tiled swimming pool on the lower deck. More charmed lanterns floated in the pool's crystal-clear water.

Scattered across my grandmother's backyard, witches, necromancers, and shapeshifters chatted quietly in small clusters. Dressed to the nines and with their magic politely tucked away at Pearl's request—and under the weight of the multitude of wards encasing the property—they nibbled on treats, watching the sun slowly setting over English Bay.

Some of Gran's guests were local. Some had traveled to Vancouver from various points in the Pacific Northwest. A couple of Convocation members had come from Europe and beyond. Even the caterers had been flown in from Toronto. With this many Adepts gathered in one place, Gran thought it best to have the chef and her staff be of the magical persuasion. Or, in this case, nonpracticing but from a witch lineage.

Initially, Gran had been pushing for a witches-and-honorary-coven-members-only event. But since neither Warner nor I were actually witches, Scarlett's pragmatism had easily won out. Thankfully, the pack had been content to be represented by Kandy, though Desmond and Audrey had both been invited. My werewolf BFF had also been muttering about inviting the beta and Lara for the bachelorette party. But keeping a polite distance from the pack in general was probably a good thing. I had a terrible habit of getting people hurt and ruining relationships. It went without saying that my mother was the diplomat in the family.

Though I'd been formally presented to each and every one of the guests as they'd arrived, I knew it was going to be a stretch for me to recall even half of their names and titles.

I hadn't been bothering to introduce myself as anything other than Jade, Pearl's granddaughter. My other titles and talents—alchemist, dragon slayer, and the wielder of the instruments of assassination—were known by very few in attendance. And since I generally declared those addendums only before I was about to kick serious ass, it really wasn't necessary to trumpet them at Gran's party. Unless maybe the chocolate fountain ran dry and a brawl broke out. But my fingers were crossed that that wouldn't happen—not only because I hadn't managed to make my way over there yet, but also because Gran would be peeved if I pulled my knife.

She had planned the most perfect engagement party, after all. And the only thing unaccounted for?

My fiance.

Yep, Warner was missing in action.

Though not literally, I hoped.

But with dragons, I never knew from one moment to the next.

"If he doesn't show, I'll give you first pick," Kandy said, brushing her shoulder against mine as she pressed a flute of champagne into my hand.

The taste of her red-berry-infused dark-chocolate magic slipped past my personal magical barriers. I was keeping all my magic tucked away tightly and my senses muted for the night, due to the number of Adepts gathering around Gran's pool.

"I've got my eye on the tall, skinny witch in the orange muumuu," my best friend said, directing her gaze across the pool at her prey. "I like her bangs. But I'm willing to negotiate."

I laughed, involuntarily snorting into my champagne as I took a sip of its sparkling sweetness. Choking as effervescence shot up my nose, I flashed a genuine grin at the decked-out green-haired werewolf.

Gran had insisted on enforcing a dress code for the party—cocktail attire—and no one but me had complained. Then Kandy had gone out and found me a dark-green silk dress that twirled around my knees when I walked, so I'd had to stop griping. Though she personally favored Lycra shorts and obscene T-shirts, the werewolf had a fantastic fashion sense when it came to clothing other people. Plus, the halter neckline, with its subtly sequined edging, looked fabulous with the black-leather patent-toe asymmetrical pumps—aka Big Presence Earharts—that I just had to buy from Fluevog.

"Only you would think the cut of a witch's bangs was a reason to date her," I murmured, eyeing the witch in question. Gran had introduced us about ten minutes earlier, before she went inside to check on the caterers. Her name was Olive … something. Magically gifted with plants—especially citrus fruit, which was normally impossible to grow at our latitude.

She was a member of the Godfrey coven and had helped save the lives of probably a quarter of the guests in attendance—holding a shield with my mother and Gran against a horde of demons on a beach in Tofino. I had also tasted her magic while casting the grid the previous night.

"Not all of us are the marrying kind," Kandy said, sniffing as though I'd insulted her.

My werewolf BFF was literally swathed in black sequins, including her skintight dress and speckled custom sneakers. A series of antique hairpins held her almost-chin-length hair back in twisted rows. She'd been liberal with black eyeliner, sparkling green eye shadow, and the deep-purple lipstick she'd pilfered from my collection.

Catching me looking at her, she pursed her lips prettily, then snapped her teeth in my direction. "Looking is free, dowser," she said, wagging her eyebrows. Then, abandoning me to my post at the head of the currently empty greeting line, she sauntered off toward the orange-clad witch.

The magic of Gran's wards shifted behind my right shoulder, and the taste of burnt cinnamon toast tickled my senses. I sighed, knowing before I'd even looked that a deep, misplaced shadow had appeared along the top edge of the fence.

Drawn by the abundance of magic gathered in Gran's backyard, but wary of the sun even as it was setting, the shadow leech was able to get through the substantial wards that encased the property because of its connection to me. Or, rather, its connection to the magic I'd absorbed from Shailaja.

I glanced over my shoulder. The leech slipped down the fence, latching onto one of the strings of lights, then slowly siphoning off the bright-blue magic my mother had spent hours casting.

I seriously refused to call the little demon spawn 'Freddie.' No matter how strained my relationship was with Mory, I wasn't going to encourage the befriending of wicked little monsters.

The string of lights flickered, then died.

"That's enough." I put as much steel as I could into the whisper. "Don't make me vanquish you."

The shadow watched me with its blood-red slitted eyes. Then it opened its dark, needle-toothed maw and chittered discontentedly.

My mother, deep in conversation with a group of witches near the chocolate fountain, turned her head at the sound. Not many Adepts could see the shadow leech, but apparently my mother could hear it. Her strawberry-blond tresses cascaded across her back. She was wearing a rose-gold dress that flared out at the waist and ended just below her knees.

Catching sight of the dead lights, Scarlett reached up and touched the bulb nearest to her. The taste of strawberry replaced the burnt cinnamon lingering on the tip of my tongue as she effortlessly imbued the string of lights with new magic.

The leech chittered again, this time almost happily. It reached for my mother's magic as it coursed down the cord toward it, lighting one bulb after the other.

"No," I whispered. Then, once again feeling guilty that a sentient being was unwillingly and unwittingly bound to me, I relented. "After. When the party is done, and everyone has gone, and before the magic all burns out. It's yours."

The leech flashed its teeth at me in what might have been a smile—if I'd been willing to admit it was capable of expressing emotions. Then it settled contentedly back in the crook of a tree limb to oversee the gathering.

Lovely.

No fiance yet, but the insatiable shadow leech had made it to the engagement party on time.

I was halfway through my second glass of champagne and more than ready to abandon my post for the chocolate fountain, when the magic of the wards shifted and hints of tart apple and cayenne-spiced chocolate rolled across my tongue.

Kandy appeared at my side just before a white-blond, gray-eyed woman stepped around the house, directed from the front walk to the backyard along glowing patio stones that were also of my mother's crafting.

Rochelle.

The oracle had arrived.

I hadn't been sure she would come, not with all the other Adepts in attendance. Even though I knew the large raw-diamond necklace she wore, practically falling to her belly button, should have shielded her from picking up random visions unless she accidentally touched anyone.

Her delectable, mocha-skinned husband prowled a step behind her, taking in every Adept arrayed on both tiers of the patio with a sweeping glance. The green of his shapeshifter magic obscured his normally dark aquamarine gaze. Beau was in full protection mode, which, given the rarity of his wife's magic, made sense. Except no one was going to accost anyone at a gathering hosted by my grandmother.

Rochelle was dressed in the most adorable pieced-together black silk dress, with artfully frayed seams. A massive gray cashmere-and-silk lace stole was wrapped around her shoulders. The series of black-inked tattoos that covered both of her arms and upper back could be seen through sections of the open lace. Gran had given the stole to the oracle last Christmas, and I knew she'd be pleased to see Rochelle wearing it. The lacework was completely contrary to the oracle's low-key personal style. And since Rochelle never seemed to do anything for show or anything that was expected of her, I had been surprised that Gran thought it a fitting gift.

I'd been wrong.

And probably not for the last time.

Beau was epically gorgeous in a black suit, charcoal shirt, and gray-and-white striped tie. The ensemble fit him like he modeled for a living, rather than spending his days helping with Rochelle's chickens, rebuilding cars, and updating their property in Southlands.

I might have been with Warner in every sense of the word, but based on the way Kandy's toothy grin sharpened as the werecat approached, I wasn't the only one who noticed the raw beauty stalking toward us.

Of course, the green-haired werewolf might simply be gleefully anticipating exerting her dominance. As a younger shapeshifter, Beau was firmly below Kandy in the pack order, in Vancouver and in Portland.

The hush that had fallen among the gathered Adepts wasn't due only to Beau's looks. It was the oracle's growing reputation, and the rarity of her permanent place within the Godfrey coven, that had momentarily deadened the polite chatter.

Though I knew that Gran oversaw petitioners for the oracle's services, my own interactions with Rochelle had been thankfully benign, meeting up every week when she dropped off eggs from her flock of deathlayers and occasionally met with Gran. No visions or dire warnings. Not until today, when she'd sent Blossom with the obscure sketch.

As such, it was disturbing to notice that Rochelle had an art tube tucked underneath her left elbow, with the silver ribbon that adorned it clearly marking it as an engagement gift.

Not that gifts from Adepts were usually a problem for me. They almost always involved magic, and I was a collector, after all. But for the engagement party, Gran had indicated on the invitations that guests weren't expected to bring gifts.

And the problem was that any gift from Rochelle that came rolled in an art tube—rather than simply being torn out of her sketchbook—seemed certain to depict an immutable future. One that I was barreling heedlessly toward, whether or not I saw caution smudged and shaded in the pages of the oracle's sketchbooks.

Fate.

Destiny.

I wasn't a fan.

No matter what power I wielded or what magical artifacts I constructed, I wasn't capable of thwarting such things. And with the smoky pink sunset closing a day that had already been filled with too many questions, I had absolutely no desire to see a sketch that the oracle had deemed worthy of gift wrap.

That made me a coward. I understood that. But only the far seer could realign the future if he saw fit to do so. I knew. Chi Wen had used me, or what was supposed to be a future version of me—the dragon slayer—to do so. I could still feel the warmth of Shailaja's blood under my splayed palms as it seeped across the inlaid tile of the phoenix's tomb—

Kandy bumped me with her shoulder.

I focused on the tiny oracle standing before me. Her gray eyes were edged with the white of her magic. Her hair, which she had been dyeing black when I first met her, was the same pale shade, almost devoid of color. Her simmering power echoed back through the large raw diamond and the rose gold of her necklace. I curled my fingers into a loose fist, denying my urge to reach out and stroke the chain, to add more of my own alchemy into the powerful artifact. It already contained more than enough layers of protection, some of which I'd placed myself. But needless to say, it didn't belong to me.

And yes, I would just keep reminding myself of that. It was like being on a diet, except worse. Because it was one thing to indiscriminately eat food I'd rightfully purchased, and completely another to go around nibbling off other people's plates.

"Rochelle. Beau," I said. "Thank you for coming."

"Yeah," Kandy echoed, leering at Beau. "Thank you for coming."

Beau laughed, shaking his head at his pack mate. Then he bowed slightly, addressing me. "We are honored by the invitation, dowser."

"Don't open it now," Rochelle said, gruffly bypassing the rest of the formalities by practically shoving the art tube into my arms. "It's for later. For your wedding."

"Well, that bodes well." I said it with a lightness I didn't feel. Being presented with oracle sketches pertaining to my pending nuptials actually felt significantly worse than getting something possibly relevant to the weird day I was already having.

"No. I…I just don't want you to get charcoal on your pretty dress." Rochelle was smiling, but there was something about how she used the word 'pretty' that seemed almost derogatory.

I narrowed my eyes at her.

Her smile widened. "I wore a dress too."

"Did you lose a bet?"

She laughed. "How could an oracle lose a bet?" Then she relented. "Kandy made me." She glanced around. A short line of newcomers was forming behind her and Beau. "There's, um, there's something else I should tell you …"

"About the sketch you sent?"

"Ah, no. That is what it will be. This is, ah, something else."

"That sounds delightful."

"I … um …" She glanced toward the house just as my grandmother came striding through the snazzy lift-and-slide glass doors—which she had dropped some serious cash on the previous month—to make a beeline toward us. "Maybe later." She grabbed Beau's hand and tugged him in the opposite direction without further ado.

"Great," I muttered, really not at all interested in anything the oracle might have been wary of telling me. Or, even worse, what she was wary of telling me in front of my grandmother.

Kandy laughed huskily and far too gleefully for my liking. Then she took the art tube from me, freeing my hands and switching places with my grandmother.

Gran took up her post at my side, which she'd abandoned only to check on the hot hors d'oeuvres. She was resplendent in a gray raw-silk skirt and a matching short-waisted jacket. Her hair, only a few shades lighter than the skirt, was coiled in a series of thick, shiny braids. She offered her hand to the brown-haired, olive-skinned necromancer who was waiting patiently next in line.

"Teresa. Delighted. You remember my grand-daughter, Jade?" She gestured toward me.

Benjamin Garrick's mother fixed her dark-eyed gaze on me. I smiled, though my cheeks were really starting to ache, and found myself hoping that I wasn't about to have to ward off a death curse for yanking her son out of a tree and interrogating him.

Regulating the new Adepts of Vancouver would have been seriously easier if Kandy's so-called misfits hadn't come with parental units.

The receiving line eventually petered out. I had exchanged inane pleasantries with eight more guests, and Gran's backyard was getting down to elbow room only. The exterior glass doors stood open, inviting entry to the living room and kitchen, though no one had moved inside yet. But with the spectacular hazy-pink sunset kissing the mountains of the North Shore across the water and over the top of Stanley Park, I wasn't terribly surprised.

Gran wandered off with the last batch of guests—and I was more than ready to do the same—when the wards shifted, accommodating a large influx of intense magic. And bringing with it the taste of sweet, syrupy cherries topped with thick whipped cream and underpinned with deep cacao.

Warner stalked around the corner of the house as if he might have been invading the backyard, rather than showing up to a gathering in his honor.

He was glowering so deeply that the witches near the side gate actually backed away from him. Kelly, a sandy-haired witch who raised alpaca and cashmere goats on Salt Spring Island, momentarily lost hold of her glass. Thankfully for Gran's deposit, she caught it with a lick of her rosemary-infused magic before it hit the patio.

Then Warner spotted me standing just past the crowd. A smile spread across his face, transforming him from forbidding to eye-blisteringly handsome. At least to me. The gold of his dragon magic flickered in his eyes as he slowed his pace, sweeping his gaze over me.

I instinctively straightened my back, tucked my abs, and settled my shoulders to thrust my chest out. Just a tiny bit. Cocking my hip slightly, I allowed myself to take in every inch of him.

He was clad in a medium-gray suit with thin white pinstripes, a white dress shirt, and a dark-green silk tie that I would have sworn was an exact match to my dress. The suit somehow made his broad shoulders and tapered torso appear almost impossibly wide and trim at the same time.

Heat flooded through my belly. I had thought Warner sexy in dragon training leathers, but the suit brought out another side of him entirely. A smooth, barely contained sexiness that I hadn't seen before. At least not outside my bedroom.

His grin shifted into an appreciative leer as he ran a hand through his recently cropped dark-blond hair, coming to a stop a couple of feet from me.

I reached up, almost involuntarily needing to touch him, and ran my fingers across his freshly shaved jaw. He was more darkly tanned than he'd been half a day earlier. The fresh scar that had marred his face had completely faded.

"Finally, asshole," Kandy hissed, suddenly standing beside me.

Warner smothered his smile, taking a step back so as to offer me a slight bow. Then he lifted a dark-gold velvet box before him.

"Jade," he murmured. "Crafted for you."

I lifted the lid from the box, exposing yards of dark green silk embroidered with strands of pure gold. Wordless, I caressed the impossibly light rectangular stole, feeling the magic woven within it dance underneath my fingers. Witch magic by its grassy undertones. The embroidery depicted two serpentine dragons facing one another.

"Warner," I whispered, awed.

My fiance passed the box to Kandy, then took the stole from me, draping it over my shoulders. "It contains a very practical warming spell, along with some protective spells, of course."

"Of course," I echoed. Despite the extra three inches my heels added to my height, the stole's twelve-inch fringe practically brushed the ground. "It's absolutely gorgeous. But... I didn't get anything for you."

He laughed huskily, running his fingers along the edges of the stole—and surreptitiously copping a rather deliberate feel at the same time. "You are my gift, Jade. Every day that I'm privileged to walk by your side. I need nothing else."

Warmth flushed my chest. I wrapped my hand around the back of his neck, brushing my lips across his, heedless of my lipstick and the crowd that surrounded us. "Warner ..." I practically moaned his name as the taste of his black-forest-cake magic flooded through my mouth, filling my senses.

"You can thank me properly later," he said saucily. But then, disappointingly, he stepped back, shifting to my side and giving me a clear view of the length of the pool.

The fire breather and her ward were strolling regally along the wood deck toward us.

My heart rate ratcheted up even faster, but in a completely different—and completely uncomfortable—way.

Suanmi, the guardian of Western Europe, had her arm laced through Drake's. And while the apprentice to the far seer was grinning madly, the fire breather's disdain was evident in every four-inch-heeled step she took.

All at once, Warner's tardiness and his deep glower upon finally arriving made absolute sense. He'd been waiting on the guardian.

The fire breather had crossed through my grandmother's wards as if they didn't exist. She was only a half-dozen feet away, but I couldn't taste a drop of her magic, even as Drake's honey-roasted almonds rolled around the both of them.

Warner cleared his throat, casting his voice low. No matter that if she'd wanted to, Suanmi could have heard us whisper from the street, even over the steady traffic that filled Point Grey Road deep into every evening. "Now you see why I was late."

I tucked my hand into his elbow. Then we faced the new arrivals as if they were a firing squad. Because maybe they were. I was never certain whether the fire breather was friend or foe.

Suanmi wore a sleeveless chiffon dress that hugged every lithe curve, graduating from the deepest of blacks to the brightest of reds around her ankles. Her red-soled, four-inch, black patent-leather Louboutin heels brought her height almost up to the top of Drake's ears—and he was over six feet. A ruby-and-diamond cornet, only a step away from being a tiara, was nestled in her silky dark hair.

Drake was decked out in a black suit with black-satin lapels and a black dress shirt. No tie. The fledgling guardian's short, dark hair was smoothed back from his wide brow, and his dark eyes danced with mirth. But then, Drake was always delighted by dangerous situations. Being a practically immortal seventeen-year-old probably had a lot to do with his attitude.

My father, Yazi, dressed in a navy suit, was a dozen steps behind Suanmi. Hanging back. And I seriously hoped he was the final guardian planning to grace my engagement party with his or her presence. He grinned easily, ignoring the other Adepts as they turned to gawk at all the new arrivals. Then he sought out and found my mother beside the buffet tables.

"What the hell is going on?" I muttered.

Warner didn't answer as Suanmi paused before us. The guardian's gaze was on the long length of my necklace—but I was certain it was the instruments of assassination tangled and clipped to the chain that had her attention. I hadn't been face-to-face with her since I'd inadvertently claimed the instruments for myself in the treasure keeper's chamber.

The fire breather's hazelnut-whiskey truffle magic momentarily shifted around me. And even with the tiniest of tastes, I knew that as heavily armed as I was, she could have burned me to a crisp before I could lay hand to any weapon.

"Suanmi," I blurted, forcing myself to move beyond the moment. Beyond the uncertainty evoked by her appearance in my grandmother's backyard. "Guardian. You bless us with your presence."

"Oui, oui," she replied in her native French. But then something very close to awe caused her to switch to English. "What is that?"

I followed her gold-flecked, hazel-eyed gaze to the three-tiered chocolate fountain. "Dark chocolate, guardian. With strawberries … pineapple, marshmallows … and cookies to dip in it."

"Marshmallows," the guardian of Western Europe murmured. "For … dipping." She returned her gaze to my necklace, then addressed Kandy at my side without looking at her. "Your shoes are an interesting choice, wolf."

"I like to run."

"Which you would likely do better barefooted."

"I do a lot of things better bare … footed."

Suanmi tilted her head, finally turning her gaze toward Kandy. Then she laughed. The sound rang across the backyard like a series of husky wind chimes.

"Wolf. You shall present me to Jade's grandmother. And then escort me to the fountain of chocolate."

A fierce grin infused Kandy's face. Completely fearless, the sequin-swathed werewolf stepped forward, elbowing Drake out of the way and offering her arm to the fire breather.

As far as I knew, the only other time that Kandy had been anywhere near the guardian of Western Europe had been the night she was almost mortally wounded in a parking garage in London. The fire breather had refused to help us then. Okay, she'd specifically refused to help me. Kandy apparently didn't carry a grudge, though.

Or the werewolf was hatching an elaborate revenge plan and Gran's patio was about to become a battlefield.

I ignored the tiny thrill of anticipation that came with that thought.

As they stepped away, Suanmi's gaze dropped to the thick, rune-carved gold cuff Kandy wore. Then she lifted her chin offishly, lightly resting her hand on Kandy's forearm.

Kandy glanced back at me over her shoulder, taking in my shocked expression with one of her patented predator nonsmiles. "The witch is all yours."

Warner looked at me questioningly.

I shook my head. "It's nothing. Just a contingency plan. You know, in case you didn't show."

Drake was absentmindedly rubbing his stomach where Kandy had elbowed him, and gazing after the fire breather. "I didn't know they knew each other."

"Well, there was London. But Kandy was probably unconscious at the time."

"Ah, yes. London." Smiling, Drake leaned in to kiss my cheek. "I wish you peace and prosperity, Jade Godfrey …"—he reached over to shake Warner's hand—"… and Warner Jiaotuson."

A white-clad server crossed out from the kitchen, carrying a tray of what appeared to be stuffed puffed pastry of some sort. Possibly dungeness crab, if I correctly recalled which of the five possible menus Gran had finally settled on. Drake abandoned us without another word, cutting off the server's progress across the patio as though he were about to kneecap an enemy.

My father stepped forward, sweeping me into his arms before I could offer any commentary to Warner about the possibly volatile foreplay between Kandy and Suanmi. Or even to ask why the fire breather was in attendance at all. For a moment, my father's intense magic thundered around me, and I had the inexplicable urge to pull my knife and run into battle by his side. Then he was clapping Warner on the back, proudly but slightly too hard—based on the wince of pain my fiancé attempted to conceal underneath a grin.

"As we discussed, sentinel," he bellowed. Then he practically leaped across to the buffet tables, inserting himself between the fire breather and my mother.

I met Warner's gaze, reaching out to lace my fingers through his. "Is it later now?" I whispered.

"Most definitely."

And with that infinitesimal amount of encouragement, I tugged him up the steps and into the house, completely abandoning my obligations, along with all the extra introductions that would need to be made now that my fiance and my father had shown up.

Utilizing the stealthiest ninja moves in our collective arsenal, Warner and I snuck upstairs. Sadly, those moves were mostly wasted, because the house was empty other than the chef in the kitchen and the servers coming and going with appetizer trays. But we made it into the black-and-white hexagon-tiled and wallpapered powder room off the main staircase either way. And then we proceeded to tangle more than just fingertips, until my dress was up around my hips and my pretty lace panties were hanging from one ankle.

"One of the bedrooms would have been more comfortable," Warner murmured, pressing kisses around the invisible sheath strapped to my right thigh.

I gasped as his kisses turned to nipping, then moved higher. "Gran's got people staying in all the guest bedrooms," I said, trying to not moan as his mouth found his target. "And that's just rude, isn't it? To use someone else's bed?"

Warner chuckled huskily, sending waves of his black-forest-cake magic radiating up and through my belly. My nipples hardened eagerly. I curled my fingers in the thick hair at the back of his neck, tugging lightly, then more insistently when he ignored my prompting that I wanted to hurry along the sexual proceedings.

I might have been all about the icing when it came to cupcakes, but I was definitely a cake girl when it came to sex.

Warner lifted me without warning, attempting to settle me down on the edge of the delicate pedestal sink.

"It won't hold my weight," I cried. Explaining how we'd broken the sink to Gran was seriously on the bottom of my things-to-do-before-I-die list.

"I'm the one holding you now, Jade."

A flush that had nothing to do with sex and everything to do with being loved by this man, this dragon, warmed my chest. Capturing his mouth in mine, I wrapped my thighs around Warner, twining my ankles behind him—but leaving myself room to get his pants off.

He balanced me against the lip of the sink, cupping my ample ass and thighs in his hands effortlessly. Then he groaned as I freed him from the confines of his dress pants with a few swift strokes.

He slipped between my legs without further prompting, but then immediately tried to slow the pace. Pinned against the delicate sink, I didn't have any leverage with which to urge him on.

I laughed into his mouth. And he grinned wolfishly.

"Captured me, have you?" I whispered provocatively. "Will you carry me off to your cave now? Chain me up alongside your treasure hoard?"

The gold of his dragon magic glinted across his blue-green eyes as he increased the pace of his thrusts, momentarily dizzying me with pleasure. "No," he said, far too seriously. "I would never attempt to keep you without your leave, Jade. I pity anyone who would try to subjugate you."

"Because you'd tear them apart?"

He laughed, sounding shaky though his feet were planted firmly on the floor. "I'd destroy them. Eviscerate them. Eradicate them."

I arched into the knot of pleasure building between my legs. His teeth scored my neck as I angled my hips sharply forward, so that he was making contact with my very center with each thrust.

I shuddered, pleasure taking my voice and scrambling my thoughts.

Warner growled, practically bruising my lips with kisses between his words. "But you wouldn't give me the chance, would you? I'd have to make do with the remains of your fury. I'd have to wait for your leave to exact my revenge. Wouldn't I, dowser? Wielder of the instruments of assassination? Dragon slayer?"

I wrapped my hands around his face, gripping and twisting my fingers within his hair. "Warner," I whispered, darting my tongue into his mouth. "Warner …"

"Yes?" he asked teasingly. "Is there something I can do for you, my Jade?"

I reached between us, timing the movement between his thrusts, and tightly wrapped my forefinger and thumb around the root of his girth.

He groaned, then shuddered, burying his face in my neck.

I laughed, pleased to have pushed him over the edge of his steady control. In reaction to his unfettered desire, the warmth simmering in my belly burst into flame, fanning up my torso and curling down my legs to pool in the bottoms of my feet. I relaxed into the feeling, allowing my orgasm to—

Someone rapped sharply on the bathroom door. "Jade? The guests are looking for you. And Warner."

Gran.

Jesus.

I laughed breathlessly, pleasure tightening across my lower belly as Warner didn't bother acknowledging the interruption. "I'll be right there, Gran," I said, panting. "I'm just coming."

Warner chuckled, completely chuffed with himself.

On the other side of the door, Gran huffed in a most disgruntled way, grumbling as she retreated down the hall. "You two are impossible. You know you have responsibilities."

I grinned at Warner, who winked. Holding his gaze, I climaxed, throwing my head back as shudder after shudder racked my body. Through it all, Warner held me steadily aloft.

Then, with a self-satisfied sigh, he followed me over the edge, milking almost painful bits of lingering pleasure from me with his final strokes.

"Why does it feel as if I'm standing inside a birthday gift?" he muttered into my neck, still holding me tightly against him.

I laughed, opening my eyes to gaze up at the ceiling. It was wallpapered in black-and-white diamonds, matching the walls. "I think that was the idea."

After Warner helped me tidy my hair and I straightened his tie—along with various buttons and zippers—we stepped out of the house, hoping to slip into the crowd unnoticed. Unfortunately, Gran was waiting. Well, unfortunately for Warner, since she simply gave me a quelling look, then took my fiancé's arm and began introducing him around the party.

The sentinel, who wasn't particularly jovial unless he was running his knife through someone or watching an '80s comedy with Kandy, smiled affably, allowing Gran to show him off.

Something about the sight of him bending to listen carefully to introductions as my Gran made them pinched my heart, triggering another heady flush. I had never known that loving someone so much could be painful. That the tiniest of gestures would turn my knees to mush or cause my heart to swell with joy.

Warner glanced back over his shoulder, winking when he caught me watching him. A wide, wholly genuine grin spread across my face. Then, allowing my smile to turn wicked, I recalled his grip on my hips and his mouth on my neck.

Warner's look turned smoldering. Gran touched his arm, calling him back to the present. He actually had to shake his head to clear it.

I laughed, making a beeline for the chocolate fountain even though it appeared to have been commandeered by the fire breather. Suanmi was imperiously gesturing toward pieces of fruit, then waiting rather impatiently as Kandy covered her selection in melted chocolate and placed it on the guardian's plate.

I stifled another laugh. Given how long Warner and I had been upstairs, I would have expected Kandy's attention span to have been seriously tested by now. Apparently, I had underestimated her ability to relish stalking large predators. The green-haired werewolf was a fan of games, and if the fire breather wanted to play, Kandy would eagerly pretend to be servile for just long enough to lull her prey.

The faint taste of peppermint tickled my senses. I paused, scanning the immediate area with more than just my eyes—and noting as I did that every other predator on the patio did the same, including my father, Warner, Drake, and Kandy. Though at a guess, they had probably picked up on the change in my demeanor, rather than catching the same scent of magic.

That magic wasn't present within the warded backyard. Meaning its peppermint-tinted power was something I shouldn't have been able to taste on the other side of the magical barrier that warded the house and property. Except I didn't have a lot of *shouldn't* in my life anymore, and I was particularly attuned to this magic, which I was fairly certain was coming from the direction of the beach.

I smiled, letting the others who were primed to draw weapons and grow claws know that everything was okay. Crossing to the gate at the far corner of the patio, I slipped away from the party, practically dashing down the wooden stairs beyond.

Pausing to tug off my shoes, I skipped across the boulders and the sun-bleached logs that edged the beachfront. The taste of peppermint intensified as I crossed through Gran's wards, my toes sinking into the wet sand.

A vampire wearing a pale-gray, slim-fitting suit stood at the edge of the surf, the lowering sun setting his pale skin and white-blond hair aglow. He was alone. I couldn't taste Jasmine's sweeter magic anywhere nearby.

I closed the space between us. "Kett."

"Jade." His cool tone didn't betray a hint of joy. But then a quick quirk of his lips let me know he was pleased to have been invited to the engagement party. Still, I was pretty sure loitering just outside on the beach probably wasn't what my mother had had in mind when she'd insisted on the executioner of the vampire Conclave being included on the guest list.

I brushed my hand across his cheek questioningly, and his icy blue eyes warmed.

"All is well," he murmured, answering my un-voiced concern.

"Jasmine?"

"I thought …" He glanced up at the patio jutting out over the beach behind me. A patio filled with Adepts. "The magic gathered might be too much for her. For the present."

Kandy burst through the ward line shimmering with witch magic behind me, landing a few steps in front of the vampire. Kett's lips twisted again in what might have been a smile, but was possibly also a snarl. He stepped back, risking ruining his shiny dark-gray Oxfords in the salt water lapping at his heels.

Kandy cackled. "You afraid to come in, ancient one?" She set her hands on her hips, glancing around. "Where's your baby girl?"

Kett opened his mouth to speak, but shook his head instead, uncharacteristically running a hand through his hair. Then he stilled in midmotion, slowly lifting his gaze to the house looming behind us.

A perfectly coiffed blond swathed in navy silk stood on the edge of the patio, gazing down at us.

At Kett, specifically.

Wisteria.

A well-tanned, utterly imposing man loomed next to the reconstructionist. His sunglass-shaded gaze was pinned to the vampire on the beach.

Declan.

Kett hadn't moved. Hadn't dropped his hand. His face was expressionless, his cool peppermint magic coiled tightly around him.

Kandy glanced up at the witch on the patio, then back at the immobile vampire. Dark laughter rose up from somewhere deep within her belly. "Centuries old but still human enough to want what you can't have. Eh, vampire?"

Kett dropped his hand, lifting his lip in a halfhearted snarl. But he didn't dispute Kandy's glib conjecture.

The werewolf snorted, snapping her teeth at Kett playfully.

I looked back toward the house, watching Wisteria glancing around, then moving for the gate that led to the beach. Declan remained behind.

"So ... Wisteria too?" I whispered.

"It's not what you think, dowser," Kett said stiffly. "Or ... it might have been. But it isn't now."

"And the tasty morsel with her?" Kandy asked, feigning ignorance in order to needle Kett. "He doesn't appear to be a fan."

"Declan Benoit." Kett spoke the name as if it had been dragged from him. "Her childhood sweetheart. Her betrothed. And Jasmine's half-brother. In another lifetime, at least."

Kandy gave me a look that I returned. None of that information was news to either of us, of course. But Kett's reaction was.

Wisteria stepped into view, pausing at the base of the stairs. After carefully assessing the beach for potential hazards, her gaze returned to the vampire at my side.

"Don't make her walk across the sand in those shoes," I murmured. The reconstructionist was wearing shiny, open-toed navy sandals with spiky heels.

Kett flinched as though I'd pinched him—and he had somehow felt it through his iced-carved physique. Then he stepped across the beach, reaching for the reconstructionist.

The surprise that flitted across Wisteria's face informed me that he'd moved quickly. To her senses, at least.

But it was the kiss that Kett pressed to the witch's cheek that was surprising to Kandy and me. The green-haired werewolf's eyes narrowed in dark assessment. She wasn't the reconstructionist's biggest fan, and I could easily guess that the circumstances tying Kett to the Fairchilds through Jasmine were bothering the were-wolf as well. But then, Kandy didn't really like anyone. Other than those few people she would die to protect.

I followed Kett, Kandy moving beside me. Wis-teria appeared completely composed, even emotionless, matching the vampire's cool aspect almost perfectly. But her nutmeg-scented magic churned around her.

They hadn't exchanged a single word. At least not out loud.

"They're an interesting match," Kandy murmured. "Boring to the extreme."

Kett offered his arm to the reconstructionist as we drew closer, preceding us up the steps and back to the party. Whatever had stopped the vampire from crossing through the wards previously had apparently been nul-lified. Perhaps by Wisteria's appearance, and her silent acceptance of his presence.

I paused to brush sand off my feet. Kandy didn't seem to care. And somehow, the vampire didn't have a speck of sand on him.

By the time I made it to the top of the stairs, the party was down to one dragon. Warner.

"Wily guardian," Kandy muttered, scanning the patio and pool for Suanmi. "Slipped my net."

I chuckled. I couldn't help it. Only my werewolf best friend would decide that stalking one of the nine most powerful beings in the world—one who could incinerate a demon with a whispered word—was a fun pursuit.

Drawing startled gazes his way, Kett weaved through the few Adepts near the top of the stairs, Wisteria's hand still resting lightly on his arm. I'd never seen the vampire willingly touch anyone for such an extended period of time.

I latched the gate behind me, seeking out Warner, then meeting his questioning gaze with a smile.

The odd couple paused before Declan where he still stood on the patio. Kett offered his hand to Wisteria's betrothed. Magic full of the taste of burned sugar raged around Declan, and for the briefest of moments, I thought he was going to attack Kett.

Because I apparently took after my father more than my mother when it came to such things, my palm itched for the grip of my knife hilt. Even without my father, Suanmi, and Drake present, there were still a lot of powerful people gathered on my grandmother's patio. A brawl would have been epic.

But Declan simply grasped Kett's hand, offering a stiff nod instead of a smile. His magic settled back into the taste of bread pudding soaked in caramel sauce.

Wisteria dropped Kett's arm, stepping to Declan's side. Then she locked her gaze to me.

I sighed. Disappointed.

No brawl, then.

Kandy chortled under her breath, flashing me a grin. Then she slipped off into the crowd to waylay a server who appeared to be carrying an Asian-inspired spot-prawn appetizer. Abandoned to deal with Wisteria, Declan, and Kett on my own, I plastered a smile over my inappropriate disappointment.

The vampire turned to look back at me over his shoulder, lifting his hand to invite me to join them. Another unusual display of forthright affection.

Then I put the three of them, along with Jasmine, together with the rumors that had filtered through the Convocation, Gran, and Scarlett. The reconstructionist had recently taken the reins of the Fairchild coven, and at least three witches had died in the transition—including the now-remade Jasmine. As far as I knew, the Convocation had accepted the official statements that the Fairchilds had provided, and no tribunal had been called for.

If anyone had asked me a day earlier whether Wisteria was capable of murder, I would have said no. Utterly and unequivocally. But I could have easily imagined that most people would have said the same of me. The cupcakes confused people, as the cool, perfectly put-together facade that Wisteria projected no doubt did as well.

The executioner of the Conclave didn't become enamored of the ordinary. Of course, neither did I—so that wasn't judgemental of me, but simply an observation. But the timing of Wisteria's elevation within the Fairchild coven, her obvious connection to Kett, and the fact that whatever had happened resulted in Jasmine becoming a vampire—all of it seemed to indicate that the executioner had been involved in the upheaval.

I stepped forward, placing my hand lightly into Kett's cool grasp and meeting his icy-blue gaze.

So … okay. The executioner of the Conclave was infatuated with a witch betrothed to her childhood sweetheart. And Declan, based on the taste of his magic, wasn't to be toyed with. But with her newly settled power, neither was Wisteria. In fact, I was fairly certain that given enough notice, either of them could seriously harm Kett if they were so inclined.

My vampire BFF squeezed my hand lightly, perhaps letting me know that I'd been staring at him too long. I turned to Wisteria. Even with both of us in heels, she stood about two inches shorter than me. A ring of bright-blue witch magic almost obscured her dark-blue eyes, informing me that my smile had taken on an edge at the thought of her hurting Kett. But her expression was otherwise placid.

"Jade Godfrey," Kett intoned formally, not knowing that I had already met Declan. "Dowser. Alchemist. Wielder of the instruments of assassination. Dragon slayer."

Still, I could see in Declan's reaction that this was the first time he realized exactly who I was—and all the terrible I was capable of. His shoulders stiffened, then angled slightly as if he might have been preparing to throw something at me. Based on the tenor of his magic and Kandy's comment about him singeing Gran's rug, I gathered that whatever spells he wielded were volatile.

My smile widened. I was a fan of new magic.

"Declan Benoit," Kett said, blithely continuing as if I wasn't egging the witch on just a bit. "Convocation extraction specialist. Of the Fairchild coven."

"Declan," I said, unintentionally purring his name. Then I added for Kett's benefit, "We met at the bakery earlier today."

Wisteria flinched, drawing my attention. Then I felt a flush of shame. The two of them were guests of my grandmother, and obviously friendly with Kett. My edginess was completely uncalled for.

I swallowed, consciously willing my magic to settle underneath my necklace and knife, though it usually did so naturally. "My apologies." I glanced at Kett, who was watching me closely. "There is rather a lot of magic … in the air."

"Indeed," the vampire murmured.

Wisteria smiled tentatively. And I realized that the witch was nervous, as if she were worried about something. Perhaps of how I would react to her obvious connection to Kett?

"Congratulations on your engagement, dowser," the reconstructionist said formally.

"And you as well." I nodded toward Declan, who acknowledged me with another of his stiff nods. But I was fairly certain it was the vampire by my side who was the source of his conflicted feelings, not me. And that wasn't any of my business. At least, I wasn't interested in getting entangled in any of it.

"Well … um …" I spoke before the silence could get any more strained. "I should introduce you to Warner."

"We've met." Wisteria smiled politely. "Twice now."

Nodding as I remembered her reference to meeting Warner in Seattle while we were first hunting the instruments, I glanced sideways at Kett. "And you should say hello to Gran."

The vampire nodded, almost imperceptibly disconcerted at the suggestion.

Wisteria laughed quietly again, obviously picking up on Kett's dismay without effort. Well, that was surprising.

"Will I see you later?" I asked the vampire.

His gaze flicked to Wisteria, then to Declan before he dipped his chin in a shallow nod of acknowledgment. I brushed my hand against his forearm as I turned away, intending to finally set up camp beside the chocolate fountain.

"Is she here?" Wisteria whispered tensely almost the moment my back was turned. "Kett? Can we see her?"

I didn't glance back, nor did I hear Kett's answer. But then, the vampire would have known how many sensitive ears currently surrounded him, more so than the two witches would have. And Jasmine was a secret he would want to keep to himself for as long as possible.

In all honesty, I wasn't sure I wanted to know all the gritty details. Unless Kett wanted to tell them, of course. But I knew that it would be better to move forward, hoping my vampire BFF remained in Vancouver despite how firmly he was now tied to the Fairchilds. I couldn't shackle him, or even Kandy, to the city just because I chose to stay, though.

Life changed, didn't it? But that didn't mean I had to like the prospect of losing those I loved if they moved on.

# Chapter Ten

*I* slipped away from the engagement party, mournfully leaving the chocolate fountain behind but needing a reprieve for a few moments. I wasn't certain why I still felt so edgy. Nothing had really happened. Yes, the day had been filled with a series of minor revelations and magical blips. But that was nothing compared to what I'd faced in the past. So why was my chest tight and my smile so strained?

Had my tolerance for stress dropped to such a supremely low level? Was I that weak? That inflexible?

I had thought of simply stepping outside the wards that coated Gran's property for a moment. But instead, I found myself walking down and around the block. Then, wrapping the comforting weight of Warner's gloriously soft stole around my neck and shoulders, I strolled through Tatlow Park. Avoiding the forested edge where Sienna had dumped Hudson's body.

That terrible moment of discovery and betrayal felt as though it had occurred two lifetimes ago. The remembrance was still saddening. Mournful. But also muted.

But that wasn't what was bothering me. That wasn't responsible for the edginess I was having a hard time denying and brushing away.

I had relentlessly avoided introspection since I'd murdered Shailaja and absorbed her magic. Since I'd become the dragon slayer, perhaps decades before I'd been destined to wield the instruments of assassination. I thought I'd accepted the idea of that accelerated time-line, but perhaps I still hadn't digested it fully. Perhaps I still hadn't figured out how to fit back into the box I'd built for myself, with the bakery and everything.

I had wedged Warner, and Kandy, and even Kett into that box. Yet we really didn't fit. And now there was Jasmine … and Wisteria … and all of Kandy's misfits.

And that was all I had. All I could come up with to justify my mood. An observation. An idea that something was going on with me, and with the city itself. But with no firm understanding of what it was or might be.

Preceded by the muted taste of his magic, Warner crossed through the shadowed playground. I had paused by the yellow plastic slide without noticing. He twined his fingers through mine when I reached for him, and together, we meandered out of the park and onto West Third Avenue without speaking.

With that simple gesture—his hand offered and accepted—Warner had anchored me back in the present. "Do I do that for you?" I whispered. "Make you … settle with just a touch?"

"Yes," Warner said. "But I know that some part of you still worries that I've reinvented myself. That I've conformed to the present, which includes marrying you. Rather than truly wanting any of it for myself."

"I know that isn't it," I said. "Or that it isn't all of it, at least."

"Being a dragon is all about duty and honor. About might and justice. And enforcing rules and regulations."

"I know."

"But…I would throw all of that over if doing so was necessary to save you."

I stopped, gazing up at the ever-darkening sky above the tightly packed houses that lined the narrow road. I couldn't see the moon, but the lights from the homes to either side kissed the neighborhood with a comforting glow. "When I thought you were dead …" I found myself struggling to find the words. "In the tomb of the phoenix…all I wanted to do was join you. And…and when I knew you were still alive, but…the far seer had…but I knew I was dying, all I wanted to do was live. To survive. With you. So I took the power. I took it. I murdered Shailaja—"

"To prevent her from killing Drake and me."

I nodded, acknowledging him but needing to get out everything I hadn't said yet. Everything I hadn't said out loud. "And then I walked away. I've walked away. No trial. No ramifications. Just a whack of power, and the only three ways to kill a guardian dragon hanging off my necklace."

Warner laughed harshly. "Isn't that enough of a punishment? That responsibility?"

I looked over at him. He was leaning into me—not touching except for our intertwined fingers—but there if I needed him. His broad shoulders turned as if offering to shelter me, or even carry me, if I needed it.

He smiled sadly. "You are so strong. Mind-bogglingly strong. Chi Wen forces this metamorphosis on you, and you barely blink. Pearl decides to erect a magic detection net solely because you are here to fuel and enforce it for her."

"I don't think—"

Warner pressed a finger to my lips softly. "I'm sure she has other reasons as well. But many cities host diverse Adept populations without a coven of witches attempting to govern all their behavior. They police themselves, as it has always been. Even the party tonight was a parade of power. How many of the guests would you call your friends? And it was supposedly our engagement party."

"You know that was just to get her off my back about not having a huge wedding …" What Warner was trying to say slowly sank into my thick head.

That was why I was so tense, why I'd been so tense the past few days. I was doing things for other people. Out of duty, not choice.

"There has to be a balance," I murmured. "Vancouver is my home."

"Our home."

I grinned at him. "So … we have to make it work here."

"Of course. But it's also okay to take a break, or even say no. Or to get mad at what's being carelessly asked of you."

"I said no to the guardians, didn't I?"

He laughed quietly. "Yeah. Right up to the moment they actually need you." He brushed his fingers through my hair, then pressed a tender kiss to my forehead. "Don't get me wrong, Jade. I love that about you."

"I still need to help recast the grid tonight," I said stubbornly. "I'm seriously tired of getting itchy feet whenever a fledgling's magic goes wonky."

Warner stilled. "Whenever? It happened to someone other than Mory, you mean?"

I nodded, tugging him with me as I continued to meander up the block. I hadn't had a moment to update him about the last twenty-four hours yet.

"Like what? A burst of power?"

"Yeah. Why?"

"Nothing. It's just that I've encountered a number of magical power surges in the last few weeks."

"With Adepts?"

He shook his head. "No. Certain locations. Magical fortifications. Pulou has had some of us, your father and Haoxin included, checking on various places. Dimensional rifts and such. That was why the others were called away. Something happening in Europe."

"Called away from the engagement party?"

"Yes. Yazi invited me to come along. But then Pearl had words with him about my almost missing the party in the first place."

I laughed at the idea of my father going toe-to-toe with my grandmother and trying to justify Warner leaving so soon after just arriving. Still, the guardians were off saving the world from disaster while I complained about itchy feet. But I quashed the thought before its critical tone could take hold of me.

"Needless to say …" Warner smiled tightly. "Yazi graciously suggested I stay."

"I imagine he did."

A comforting silence settled between us. And for the briefest of moments, I managed to enjoy the warmth of Warner's hand in mine and the feel of my silk skirt shifting around my knees as we slowly traversed the sidewalk.

Then the rest of Warner's comments about 'power surges' sank in. "Power surges at fortified places? Such as the tomb of the phoenix?"

"No," he said. "More like the dimensional pocket we found within the lighthouse." He was referring to Hope Town in the Bahamas, where I had collected the first instrument of assassination for the treasure keeper. And where we had inadvertently freed Shailaja in the process.

"Sorcerer constructed?"

"No, all dragon wrought. The dysfunctional magic appeared to be drawing undesirables."

"Like what? Demons? And the elf with the blade that cut you so badly?"

Warner nodded, but he didn't elaborate. Though he appeared more thoughtful than secretive.

We reached the corner at Macdonald. From there, turning left would circle us back toward Gran's, while continuing straight would eventually lead to the bakery.

"Let's set a date," I said. "For the wedding."

"What about tomorrow?"

I laughed. "That doesn't give me much time to plan."

"But it'll be done your way, not your grandmother's."

"She had the engagement party. The wedding is ours."

"I will walk down the aisle wherever and whenever you wish."

"How about December 21st?"

Warner grinned, brushing a kiss across my knuckles. "The winter solstice it is. Shall we book a church? Or find a secluded beach?"

I shook my head. "I'm not sure yet. I just … I just want to marry you. However we decide. No uninvited guests, no securing of alliances. Just you and me and everyone who truly matters to us."

He tugged me toward him, pressing his lips to mine. I wrapped my arms around him, holding us within the moment for another soft, lingering kiss.

"Speaking of uninvited guests," he murmured. "I wasn't quite sure how to refuse Suanmi when she demanded that Yazi and I escort her and Drake to the party. In fact, I'm fairly certain that Haoxin and the healer were planning to show up as well. They must have been called away."

"I don't want to talk about guardians right now." I smiled teasingly. "And I don't want to go back to the party."

"Shall we run away together?"

"Yes. Straight home."

"And into bed?"

"What do you think? You still owe me two more orgasms. That's one of your rules, isn't it? That I get three to your one?"

Warner threw his head back and laughed.

I smiled, letting his unbridled joy carry me all the way out of my head. Whatever was really going on around me would soon reveal itself. And it wasn't likely to do so any quicker just because I was obsessing about it.

Maybe, just maybe, we would recast the grid at midnight and everything would settle. The rain would come and clear away the smoke. And I could focus on opening the bakery in Whistler, and on getting married.

By unspoken agreement, Kandy met Warner and me in the bakery kitchen about twenty minutes before midnight. All three of us had swapped our finery for jeans and T-shirts, but Kandy and I hadn't washed off our makeup yet. With the combination of her thick eyeliner, gold cuffs, and a plain black T-shirt and jeans, Kandy looked seriously badass.

Of course, the cake crumbs across her chest kind of ruined the image.

"Where did you get the cupcakes?" I asked, hopeful that there were more.

"All gone now," she said, still chewing her way through the last bite. Then she reached down to grab the purple dinosaur backpack resting at her feet. "I had to occupy myself somehow. You, Warner, and Kett completely abandoned me at the party."

"At the party where there was copious food, you mean?"

I opened the back door and wandered out into the dark alley.

Warner chuckled quietly to himself, tucking his hands into his front pockets while he trailed behind Kandy and me onto Yew Street and down the hill.

"Still. Abandoned, dowser. Not cool."

"Where did Kett go?" I asked.

Kandy snorted, displeased. "Off with you-know-who. Times two."

At the crest of the hill, I paused to let a car pass, gazing out at the dark mountains. The sky was a mixture of deep blue and dark gray, not a hint of light remaining. "To meet up with Jasmine, maybe," I murmured, stepping off the curb and continuing down the hill toward the beach.

"Jasmine?" Warner asked.

"Kett's new vampire baby," Kandy said. "Wisteria Fairchild's cousin."

"What?! The vampire turned a witch?"

"He had permission," I said mildly. I eyed Kandy, who was grinning to herself with much satisfaction. "Are you going to hold it against him for long?"

She shrugged. "I might."

I shook my head, glancing back over my shoulder at Warner. "A lot's been revealed in the last twenty-four hours. A lot of little things. Little annoying things."

He rubbed the back of his neck. "It felt like more than a day for me."

"Tell me about it," Kandy grumbled. Then she wove her arm through mine and leaned her head against my shoulder. The werewolf really wasn't a fan of change, or of being out of control.

"I'm sorry we all abandoned you at the party," I said.

"Whatever. I was doing nothing but fending witches off anyway. Once you go guardian, you don't go back."

Warner sputtered out a laugh from behind us. I couldn't help but chuckle myself, even though I seriously hoped that Kandy wasn't serious about pursuing the fire breather.

As we stepped off the curb, crossing West Second Avenue, one of the puffy spikes on Kandy's backpack pressed against my side.

"Seriously, wolf," I said. "What the hell is up with the backpack?"

She huffed. "You won't like it."

"Well, I'm not sure it suits you. But if you like it, then fine."

"I was … Drake gave it to me. From Chi Wen."

I paused, looking at her in the light of the overhead streetlamp—to see if she was serious. "Chi Wen?"

"Yeah. You know, like with the cuffs." Kandy raised her arms, and magic glistened across the diamonds embedded in the gold of her rune-carved cuffs.

"The far seer asked you to wear this hideous backpack?" Warner asked doubtfully. "And he gave it to Drake to deliver it?"

"Yeah," Kandy said, getting testy. "So?"

"What exactly did Drake say?" I asked.

"He said, 'The far seer would like to see you wearing this backpack.' I assumed it was probably only necessary when I was with you, dowser. Since you're the one who gets in all the trouble."

I glanced over at Warner, struggling and failing to quash my grin as I figured out what was going on.

Warner threw back his head and started laughing.

"What?" Kandy cried.

Giggling myself, I said, "'The far seer would like to see you wearing it.' 'See,' not 'sees.' Not 'The far seer sees you wearing this backpack.'"

Kandy glowered, thinking fiercely. Then she snarled. "Asshole. Thinks he can prank me, does he?"

"Who?" Warner asked, still chuckling. "Drake or Chi Wen?"

"Either one," Kandy snarled. "It's so on now."

"Didn't you start it?" I asked. "With the T-shirt? The one with the three bananas that you made Chi Wen wear?"

"That was punishment." Kandy pointed at me. "And you stay out of it, dowser."

I raised my hands in surrender.

Kandy shook her head, still peeved. Then she checked the time on her phone as we passed a closed Starbucks on the corner of Yew and Cornwall. "Enough dillydallying, my beauties. Time to run freely."

And with that pronouncement, she darted across the street against the walk light, heading into the darkened park beyond.

Warner laughed, swept me forward into a blistering kiss, then took off after the wolf.

Apparently, we were jogging the rest of the way.

Burgundy was already waiting at the grassy park off Ogden Street in Kits Point. Warner, Kandy, and I strolled across the short brown grass at exactly ten minutes before midnight.

The witch had pulled back her blue-streaked brown hair into a loose bun, and was wearing jeans paired with a dark-blue hoodie. She settled her gaze on me and didn't look away. And it wasn't because she found me the most reassuring. She was nervous, repetitively petting a smooth rock about the size of her palm.

"Burgundy." I smiled.

She bobbed her head, glancing briefly toward Warner and Kandy. Neither offered a greeting, so she returned her gaze to me. Her feet were already bare, her socks and shoes neatly tucked beside a small satchel in a crook of the large roots of a chestnut tree about a dozen feet away. Since she was standing practically on top of the anchor point, she'd presumably been walking around and feeling for its energy. Her own green-watermelon magic flickered around her hands.

To our far right, the Maritime Museum was a large, peaked shadow on the edge of the shoreline, with the lights of the city spreading beyond the beach across the water.

Kandy pressed the crumpled piece of paper containing the runes I was supposed to reuse into my hand. Then she and Warner peeled off in separate directions, prowling the edges of the park.

"We're going to take down the grid in a couple of minutes," I said. "Then you'll step in and take my place."

Burgundy swallowed. "Yes. Scarlett … your mom called me."

"I have to replicate the runes I used."

Burgundy stepped forward onto the grass, leaving the paved seawall open for me to chalk. Behind the junior witch, the lights of the city blazed against the deep blue of the mountains. A quarter moon had made an appearance over the bay, and the wind coming off the water informed me that it was definitely going to rain tomorrow.

Finally.

"I brought water," Burgundy said, babbling a little as she hustled over to grab a bottle from her bag. "And a drying spell. So I can chalk a simple circle in place of yours. If I move quickly enough, the drying spell should fade and not affect the grid casting. But I was worried about chalking a circle on a wet surface."

"Okay. Sounds good." I crouched down, feeling the magic of the grid where I'd anchored it to the concrete. Retrieving the pink chalk from my satchel, I set out to carefully replicate the symbols my mother and Gran had fought over, including the extra flourish on the one that looked like a triangle with feet.

Burgundy watched my every stroke, turning the rock over and over in her hands.

"Is that a focal stone?" I asked, making conversation because the night was dark, Warner and Kandy had wandered far, and the witch was nervous.

"Oh. This?" Burgundy sounded surprised that I had noticed the stone.

I glanced up. Her face was deeply shadowed, but I could see a starburst of her blue witch magic softly glowing around each of her irises.

"Right. Dowser," she murmured, curling her toes in the grass. "Yes. I've lived in the same place my entire life so far. In Dunbar. Though I was thinking of moving into residence at UBC. And, um, Scarlett...your mom...thought that a touchstone might help me access my, um, latent magic."

I nodded, still chalking the runes. "I met a witch in Scotland once who worked with a set of stones like that. Creating circles and such."

"For casting?" Burgundy had gone a little breathless. "Like instead of chalk?"

"Yeah. She was waiting behind a shield spell when we met."

"Invisible?"

"Yes."

"But you saw her?"

"Tasted. But then, it's difficult to hide from me, and she was acting contrary to protocol."

Burgundy thought about that for a while. I double-checked the runes I'd chalked.

"She was probably full-blood," the junior witch finally whispered.

I straightened, stepping into the circle of pink runes. "We all have different talents. And not all magic is tied to ancestry."

Kandy appeared out of nowhere beside Burgundy, who squeaked but held her ground.

"Ready, dowser?"

"I'm standing, aren't I?" I flashed a saucy grin at my werewolf BFF.

"But you're wearing things you shouldn't be."

Burgundy frowned, first confused, then concerned—like she was thinking that Kandy meant my clothing, rather than my necklace and knife.

"I'm pretty certain that breaking the grid is different from calling it forth."

Kandy sniffed, glancing at her phone. "Thirty seconds."

Burgundy tucked her focal stone in the pocket of her hoodie. Then, juggling the bottle of water, she pulled a piece of white chalk and a small white rock—tasting of my grandmother's lilac magic—out of her bag.

At the last second, I reached for the bottle of water, and the witch dropped it into my hand without hesitation. Magic sprang forth under my feet as the other twelve witches activated their individual circles around the city. I responded with a slight push of my will, adding my own magic to the mix with a long, sustained exhalation. My rune-marked circle sealed itself.

I tasted lilac, strawberry, nutmeg, orange, rosemary, and fresh-baked bread…then the power abated to a simmer that simply tasted of grassy witch magic.

Before I could become giddy off the energy, I uncapped the bottle and carefully sloshed water over the pink-chalked runes encircling my feet.

The magic died instantly, severing my connection to the grid. The other witches would wait for Burgundy to take my place, then would reestablish the anchor point.

I poured out the remainder of the water, pushing the residual pink chalk to the edges of the path. Then I stepped onto the grass.

Burgundy rushed forward, placing the white rock in the center of the wet area.

"That's it?" Kandy asked.

I shrugged. "I can't feel the magic anymore. But it isn't a done deal until Burgundy claims the anchor point for herself."

The junior witch pressed a finger to the rock, murmuring something under her breath.

Nothing happened.

She moaned nervously. She tried again. Still nothing.

"Your focal stone," I whispered, prompting her.

Burgundy dug the stone out of her pocket. Then, holding it in one hand, she tried to trigger Gran's pre-made spell again.

A small burst of magic flashed out from the white stone on the ground, drying most of the wet path.

Burgundy muttered excitedly, already stepping forward. Placing her chalk to the concrete, she spun clockwise, forming a perfect circle.

Kandy grunted in approval as Warner appeared beside me.

"Where have you been?"

He flashed a grin at me, then nodded toward the large building that housed the Maritime Museum. "Looking at boats."

"You broke into the museum?"

He shrugged. "They'd left an upstairs window open."

Kandy laughed huskily.

Energy shifted around Burgundy, stirring her hair and amplifying her watermelon magic.

"Oh," she cried, reaching out to the power now coursing through the circle and allowing it to play through her fingers. Her eyes were shining bright blue.

Standing back from the circle, I could actually see the streams of magic in a way that I hadn't been able to on the night I cast—emanating out to the left, to the right, as well as straight out through the park. The third stream cut between Kandy and me, just a foot or so away from where I stood.

Something about that was wrong.

"Each point links to three others?" I asked.

Kandy nodded. "They all link to the anchor at Pearl's, then to whatever points are next to them."

"Okay, so …" I gestured from Burgundy along the seawall to my left. "This section anchors to Gran's directly to the west. And then this …" I gestured to my right, tracing the second stream of magic. "This connects somewhere on Boundary Road on the east edge? Yes?"

Kandy nodded. "At the base of Second Narrows Bridge."

"So what's the third point?" I traced the beam of magic simmering before me, cutting through the park and the houses of Kits Point. "What is it anchored to?"

Kandy shook her head, looking confused. She pulled out her phone and a copy of the map she and Gran had slaved over for months.

Holding my arm aloft and following the path of the third stream of magic, I tried to imagine where it might have been pointing. "There should only be two connecting points for this anchor, right? Not three. Because this is the anchor point east of Gran's, it doesn't need to connect separately."

"Southlands?" Kandy asked. "That would be Rochelle's place. Scarlett is anchoring the grid there. Maybe your magic was somehow drawn to your mother's as well? Except … you should have just severed your connection … I felt the anchor point disconnect."

"No." Dread settled in my belly as I picked up a familiar tenor in the power stream. "Not Southlands." I met Warner's shadowed gaze. He was watching me intently. "The bakery. Did I somehow anchor the witches' grid to the bakery?"

Kandy shook her head insistently. "Even if that was the case before, that should be canceled out now. Burgundy has reconnected this grid point."

She nodded toward the witch, who was now floating a couple of inches off the path, just as I had.

Burgundy had clearly successfully cast and triggered this particular anchor point.

"Plus," Kandy said, "Scarlett was really clear that we couldn't use the bakery, like Pearl originally wanted. Because of …" She looked at me, an understanding dawning. "Because of your blood wards."

"It's not just the wards that reside there," I murmured.

"The portal," Warner said, far too matter-of-factly.

"Can you see it?"

"I feel it." He glanced over at Kandy. "Have the witches keep their individual circles and the grid active." Then the sentinel slipped off into the night, moving faster than even I or Kandy could have as he traced the magic back to the bakery. Or worse, to the portal, if that was where it had inadvertently anchored. Because even with my limited knowledge of such things, pulling power from a magical transportation hub created by a guardian dragon seemed like a seriously bad idea.

The kind of bad that might trigger all sorts of other things … like random flare-ups of other Adepts' magic.

Kandy started texting. "The witches want to test using the grid as a defensive shield."

"Magically sealing the entire city? How the hell would that work?"

Kandy shrugged. "Don't know. But it gives them something to do while the sentinel is scouting."

"Is something wrong?" Burgundy asked.

I glanced back to the witch, who was standing on the ground once again. I shook my head, ready to assure her that everything was okay.

Then a rush of power exploded from within a house almost directly across the park from us.

Kandy and I whirled toward the four-storey Crafts-man in the center of the block. Its recently painted red siding appeared almost burgundy in the night—except for where a brilliant white light pulsed out from the partially below-ground basement windows.

"What the hell is that?" I could see where the third stream of magic from the anchor point—the stream Warner was currently tracing—touched the very edge of the house.

"That's the Talbots' …" Burgundy whispered from behind us.

"That's the Talbots'?" I echoed, just on the unbecoming edge of screeching.

Kandy nodded in rueful confirmation.

"You've got to be freaking kidding me."

"I was just there," Burgundy cried, becoming distraught. "I mean, we were all there. All the others. They're holding my place in the game."

"Can you see the bright light from the basement windows?" I asked Kandy, ignoring the babbling witch. I was fairly certain I was seeing magical energy.

She shook her head. "I can smell the magic, though. Can you taste it?"

"Not yet." I took off across the grass. Kandy followed.

"Wait!" Burgundy cried out behind us. "What should I do?"

I glanced back at the terrified witch. "Stay in the circle! Keep it active until Warner comes back."

She nodded, crouching down to retrieve her focal stone and cradling it in her hands. Fear shot through my chest at the sight of her alone, perched on what appeared to be an island of land and light within the surrounding darkness. All I could think about was that I should have added some protections to the stone. I should have offered my magic freely. I should have been the one in the circle.

No.

I shouldn't have been the one standing in the circle in the first damn place.

I should have been able to understand my limitations, rather than powering through them. I should have been able to get past the fear of disappointing my grandmother. So what if I wasn't the witch she wanted me to be? I never had been.

I never would be.

But trying to hide from that meant that I just might have anchored a massively complex witch spell—an ongoing spell, actively working—to a guardian portal.

I yanked my attention back to the present as I hit pavement, charging across the narrow road. Kandy matched me step for step.

I felt wards on the Craftsman, but they were dormant. Sorcerer magic, waiting to be triggered but not currently live. The white energy still streamed out from the basement.

"Is there a basement door?" Kandy would have fully scouted the Talbots' property when she visited earlier that day.

"Around the back," the werewolf said.

Forgoing the front steps, I tore along the path at the side of the house, planning on going through the basement door, then through the upper floors of the building if necessary. The bright energy lit the stone pathway and the tall cedar hedges along the edge of the property. Kandy was a silent shadow, so close that I could hear her slow and steady breathing. We ran through magic that tasted of everything and nothing at all. Too many flavors mixed together.

I rounded the corner—and almost fell into an old concrete stairwell that didn't have a safety rail. Even at the back of the house, the basement was still partly below ground.

"Jade," Kandy hissed. She grabbed my arm, pulling my attention to the foliage that dominated the backyard.

Things were crawling out of the ground.

Dead things. Rodents … snakes …

I caught a hint of toasted-marshmallow magic.

"Mory," Kandy murmured.

I looked away, not wanting to see the full scope of what might have been buried in the yard of a house that was easily a hundred years old.

I jumped down, landing at the base of the stairs and kicking through the door in the same motion.

An open area of unfinished basement before me was dark. But the white magic was flooding past the edges of a closed door on an inside wall halfway through the house.

I pulled my knife as I slipped across the door I'd kicked to the ground. Slowly stalking toward the glowing door, I passed laundry facilities on my left. Someone was drying lacy underwear and bras on a clothesline over a free-standing laundry sink.

Kandy picked up the door behind me, placing it back to cover the opening to the yard even though I'd ruined the hinges and the lock. Still, we'd hear it if anyone came in behind us.

The hot water heater and a pair of bicycles were tucked up against the open-stud walls to my right. I continued stalking toward the closed door, giving my senses time to adjust to the magic emanating past it.

Above and to the right, I heard a door open. Another light source flooded down into the basement, revealing a stairwell descending from the main floor.

"What the hell is going on down there?" a woman's voice called. "I heard a crash."

Recognizing the accent, I glanced back at Kandy, whispering, "Angelica Talbot."

She nodded. As I reached the door outlined in white magic, the werewolf veered off to the right, sticking to the shadows but setting herself into position to cover the stairwell at my back.

"Tony?" Angelica called again.

I touched the closed door, again picking up a hint of Mory's magic. Probably because I knew it so well. But her necromancy was layered within too many other tastes and tenors. The door itself wasn't spelled, though. It also opened out, rather than swinging in.

Angelica sighed like only a long-suffering mother could. Then she started down the stairs.

I opened the door, stepping to the side as I did.

A six-foot-tall snarling monster barreled through the doorway.

Bitsy.

I slipped my foot forward, intending to trip her as benignly as possible. Unfortunately, she didn't fall for that move a second time. At least not completely.

Tangling her leg around mine, she tumbled forward, hooking her claws into my ribs and dragging me with her. We fell together—head first into the water heater. Denting it so badly that the metal folded inward.

Angelica Talbot cried out, stumbling down the rest of the stairs and right into Kandy's arms. My werewolf BFF snatched the sorcerer out of the darkness, clamping one hand over her mouth while pinning her arms with the other.

Scalding-hot water erupted from the tank, soaking me as I thrust my forearm up to block the partially transformed werewolf from tearing out my throat.

Snarling madly, Bitsy clamped my arm between her jagged teeth and twisted, doing her best to rip the limb from my body.

"Gentle, Jade," Kandy cautioned from somewhere below my feet. It was difficult to see through the steaming water spraying everywhere.

"I'm letting her chew on me, aren't I?"

I got my knees up underneath Bitsy's torso, easily tossing her off me and to the side. Then, before she could recover and come at me a second time, I gained my feet and cold-cocked her.

She fell heavily to the floor, like a bag of cement. Unconscious.

Kandy made a quiet mewing noise. I threw a glare at her through my wet hair as I stepped over to check on the downed werewolf.

Bitsy's chest rose and fell steadily. She wouldn't be getting up any time soon, but I hadn't broken her neck.

More eager to get out of the ill-timed hot shower than to face whatever awaited me in the room beyond—and trying to ignore the guilt that came with being bigger and badder than everyone else, even when I was pulling my punches—I stepped through the white energy streaming out through the door. Kandy followed, shoving Angelica before her, but pausing within the doorway behind me.

Gabby Talbot was standing in the center of what appeared to be a recreation room. Her light-blond head was thrown back and magic was streaming out of her, spiraling around the room, then feeding back into the amplifier.

And she had somehow caught all the other Adepts in the room directly within that looped river of energy.

Peggy was curled in a ball on the floor in the far corner to my right, clutching her head and muttering.

Mory was directly across from me, tucked into the opposite corner of the room from Peggy. The necromancer's eyes were closed as she clenched her necklace in one hand—and held what appeared to be a reanimated red-eared slider in the other. All of the magic in the room was combined into a whirlwind of untapped power, including Bitsy's cacao nibs and toasted walnuts, even though the werewolf was still unconscious and outside the stream.

Mory was desperately trying to control her necromancy—and failing miserably, judging by how she was in the process of being swarmed by a pack of dead mice and more than a few rats. I was also pretty sure that two zombie cats—and possibly a small dog—were banging against the window above her head.

"Mory!" I snapped. "That's just creepy as all hell."

The petite necromancer's eyes snapped open. "Jade!" she cried, visibly relieved to see me. Then, reverting to her regular disgruntled tone, she added, "Why are you all wet?"

"How about we focus on what's immediately relevant?"

"Fine," she mumbled. "But your makeup is running."

I threw my hands up in the air, glancing back at Kandy and seeking commiseration.

Then a fourth person in the room popped up from behind an overturned sectional, hitting me with some sort of electrical pulse. Straight to the neck and chest.

I stumbled, hearing Angelica gasp, "Tony!" from behind me. Pain radiated through my upper rib cage, down and across my torso, and out through my limbs.

I lost hold of my knife. And for just a moment, I thought I might go down.

Instead, I gritted my teeth, reached for the lightning-like sorcerer magic attempting to attach itself to me, and ripped it from my chest. The electrical energy twined around my hand, still feeling as though it were cutting into my skin, but my eyesight cleared. And I found myself facing off against a shaggy-haired, eighteen-year-old sorcerer wearing a T-shirt inspired by the old *Legend of Zelda* video games. I recognized the red sword.

The sorcerer was a younger, slighter, male version of his mother, and was clutching what appeared to be a series of electronic items. I could see a laptop, a game console, and an iPad among his collection.

"You must be Tony," I snarled in pain, though I'd been going for snark.

His eyes widened, glancing down at the magic I held in my hand—his sorcerer magic, which was obviously connected to technology somehow. "You ... you ... you're hurting my sisters."

"It isn't me, you ass. I'm here to fix it. Let's start with giving this back to you."

I stepped forward swiftly, slamming the palm of my hand and the spell I held against the wall of electronics he was clutching to his chest like a shield.

Tony flew back, crashing against a large-screen TV on the far side of the room, then falling to the ground insensible. Thankfully, the shattered TV stayed attached to the wall. Accidentally murdering fledgling sorcerers possibly not in control of their magic wasn't on my to-do list. Not at the moment, at least. But it seemed too likely, painful lesson or no painful lesson, that Tony Talbot was stupid enough to try to draw my attention more than once.

Yeah, I really was prejudiced against sorcerers. But seriously, given what I'd been through, who would have blamed me?

I glanced back at Kandy in the doorway. The green-haired werewolf was pinning the terrified Angelica by both wrists, grinning viciously. Or was that victoriously? The magic the sorcerer carried in her multiple bangles rose up, but was countered by the power of Kandy's cuffs before she could actually wield it.

"What the hell is it with you Talbots?" I snarled. Again, still in pain. "Throwing magic around before you even say hello?"

"I…I …" Angelica stuttered.

Kandy laughed.

"You are far too delighted for someone who just watched her best friend take an energy spell to the chest, werewolf."

Kandy sneered. "You love a challenge, dowser. You've been complaining about it all day."

"Not out loud."

"I can read you like a book."

I shook my head, laughing quietly. The pain in my chest eased. Then I returned my attention to the remaining issue, willfully stepping into the magic that was still pouring into the room from Gabby.

My mouth flooded with the taste of tart raspberry jam, so intensely that I momentarily worried about—

"… getting seeds stuck in my teeth," Peggy said, completing my thought. She was still curled up in a ball on the floor, clutching her head.

Jesus, I thought. The telepath—

"… is in my head." Peggy pressed the heels of her hands to her forehead harshly, continuing to speak my thoughts out loud.

Though why she was—

"… cueing into me instead of Gabby or Mory, I didn't know."

Yeah. That wasn't—

"… especially creepy at all," Peggy said.

Mory started laughing, on the edge of hysterical.

I deliberately looked away from her and Peggy, focusing on the amplifier currently causing all the mayhem. My walking into the magic streaming from Gabby must have inadvertently forged a connection to her sister, Peggy. Hence, the telepath reading my mind.

"Plus," Peggy said conversationally. "I really didn't want to see what else the necromancer had awoken."

Jesus. I talked to myself a lot.

Trying to clear my mind so the telepath would stop narrating my thoughts, I stepped closer to Gabby.

The amplifier was completely in thrall to her own magic, which was still trying to attach itself to me, but was being rebuffed by the barrier made by my necklace and knife.

"Except that was about to change," Peggy whispered.

Right.

"Gabby?" I asked.

The amplifier didn't acknowledge my presence.

"I was going to have to touch her," Peggy narrated.

Kandy laughed. "Let's keep the telepath around, Jade. She's fun."

Ignoring the werewolf, I pressed my hands to either side of Gabby's face. The amplifier was the same height as me, her in sock feet and me in one-inch heels.

Gabby immediately grabbed both of my wrists, her magic snapping to me, attempting to pull my power into the maelstrom looping around the room.

So, not knowing how else to stop it, I allowed her amplifier power to stream through me. I let it mix with my own magic, filling the bottomless reserves of my knife and necklace.

For the briefest of moments, I could taste dark, deep cacao with hints of possible fruit notes…maybe even sweet, juicy strawberries…but underneath it all was that spice that reminded me of—

"Chinese food," Peggy whispered.

Oh, god. I was tasting…I had never tasted—

"…my own magic," Peggy whispered reverently.

Then the energy flowing between Gabby and I shorted out. I carried too much power for the amplifier to handle, even without me taking any for myself. She fell forward into my arms, convulsing wildly.

I carefully lowered her to the ground, realizing that the rug underneath her had gotten tangled in her feet.

Angelica, after being freed by Kandy, dashed over to us, kneeling and reaching out for her daughter. Gabby stopped convulsing. I laid the amplifier gently across her mother's lap.

Peggy, weeping, slowly crawled toward us. She began to caress her twin's arm the moment she was within reach.

"Put the crawlies back," Kandy growled above my head.

"Already am," Mory said snottily.

"What happened?" Angelica asked. "What happened? What is going on?"

No one answered her.

Tony moaned from where he'd fallen to the floor.

I rose, ready to put the tech sorcerer, or whatever he was, down again.

Then I tasted it.

Strong black tea, topped with a dollop of cream and…something else.

I spun around in a circle, trying to track the magic I hadn't noticed underneath everything else whirling around the room.

Cloyingly familiar magic that I couldn't quite place.

"What is it, dowser?" Kandy asked.

I reached down and flipped the corner of the rug back, exposing a crack in the concrete floor. "Magic that shouldn't be here."

"Get back," Kandy snapped at the Talbots.

They scrambled to comply, Angelica and Peggy dragging Gabby until they were huddled against the wall with Tony. The sorcerer's medium-brown hair had fallen all around his face. He sorted through the shattered pieces of his electronics with so much dread etched across his face that they might as well have been forever-lost family members.

Kandy tugged the rug out from underneath a snack-littered coffee table that had somehow remained upright, then from under the sectional couch.

The crack in the concrete bisected the room. I traced it back to the wall Mory was still huddled against. Thankfully, all the zombie animals she'd called forth were gone, except for her dead pet turtle.

Ignoring Ed, I shooed Mory out of the way, crouching to taste the magic emanating from the fissure. It was abating, but as far as I could tell, it hadn't actually come from underneath the house.

I straightened, contemplating the wall before me, then pointing at it. "The park lies in that direction, yes?"

"Yes," Angelica said. "That's the front yard, leading to the road, the park, the seawall …"

I glanced over my shoulder at Kandy. My werewolf BFF looked grim. "And the anchor point for the witches' grid. My anchor point."

"Does it taste like witch magic?" Kandy asked. "Like the grid magic?"

I shook my head, crossing out of the room without another word.

"We should check the rest of the house," she called after me.

Damn it. She was right.

I took the stairs instead of the back door, with the green-haired werewolf at my heels.

# Chapter Eleven

*K*andy and I split the floors of the house between us, but our careful search found nothing that could have explained the magic seeping through the crack in the basement. While we scoured the Talbot home, Angelica gathered all her children into the kitchen. I had checked in on them, seeing Tony pressing frozen peas to Bitsy's forehead, while holding what looked like frozen mixed berries to the back of his own head. Thankfully, the werewolf had reverted to human form while unconscious, and neither she nor her brother were seriously injured.

Kandy and I regrouped on the front patio. A glance toward the park confirmed that Burgundy's circle was still active and glowing softly blue, but I couldn't see the junior witch herself from this vantage point.

"Should we get them out of the house?" I asked as soon as the front door latched closed behind us and we had a modicum of privacy. "As far as I can tell, the magic that might have been triggering the amplifier has completely faded."

"Until we find the source and figure out how to cut it off, I'd suggest they stay out of the damn basement," Kandy growled. "Some people's kids, right? I mean, how didn't they notice magic seeping into the basement?

Then those two morons attack you instead of figuring their shit out."

She meant Bitsy and Tony, of course. And honestly, my chest was still a little sore from whatever the sorcerer had hit me with. In retrospect, it hadn't felt like pure magic, and if that was what being electrocuted felt like, I really wasn't a fan. But since Bitsy and Tony would both eventually regret what was probably an instinctual need to protect their sister, I opted to let it go. For now. "Angelica didn't seem affected."

Kandy chuckled darkly. "I could have taken her without the cuffs."

I didn't offer an opinion. But it didn't seem likely to me that Angelica Talbot collected magically challenged teenagers—for lack of a kinder phrase—without the ability to handle them and anything else the Adept world threw at her.

Except us, of course. But perhaps the Talbots' relocation had been more about not having to be constantly at war, rather than a lack of ability to protect their brood. In Vancouver, that job belonged to Kandy and me.

A second after I tasted his magic, Warner stepped out from the shadows onto the path from the sidewalk. He eyed Kandy and me hanging around on the patio. "Why does it look like you had more fun than I did?"

I glanced down at my waterlogged jeans and T-shirt, seeing no evidence to suggest I'd had any sort of so-called fun. Digging into my satchel, I pulled out some Kleenex and attempted to do something about my apparently runny makeup. I adored being made to feel inadequate by a teenage necromancer. Especially while I was saving her ass.

The sentinel jogged up the stairs. Kandy, who had managed to avoid the hot shower, was texting with someone.

"Did the magic of the grid extend all the way to the bakery?" I asked Warner.

"It thinned, then dissipated before I got there," he said. "But I checked the bakery and the portal. Both appear undisturbed."

"I don't get it," I muttered.

Kandy glanced up from her phone. "Huh. Something happened. The witches had to drop the grid ... some sort of weird feedback. A couple of them, Olive and Kelly, fainted while they were trying to test out the barrier spell."

"Like there was another magical surge?"

Kandy grunted in the affirmative.

"Fantastic." I gathered my curls into a ponytail, trying to wring the rest of the water out of my hair—or whatever hadn't already been absorbed into my T-shirt, at least—while I filled Warner in on our hijinks with the Talbot crew. "We felt magic in the basement here. By location, it seems like it should be tied to the grid, or at least to the arm that you traced back to the bakery. But it doesn't taste like—"

Movement in the park drew my attention. Warner and Kandy followed my gaze. I stepped down two steps, clearing my view of the leafy branches of a cherry tree at the front edge of the property.

Across the wide stretch of park between the road and the seawall, an exceedingly tall, white-clad figure was slowly circling Burgundy. The junior witch was still within her softly glowing witches' circle, but she appeared to be curled up on the ground.

I was too far away to see the figure's face, but its pale skin and white hair were almost iridescent, picking up and reflecting the blue of Burgundy's magic.

"Who the freaking hell is that?" I was already stepping down onto the front path as I called my knife into my hand.

Warner touched my shoulder, lightly holding me back. "Don't run …"

"What? He's attacking Burgundy!"

The sentinel shook his head grimly. "It is better to approach this creature with caution. Calmly communicate, if possible. It will perceive any rushed movement as an attack and perhaps kill the witch before we can draw it away from her."

"This creature?"

"An elf."

"Elf …" That gave me pause. "As in, your dimensional interlopers? Possibly wielding knives capable of harming a dragon?"

"Add in martially inclined and constantly looking to expand their territory, according to the treasure keeper. And yes." Warner's magic rolled up and over him, leaving him clad in his dragon leathers. His knife was openly displayed in its built-in sheath.

"Oooo," Kandy crowed. "Is it powering-up time?"

"Your power-up is a little obvious for a residential area," I said, carefully watching the elf as it jabbed at Burgundy's circle—with some sort of weapon that I could only barely see, like it was made from rippling air.

Kandy pouted playfully. But like Warner and me, her gaze was riveted to the new predator who had just appeared on the scene.

"All right." I slipped my knife into my sheath. The fact that Burgundy's circle was still intact meant that the witch was still somewhat protected. For now. Though why the elf had decided Burgundy was a threat, I had no idea. Possibly it was the witches' grid in and of itself that bothered him. But Burgundy's circle falling would have no effect on the main grid. "I can play it cool."

Kandy snorted.

Ignoring her well-founded disbelief in my ability to be rational under such circumstances, I tried to calmly assess the situation. "It looks like the elf is favoring its left leg."

"Subtle," Warner said. "But I concur. Watch out for the blade. Calling it sharp is an understatement."

Kandy eyed Warner sideways. "Is that first-hand knowledge?"

"Unfortunately."

Angelica Talbot opened the front door of the house behind us. "Ms. Godfrey. I wasn't aware—"

"Get back inside," I snapped over my shoulder. "And Ms. Talbot? I suggest you raise your defensive wards."

Angelica's face blanked. Then she nodded curtly, slamming and locking the door.

Returning my gaze to the elf slowly circling and tapping on the magic of Burgundy's circle, I felt layers of sorcerer magic flood across the house behind me.

Walking determinedly but slowly, I strode across the sidewalk. Warner and Kandy kept pace alongside me, brushing my shoulders as we strolled across the street. I wanted to rush across the grassy expanse between myself and the elf, demanding answers. But I'd try diplomacy if that was what Warner recommended. Right up until the moment I concluded that the elf was the reason Burgundy was curled up on the ground.

The park was wider than it was deep, spreading out before us with the Maritime Museum on its far right edge and a denser treed area on our far left. From this vantage point, I could see the low bracing that had recently been installed on the First Nations-carved totem pole that graced the museum's landscaped entrance. The massive chestnut tree about a dozen feet to the right of Burgundy's circle was a dark outline against the deep-blue-black sky. Despite the glare from the city, a few stars had appeared overhead.

"Something in the dark," I murmured. "Something trying to break through."

"Or maybe something already here," Kandy added grimly.

"Explain," Warner said.

"Peggy Talbot," I said. "The telepath. She picked up something. Or someone's thoughts, I guess. Last night and earlier today. Maybe the elf?"

Warner grunted in acknowledgement.

"Who wants to bet we're about to figure out what the hell is going on?"

"Not me," Kandy said. "That's a loser's wager. And I don't lose."

"Except for that one time," I said. "You know, when you drowned."

Kandy barked a laugh. "Are you crazy, dowser? That was the biggest win of all."

Warner chuckled darkly, completely in agreement with the insane werewolf. But then, he would have known about that sort of thing, having survived being crushed by a freaking mountain.

Lovely. My companions thought that returning from the dead was all just part of the fun.

But honestly … feeling my own magic, which had already been riled up by the amplifier, surging through my necklace and flowing into my knife, I really couldn't disagree.

The elf looked like just the challenge I'd been waiting a year and a half to face. I only hoped Warner and Kandy didn't get greedy and take him out first.

The elf turned to face us when we were about twenty feet away. His movement was casual, almost nonchalant, as though he hadn't been tracking our every step since we'd hit the grass. But the wary set of his shoulders betrayed him. And yes, I was fairly certain he was male, though the sharp lines of his face and his long, plaited, moonlight-hued hair were fairly androgynous. He was taller than Warner, who was six feet four, but not as broad through the shoulders.

He was also wearing shockingly familiar clothing. Similar to the items I'd found myself wearing after Pulou had locked me away in one of his magic-nullifying cells. White cotton drawstring pants. A white T-shirt. No shoes.

Well, that was a weird complication.

"Note the outfit," I whispered.

Warner grunted in acknowledgement.

The elf's gaze snapped to me when I spoke. Now that I was closer, I could see that his white skin was finely scaled, currently reflecting the blue of Burgundy's circle where it still simmered beside him. But based on its iridescence, I had a feeling it might shift depending on the available light, possibly allowing the elf to wield some sort of chameleon abilities. Similar, perhaps, to how Warner's own magic manifested.

To literally top it all off, the elf appeared to have some sort of large gemstone, almost the exact color of his skin, embedded in his forehead. An eight-sided stone, echoing the oracle's sketch just enough to add a low murmur of caution to the gleeful anticipation I was attempting to keep quelled.

"I probably should have mentioned that Rochelle gave me a sketch today," I said.

"You opened it?" Kandy asked.

"Ah, no ... a different sketch."

"Of an elf?" Warner asked.

"Not exactly." I didn't want to be more specific in front of the elf. "I probably shouldn't have brought it up in mixed company."

The elf's gaze had locked onto the sentinel at my right shoulder, as though he might be deeming Warner to be the biggest threat among the three of us. Which was fine by me.

I still couldn't taste any magic from the intruder. At least not enough to determine whether he was responsible for whatever had rendered Burgundy unconscious. But him tapping on the witch's circle was pretty suspicious—and maybe something that could have caused the feedback that had reportedly knocked Olive and Kelly out as well.

That kind of unprovoked attack wasn't cool. It was time for him to pick on someone his own size.

Warner spoke in a language with a lot of long vowels, similar to my vague understanding of what Norwegian or maybe Swedish sounded like. But at the same time, it was nothing like any language at all.

The elf sneered at him. Apparently, disdain translated through dimensions. "Your pronunciation is atrocious, dragon." The elf's English was stilted, and—oddly—carried a British lilt.

"I didn't expect you to speak any earth language," Warner said stiffly.

"My jailor was English, after all."

Well, that explained the clothing. But not the elf's presence in Vancouver.

"This territory has certain protocols," Warner said. "You've already broken several."

The elf raised his hand toward Burgundy's circle, then shifted it as though he was feeling one of the wings of the magical grid. "Witch territory." He didn't sound impressed.

"Does Pulou know you've gone for a walk, elf?" I asked.

The elf bared his teeth at the question. They were jagged, like a shark's. "Are you so scared, so worried that your warriors cannot deal with me on their own, that you need to call in a guardian, witchling?"

Kandy laughed darkly. "You know I love it when they underestimate you, dowser. But this asshole is all bluff. I say we stuff him back wherever he came from and go for dessert."

The elf turned his attention to Kandy. "I will not be going back."

"Dead or alive. Elf, demon, or any other dimensional creep," she said. "It makes no difference to me."

Magic slipped up and then around the elf, forming the long, slim blade I'd seen before at the end of his right hand. Seen up close, it appeared to be made out of some sort of crystal substance, not air as I'd originally presumed. The already-brown grass withered even more, turning black underneath his feet.

He was pulling magic from the earth, as witches did. But his draining was destructive.

Warner and I drew our weapons, anticipating an attack. But instead of stepping forward to meet our blades, the elf spun, slicing through Burgundy's circle without effort. The severed magic rebounded off the elf, buffeting Warner, Kandy, and me as we surged forward.

The junior witch convulsed, writhing on the ground and screaming silently.

The elf lifted his blade, as if intending to bring it down in an arc that would decapitate the witch.

The shadow leech appeared out of nowhere, wrapping itself around the elf's hand and momentarily checking his attack. I ducked underneath the weapon, ceding the lead to Kandy and Warner so I could focus on the junior witch. I wasn't certain Burgundy was still breathing.

Even as Kandy stepped into the fray, she transformed in a flash of magic into her half-wolf/half-human warrior form. Standing as tall as the distracted elf, she easily caught him in a chokehold.

I darted around the elf's legs, sheathing my knife as I grabbed Burgundy's shoulders and dragged the witch out of the way.

The elf stumbled backward, trying to twist from Kandy's grasp. At the same time, he flicked his hand, throwing his blade—and the leech—directly at me.

I ducked, gently propping Burgundy against the chestnut tree. The elf's blade skewered the shadow demon to the tree trunk just over my head.

The witch moaned quietly, thankfully assuring me that she was alive. I stepped in front of her protectively, returning my attention to the skirmish.

Warner was looking for an opening, but Kandy was effectively blocking him from engaging the elf. The massive werewolf still held the creature fast in a chokehold he couldn't seem to break.

So the elf changed tactics. His magic shifted again, manifesting short, double-edged blades in both hands—at the same time as he slammed his fists into either side of Kandy's rib cage.

The werewolf howled in pain, listing to the side.

Warner slammed a kick to the elf's left leg—the one he'd been subtly favoring. The elf went down on one knee, but he managed to keep the still-skewered Kandy between him and the sentinel as a shield, held fast by his blades.

Warner slammed a right jab into the elf's face, just beside Kandy's head. Then as the elf reeled back, he grabbed Kandy and tore her from his grasp. But the blades snapped off as he did, still embedded in the werewolf's ribs.

The elf, whose face and leg had taken heavy damage from Warner's blows, twisted sideways, knifing Kandy in the stomach with a third blade that appeared out of nowhere—and which he left jutting out of her back.

Warner stumbled.

He stumbled. Trying to keep himself between Kandy and the elf, even as the werewolf tumbled from his grasp.

And in that brief moment in which the sentinel's attention was diverted, the elf reached up and snapped Warner's neck.

Bone and cartilage crunched.

Burgundy screamed, wrapping herself around my leg. With all my attention focused on the skirmish, I hadn't even been aware that the witch had woken while I stood sentry over her.

Warner fell.

It had all happened so quickly. His arms were still stretched out toward Kandy.

I didn't watch him hit the ground.

I didn't look to Kandy lying far too still on the ground only feet away.

The elf stepped through the sprawled limbs of my loved ones, sneering at me and the terrified witch latched to my leg.

I breathed, relaxing into the exhalation.

Then I let my magic loose.

All the power I held tightly within me, tucked in behind my necklace and knife. Power that recalled chaos, blood, and a sense of righteous, brutal justice.

"Let me go, Burgundy." I leaned down to pat her arm. "I have some garbage to deal with."

She gripped me tighter.

"Amy!" I snapped. "If you can walk, go to the Talbots'. If not, tuck up against the tree. I won't be a minute."

"Yes, Amy," the elf said. "I'll be saving you for dinner."

The witch moaned.

The elf sneered, snapping his shark-like teeth at me as though he might have been flirting. As though he might have been thinking of having me for dessert.

What else was new?

I sighed, allowing my power to touch Burgundy. The refreshing taste of her watermelon magic rolled across my tongue.

She screeched, letting go of me like I'd attempted to set her on fire, then scrambling back to press against the chestnut tree.

I stepped away from the witch, keeping parallel with the elf but clearing the battlefield between us.

"Your warriors are down, witchling." His English was still labored.

Directing my magic across the trimmed grass toward Kandy and Warner, I covered my uncertainty as to how badly they might have been hurt by allowing a wicked grin to spread across my face. I lifted my hands to the sides—not high enough to indicate surrender, but enough to show that I held no weapons. Well, no weapons the elf could see. Otherwise he wouldn't have been sneering quite so much.

"Hasn't it occurred to you, elf?" My magic licked against Kandy, then Warner. The intense taste of their magic confirmed that they were down but not mortally injured. Not yet, at least. "That they might have been the reasonable ones? Willing to simply stop you from harming the witch, then hand you back over to Pulou? But I hold no such loyalty to the treasure keeper. And I'm not a fan of assholes hurting my loved ones."

He laughed without any mirth. "Prove you're more than just talk, witch."

"Oh, but I have to set the scene for you." My magic curled toward him, causing me to inwardly cringe as it crossed the dead space where he had stripped magic out of the earth to manifest his weapons. "Otherwise, it'll go by so quickly that you'll miss it and just be dead."

"Bring your worst."

"Nah. You don't even get my best."

"What I am getting is bored."

"Allow me to alleviate your suffering."

Finally, I caught and captured the tenor of his magic, though not the taste of it yet. But it was enough that I could reach for the energy in the crystal blade pinning the shadow leech to the chestnut tree. With my right hand, I called that power to me. The blade shifted, ripping free of the shadow leech.

The leech fell to the ground.

The blade disintegrated into a fine white powder, coating Burgundy's head and shoulders like a dusting of snow. A triumphant look replaced the witch's terror. She clenched her focal stone in her hand, pinning her now-fierce gaze to the elf.

Then I tore the three blades from Kandy, holding them suspended before me with my unleashed alchemy.

The werewolf screamed, the green of her shapeshifter magic flooding her eyes as she reverted to her human form. Then she rolled to her side, further clearing the path between me and the elf.

"Summoner," the elf muttered. His eyes glittered like shards of emerald as he assessed me. Apparently, magic similar to mine existed in his dimension.

"I have many titles," I said. "But none of them are relevant to what I'm about to do to you. These are yours, so have them back."

I flicked the crystal blades at him.

He reached forward, grabbing one and knocking the other two away. They shattered into minuscule pieces, fluttering down around him.

He corrected his stance, protecting his weaker leg.

But he was already too late.

Too slow.

I moved.

Slipping through the wash of my magic writhing in the air between us, I moved. I wanted to take my time. I wanted to tear him apart slowly, deliberately. I wanted him to experience every moment of his destruction, just for thinking he could hurt those who stood by my side, in my territory, under my protection. But I wasn't certain how hurt Warner and Kandy—or even Freddie—really were.

So I moved.

His expression shifted. Angry transforming into disconcerted. Then tinting with the first hints of concern.

Yeah, he'd underestimated me.

What else was new?

The elf brought his blade around, even as he formed a second weapon in his left hand. He raised both, crossing them in front of him in a scissoring motion, intent on decapitating me.

I threw myself backward at the last moment, arcing underneath his knives as they closed over me. Pivoting on my left leg, I snapped a harsh kick to the side of his already-damaged knee.

A curl of blond hair fluttered down to the ground beside me.

He'd cut my freaking hair.

Okay, now I was seriously peeved.

The elf stumbled, going down on his good knee, but he didn't drop his weapons.

Touching down with both feet, I tucked my knees to my chest, pushing upward to flip over his blades. Then, on the downward arc, I slammed both feet into his chest, riding him down as he crumpled to the ground.

He lost hold of his knives midfall. I crushed the magic of the weapons with my alchemy without a second thought. Fine particles of crystal coated my arms, my shoulders, my face and hair …

He grabbed my calves, then my thighs as I pinned him, trying to throw me off. When he couldn't shift me, he drew on the wealth of magic in the park around him, forming two shorter blades in each hand. The perfect length for a close-in tussle.

Except—once again—he was too slow.

I raised my fist overhead, calling forth my knife as I plunged my hand and the jade blade into his forehead. Dead center through the gemstone that teemed with his power.

Very few types of creatures could survive being stabbed between the eyes. Apparently, elves weren't one of them.

Stunned shock spread across his face, just a moment before the magic deadened in his eyes. He didn't make a sound, not even in pain or death. A warrior to the end.

"Oops," I said. "Forgot to introduce myself. Jade Godfrey."

I yanked my knife from his head, instantly absorbing his magic into the blade. His viscous blood, appearing practically the same color as his skin in the dark, dried almost instantly. I was quite certain that if I were to brush it off his forehead, it would disintegrate just like his blades. So he'd manifested his weapons from or through his physical being somehow.

I clawed my fingers around the cracked gem in his forehead, then tore it from his flesh. And for the briefest of moments, I gazed down at an imperfect echo of the oracle's charcoal sketch in the palm of my hand. But while that gemstone was whole, this one had been fractured by my knife. Then the veins of magic—echoes of the severed wisps in Rochelle's drawing—that had tethered the gemstone to the elf died, crumbling into what looked like large snowflakes.

I was fairly certain it was all some sort of crystal, though. Perhaps even the solidified blood of the elf, which then disintegrated when it was removed from its host and exposed to our dimension. Demons crumbled to ash when vanquished in the same sort of way. Magic not of our world, and therefore unsustainable in this environment.

"Got you now, asshole." With the gemstone in hand, I finally tasted the elf's magic. It came with the smell of rain after a terrible dry spell…a storm on the horizon…and, underneath the wildness, sharp woodsy notes. Cedar and sap, perhaps.

A shadow crossed my knee suddenly—and a split second before I instinctively skewered it, I recognized the shadow leech, which appeared to have dragged itself across the grass toward me.

"Freddie." I scooped the leech up, tossing the cracked gemstone onto the elf's chest, then placing the little demon on top of it. "Thank you for trying to protect the witch. Feed."

Chittering almost too quietly for me to hear, Freddie latched onto the gem, then immediately flowed across the dead elf's chest, siphoning off the magic I could feel rapidly fading. Helped along by the leech, the elf would presumably also crumble into a fine crystal powder, then wash away with the coming rain.

I stood, ignoring Burgundy, who was still pressed against the chestnut tree—and was now watching me like I was some sort of viper.

Kandy had crawled over to Warner. She was sitting, silently weeping with her hand on his chest. With his neck cranked harshly to one side, the sentinel didn't appear to be breathing. But I could still taste his magic.

I crossed to them, kneeling with Warner between me and the mourning werewolf. I laid my hand on his chest, feeling his magic impotently churning inside him.

"Help me." I tried coaxing his magic up underneath my palm, then encouraging it in the direction of his neck. Though I wasn't a healer, the sentinel had his own healing power. But it was apparently being stopped up by what I assumed was a broken neck.

Kandy wrapped her arms around herself, weeping openly. "He's dead, Jade. He's dead."

"He's not dead."

She started keening, a quiet and terrible sound that burned through my chest and threatened to quash my resolve. "It's my fault. He was protecting me. And now he's dead."

"He's not dead. Damn you, Kandy. Help me."

She looked up at me, reaching across Warner to cup my face. Her hands were bloody, most likely from her own wounds. Her T-shirt was torn and badly stained. "He's dead, Jade."

"Don't make me slap you, wolf. Now straighten his freaking neck!"

Kandy looked confused, then affronted. "You can't move his head. You'll damage his spine."

"You just said he was already dead! And if we don't straighten his freaking neck, his freaking magic will heal it wrong. Do you want him to have to get it snapped again?"

Kandy dropped her hands from my face, looking down at Warner. "He's not dead?"

"He's dying. And you're the physiotherapist."

She scrambled around until she was kneeling on either side of Warner's head. She tentatively reached for him with shaking fingers.

"Just be careful with the cuffs," I muttered.

She glared at me.

Well, at least that was a step in the right direction.

Kandy slipped her fingers underneath Warner's neck, closing her eyes, then muttering to herself. She appeared to be counting.

"What are you waiting for?" I hissed.

"If I'm going to do this, I have to realign his vertebrae properly, dowser. So shut the hell up."

I clamped my mouth shut, concentrating on Warner's magic still churning underneath my hand.

Burgundy settled down beside me in the grass. She placed her hand on Warner's arm, then whispered what I assumed were healing charms under her breath. As scared as she was, as drained of her magic as she was from holding the circle against the elf, she was still trying to help. I silently bequeathed her cupcakes for life.

Warner's head shifted almost imperceptibly. Kandy grunted. "He's hard to move."

"He's a dragon," I said, as if that explained everything. "It's like a secondary protection. Making them more difficult to kill even when immobilized."

Kandy squeezed her eyes tightly shut. Then slowly—painfully slowly—she righted Warner's head, carefully shifting and aligning each vertebra as she did so.

"Come on, sixteenth century," I whispered. I brushed my palm across his chest in an upward motion, as though I could direct his magic.

Warner opened his eyes. Then that magic rolled across him in a rush. Sweet stewed cherries. Deep, smoky chocolate. And the creamiest of whipped cream.

I laughed, choking back the sobs I'd been holding at bay.

Warner placed his hand over mine on his chest. Then, croaking the words, he said, "Are you planning on kissing me, werewolf?"

Kandy's eyes snapped open, her head still hovering over his. She laughed incredulously. "Well, that's how the healer does it."

"I hate to break up the celebration," I said. "But I need to figure out where the hell the elf came from."

Burgundy raised her hand, pointing past my shoulder toward the staircase that led to the beach at the side of the Maritime Museum. "There. At least that's where I first saw him."

I nodded, meeting Warner's gaze.

"Right behind you," he whispered.

Heedless of our audience, I leaned over and brushed a kiss across his lips.

Then I left my fiance to the care of a junior witch and a seriously injured werewolf, tracing the elf's residual magic. Tracing it to a cave, hidden behind disabled wards that tasted of dragon magic, in the rocky shore underneath the seawall.

What else could I do?

Whether I wanted to be one or not, warriors only got to go home after everyone else was safe and sound.

The elf I had just murdered without a second thought knew that well. He hadn't even had the luxury of dying in his own dimension.

# Chapter Twelve

I had sand caked up to the knees of my wet jeans by the time I finally found an opening in the rocky shore. Slipping into it, I traversed a narrow tunnel carved out of ocean-smoothed rock that glistened with golden guardian-dragon magic. Defensive wards. Containment spells. Magic that I guessed was a cloaking spell. And as best as I could tell, all of it had been systematically torn apart. Though I didn't put together the 'systematically' idea until the naturally smoothed rock underneath my feet became honed stone. Until I passed two open doorways cut into white tile surrounds. Until I came to the third room.

The final cell.

And the crack that ran through its far corner.

With my knife in hand, I had briefly glanced into the first two rooms along the rock-walled passageway. Light spells, triggered by my own magic, had lit up overhead as I paused at each torn-open doorway, scanning the familiar white tile walls of the cells beyond.

The first two cells were empty. As I'd already expected. I didn't bother stepping inside.

But at the threshold of the final white-tiled prison cell, I paused for a different reason.

I knew what it felt like to be contained in one of these cells, and I'd been locked away for only a couple of days. How long had the elf languished here?

It was an easy guess, based on how far I had walked and the magic I could feel simmering in the rock and dirt above me, that I was standing near the anchor point of the witches' magical grid. The first two white-tiled rooms hadn't contained a single drop of magic, but I could feel the tiniest of trickles emanating from the third.

I contemplated setting aside my necklace and knife, not knowing what the nullifying power embedded into every eighteen-inch-square tile of the cell would do to their magic. But in the end, I was loath to leave them behind.

So I crossed the threshold, stumbling as a terrible chill washed over me, taking every drop of magic, every bit of my power. It didn't fade or ebb away. It was simply gone.

Ignoring the weakness, the feeling of vulnerability that came with having my magic stripped from me, I steadily crossed toward the crack I could see in the corner tile, crouching over it.

More than a crack, actually. But I could imagine it starting as the tiniest of fissures, seeping with the tiniest hints of natural magic. Then I imagined what must have happened when I deliberately took those two large steps before casting the previous evening, pissily realigning the anchor point even though Kandy and Gran had already set the location. Because I could feel magic better than a witch and a werewolf, and I liked to show off.

Someone—the elf I had just killed, perhaps—had systematically slammed a fist over and over again into the crack. Widening it, even as they'd left their now-dried blood behind. Blood that appeared to be lightly tinted green against the white of the tile. Any natural healing magic the elf possessed wouldn't have worked in a guardian dragon prison. Just like whatever damage he'd sustained to his leg hadn't had time to heal outside the prison cell either.

In my mind's eye, I could see the events that had been taking place underneath my feet as I haphazardly fed them with my ignorance—and possibly the magic of the bakery wards and the portal. I envisioned an extra surge of power when the witches recast the grid with Burgundy in my place. A final surge that must have been enough for the occupant of the cell to harness and use, to finally tear through the door and all the layers of magic beyond.

But none of that was the real problem.

The real problem was the three cells.

Three.

Three elves.

In Vancouver.

I pressed my hand to the shattered tile, wondering if I would have had the strength to pound away at the impenetrable as the elf had. Breaking my skin, bleeding, breaking the bones of my hand ... and doing it over and over again until I'd collected enough magic to break out of my prison.

I could still taste the muted witch magic filtering in through the fissure in the tile. But it was what I couldn't taste that worried me. My own magic. And the power I'd inadvertently tied to the anchor point—the magic of the bakery and the portal in the basement.

I might not have caused the crack in the first place, but I'd given it a boost. So much so that the magic of the prison—and of the elf as he attempted to break out—had been leaking straight into the Talbots' basement. Where it had been picked up by the amplifier and dispersed out through the other so-called misfits.

When I'd anchored the grid myself, it had resulted in Mory's magical surge. The junior necromancer had reported that she and Burgundy had been playing board games at Tony's—who turned out to be Tony Talbot. The twins and Bitsy might well have been belatedly reacting to that same event. And then it had happened all over again when Burgundy took my place in the grid.

It was all guesswork, of course. But it was the parts of the puzzle I couldn't piece together that were my primary concern. At least for the moment.

Why had one elf stayed behind? And had there been more than three? It might have been the case that there were a number of Adepts contained in the other two cells. But either way, while the others fled, the elf had remained. To deal with Burgundy?

Or to deal with Kandy, Warner, and me?

Magic shifted in the open doorway. Warner stepped onto the white tile, stumbling slightly as his magic was stripped from him. He quickly retreated, rolling his bruised neck. Keeping his feet firmly planted on the honed stone floor beyond the door, he cast his grim gaze around the white-tiled room.

I straightened from the fissure, sighing.

"Pulou," the sentinel said darkly.

"Yeah, Pulou." I gestured toward the shattered tile. "I'm thinking the cell was compromised when Shailaja took him down? Just as all the portals tied specifically to Pulou were inactivated."

"Likely."

"I'm also thinking that this breakout, this sort of thing, is similar to what you've been running around taking care of for months. With my father and Haoxin.

And whatever called the guardians away from the party tonight?"

"Also likely. Though it would have been nice to know what we were dealing with when wading in." Warner cranked his neck left, then right.

I winced at the sound of cartilage and ligaments snapping and crackling.

"He sent me a summons tonight." I sighed. "Pulou. I ignored it. Actually, I told him to screw off. Again."

"Understandable."

I laughed involuntarily. Trust Warner to back me even when I was being stupidly, willfully blind and pissy.

"I suspect Vancouver was the least of his concerns," I said.

Warner nodded his head. "He knows you are here."

I ignored the flush of warmth that came with the compliment. Pulou almost certainly didn't think of me that highly. "Do you think this is why my trial was resolved so swiftly?"

"One of the reasons. Plus the fact that it should never have been called for in the first place."

I glanced around the room, making sure I wasn't missing anything. But aside from the damage in the corner, the cell was spotless.

"Have you ever wondered why there was a portal in the basement of the bakery? A portal of Pulou's construction?"

Warner grunted. "Now we know."

"Three elves, then?"

"It would make sense. Three cells."

Silence fell between us. If there were more elves to fight, then Warner was about to be on the front lines. Elves or whatever other entities Pulou had locked away … and perhaps even more compromised prisons or dimensional doorways around the globe.

"Remember you have a wedding to attend," I whispered. Not looking at him, not wanting to guilt him. But needing to say something.

A wide grin spread across his face. And despite the pain of having the magic that was still trying to heal him stripped away, he stepped into the cell, closing the space between us in two quick steps. "I'll be there."

Lifting up on my tiptoes, I brushed a kiss against his lips. Carefully. Not wanting to reinjure his neck.

"The witch can't stop gushing about how you took the elf down. One moment you were talking, and the next he was dead."

"There was a little more in between."

He chuckled.

"You and Kandy need to train together," I said. "Seriously train."

"Yeah …" Warner rubbed his neck ruefully. "A lesson I'd prefer not to repeat."

I touched the edge of the massive bruise slowly spreading across his neck, remembering the tattoo that had once edged his collarbone. And the duties that had come with that magic embedded underneath his skin.

"Why do you think the elf stayed behind?" I asked. "To distract us so the other two could get away?"

"Again, that would be a terribly logical guess."

"He was hurt already. A long-term wound that hadn't healed, probably because they'd been locked away here … without access to their magic."

"He would have slowed the other two before he had the chance to heal. Assuming their magic works like that in this dimension."

I sighed. "Why wouldn't Pulou have killed them? Or sent them back to their own world?"

"A question for the treasure keeper. Though I'd guess that it has something to do with how they got here in the first place."

I snorted. "Do you really want me questioning Pulou?"

Warner laughed harshly. "No. But I'm certainly not going to try to stop you."

Kandy stuck her head through the doorway, then rapidly retreated a step. "Right." Rubbing her arms, she scanned the four corners of the cell, then met my gaze grimly. "So the next time either of you go missing for more than a couple of days, I should check here?"

"Yep. Apparently Pulou has a thing for imprisoning people who piss him off." I was going for a teasing tone as I said it, but I didn't make it all the way.

Kandy nodded, unyieldingly grim. "The witches are here."

"Clean-up crew," I said.

"Yeah, though the leech hasn't left anything for them."

"Just white powder?"

"Not even that. And Angelica Talbot masked the bulk of the fight. From the view of the street, at least. With a mirror spell that the witches are currently cooing over." Kandy shook her head ruefully. "Then she called in Liam. Just in case a police presence could help mitigate any neighborly concern. So I guess we owe both sorcerers our thanks." With that update abruptly delivered, she took off down the tunnel. I didn't blame her. The cells disturbed the hell out of me as well.

I reached for Warner, twining my fingers through his. "Ignoring all of this until after the wedding probably isn't going to be an option."

"Would you want to ignore it?" He grinned knowingly.

I threw my head back and laughed. I couldn't deny it. There were two more elves in Vancouver. And I'd be there the moment they stepped out of line.

Gleefully.

I was a warrior, to the bittersweet end and dragging as many cupcakes as I could in my wake. Whether I wanted to be or not.

# Acknowledgements

With thanks to:

**My story & line editor**
Scott Fitzgerald Gray

**My proofreader**
Pauline Nolet

**My beta readers**
Terry Daigle, Angela Flannery, Gael Fleming,
Desi Hartzel, and Heather Lewis.

**For their continual encouragement,
feedback, & general advice**
SFWA
The Office
The Retreat

**Meghan Ciana Doidge** is an award-winning writer based out of Salt Spring Island, British Columbia, Canada. She has a penchant for bloody love stories, superheroes, and the supernatural. She also has a thing for chocolate, potatoes, and cashmere yarn.

### Novels
After the Virus
Spirit Binder
Time Walker
Cupcakes, Trinkets, and Other Deadly Magic (Dowser 1)
Trinkets, Treasures, and Other Bloody Magic (Dowser 2)
Treasures, Demons, and Other Black Magic (Dowser 3)
I See Me (Oracle 1)
Shadows, Maps, and Other Ancient Magic (Dowser 4)
Maps, Artifacts, and Other Arcane Magic (Dowser 5)
I See You (Oracle 2)
Artifacts, Dragons, and Other Lethal Magic (Dowser 6)
I See Us (Oracle 3)
Catching Echoes (Reconstructionist 1)
Tangled Echoes (Reconstructionist 2)
Unleashing Echoes (Reconstructionist 3)
Champagne, Misfits, and Other Shady Magic (Dowser 7)

### Novellas/Shorts
Love Lies Bleeding
The Graveyard Kiss (Reconstructionist 0.5)
Dawn Bytes (Reconstructionist 1.5)
An Uncut Key (Reconstructionist 2.5)

For recipes, giveaways, news, and glimpses of upcoming stories, please connect with Meghan on her:

Personal blog, www.madebymeghan.ca
Twitter, @mcdoidge
Facebook, Meghan Ciana Doidge
Email, info@madebymeghan.ca

Please also consider leaving an honest review at your point of sale outlet.

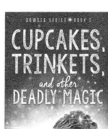

DOWSER SERIES ✦ BOOK 1

# CUPCAKES, TRINKETS,
*and other*
## DEADLY MAGIC

MEGHAN CIANA DOIDGE

DOWSER SERIES ✦ BOOK 2

# TRINKETS, TREASURES,
*and other*
## BLOODY MAGIC

MEGHAN CIANA DOIDGE

DOWSER SERIES ✦ BOOK 3

# TREASURES, DEMONS,
*and other*
## BLACK MAGIC

MEGHAN CIANA DOIDGE

DOWSER SERIES ✦ BOOK 4

# SHADOWS, MAPS,
*and other*
## ANCIENT MAGIC

MEGHAN CIANA DOIDGE

DOWSER SERIES ✦ BOOK 5

# MAPS, ARTIFACTS,
*and other*
## ARCANE MAGIC

MEGHAN CIANA DOIDGE

DOWSER SERIES ✦ BOOK 6

# ARTIFACTS, DRAGONS,
*and other*
## LETHAL MAGIC

MEGHAN CIANA DOIDGE

ORACLE SERIES ✦ BOOK 1

# I SEE ME

"Doidge merges romance, comedy, and supernatural fantasy in this effort."
— Kirkus Reviews

MEGHAN CIANA DOIDGE

ORACLE SERIES ✦ BOOK 2

# I SEE YOU

MEGHAN CIANA DOIDGE

ORACLE SERIES ✦ BOOK 3

# I SEE US

MEGHAN CIANA DOIDGE

RECONSTRUCTIONIST SERIES ✦ BOOK 1

# Catching Echoes

MEGHAN CIANA DOIDGE

RECONSTRUCTIONIST SERIES ✦ BOOK 2

# Tangled Echoes

MEGHAN CIANA DOIDGE

RECONSTRUCTIONIST SERIES ✦ BOOK 3

# Unleashing Echoes

MEGHAN CIANA DOIDGE

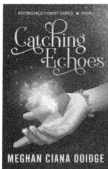